"Everything Margaret Atwood says in this book is overwhelmingly true . . . You're sure to recognize yourself somewhere."

—*Spectator*

"Margaret Atwood is a deeply serious writer who is also wildly funny."

—*Chatelaine*

"Deft, sardonic: quintessential Atwood."

—*Toronto Globe and Mail*

"She has done it again . . . *Dancing Girls* is a must."

—*Montreal Gazette*

Dancing Girls
and Other Stories

by
Margaret Atwood

SEAL BOOKS
McClelland and Stewart-Bantam Limited
Toronto

This edition contains the complete text
of the original hardcover edition.
NOT ONE WORD HAS BEEN OMITTED.

DANCING GIRLS AND OTHER STORIES
*A Seal Book / published by arrangement with
McClelland and Stewart Limited*

PRINTING HISTORY
*McClelland and Stewart edition published
September 1977
6 printings through December 1988*

ISBN 0-7704-2332-9

PRINTED IN CANADA

COVER PRINTED IN U.S.A.

U   15 14 13 12 11 10 9 8 7 6

Contents

Acknowledgements

The following stories were previously published:

TITLE	PUBLISHED BY
The War in the Bathroom	*Alphabet*
The Man from Mars	*Ontario Review*
Polarities	*Tamarack Review*
Rape Fantasies	*Fiddlehead;*
	Toronto Life
Under Glass	*Harper's*
The Grave of the	
Famous Poet	Oberon Press
Hair Jewellery	*Ms Magazine*
When It Happens	*Chatelaine*
A Travel Piece	*Saturday Night*
The Resplendent Quetzal	*The Malahat Review*
Lives of the Poets	*Saturday Night*

The War in the Bathroom

o o o

Monday

Late this afternoon she moved out of the old place
into the new one. The moving was accomplished
with a minimum of difficulty: she managed to get everything into the two suitcases and was able to carry
them herself for the three blocks that separate the
old place from the new one. She only had to stop and
rest twice. She is quite strong for her age. A man came
along and offered to help her, rather a pleasant-look-
ing man, but I have told her never to accept help
from strangers.

I think the German woman was glad to see her go.
She always regarded her with a certain amount of
suspicion. She stood on the wooden porch in her slippers, watching, her arms in their gray ravelled swea-
ter-sleeves folded across her fat stomach, her slip
hanging an inch below the figured cotton housedress
she always wore. I, for one, have always disliked the
German woman. I had become tired of seeing that
certain things in the room had been moved (though
she took pains to set them back in the approximate
proper spot, she was never quite meticulous enough),

and I had begun to suspect lately that she was looking at the mail: the envelopes had greasy thumbprints, and it is still too cold for the postmen to go without their gloves. The new place has a landlord instead of a landlady; I think, on the whole, I prefer them.

When she reached the new place she got the keys from an old man who lives in the ground-floor front room. He answered the doorbell; the landlord was out, but had told him she was to be expected. An agreeable old man with white hair and a benevolent smile. She took the suitcases up the narrow staircase to the second floor, one at a time. She has spent what was left of the day arranging the room. This room is smaller than the old one, but at least it is clean. She put the clothes into the cupboard and some of them into the bureau. There are no shelves so she will have to keep the saucepan, the cup, the plate, the silverware, and the coffee pot in one of the bureau drawers. However there is a small table, and I decided that the teapot may be left on it, even between mealtimes. It has a decorative pattern.

She made up the bed with the sheets and blankets that the landlord had provided. The room has a northern exposure and will be chilly. Fortunately there is an electric heater in the room. She has always been partial to warmth, although I myself have never been overly conscious of temperature. A compensation: the room is the one next to the bathroom, which will be handy.

The Notebook will be kept on the table, beside the teapot.

Tomorrow she must go outside for some groceries, but now she will go to bed.

Tuesday

She was lying in bed this morning trying to get back to sleep. I was looking at the clock and agreeing with her that indeed the mattress was thin and quite hard, harder even than the one at the old place. It was almost nine and I told her to reach out and shut off the clock before the alarm went off.

Someone came up the front stairs, slowly, with a limping step, and went into the bathroom, closing and locking the door. I have discovered that the walls are not thick and noises tend to carry. She was about to turn over and sleep again when the person in the bathroom began to cough violently. Then there was a sound of clearing and spitting and the toilet being flushed. I am sure I know who it was: it must be the old man from downstairs. The poor man must have a cold. He stayed in the bathroom exactly half an hour though, which is rather long; and he managed to make a number of unpleasant noises. I can see that the room beside the bathroom may have its disadvantages and I am beginning to realize why the landlord was willing to rent it so cheaply.

I finally persuaded her to get up and close the window (I have always felt fresh air to be necessary for one's health, although she is not fond of it) and turn on the electric heater. She began to go back to bed but I told her to put on the clothes: she had to go shopping, there was nothing to eat. She went into the bathroom, none too soon because there were other footsteps approaching. I thought that the bathroom could have been cleaner; however, this morning she just washed in the basin. Plenty of hot water at any rate.

She went back into the room and put on her coat and overshoes. I told her she had better put on the scarf too as I had noted frost on the storm window. She picked up the purse and went out of the room, locking the door behind her. The bathroom door was closed as she went by; the light showed through the transom. When she reached the bottom of the stairs the old man was in the hall, sorting out the mail on the small dark table that stands near the front door. He was wearing his bathrobe; below it his striped pyjamas went down, then his thin ankles and maroon-

leather bedroom slippers. He smiled beautifully and
said good morning. I told her to nod and smile
back.

She closed the front door behind her and took the
gloves out of her pocket and put them on. She made
her way down the porch steps, carefully, since they
were icy. I have often noticed that it is much less
dangerous for her to go up steps than to go down
them.

She walked along the street towards the place, a
few blocks along, where I knew there was a store. I
gloated over the houses on the street as she passed
them, fondling them, placing them in order: red brick
houses, double houses mostly, like the one that the
room is in, with twin wooden porches. The houses
near the old place had been bigger. I had been on this
street before, of course (it was not far from the old
place), but now I could regard this street for the first
time as mine, as part of the new territory through
which I could trace out pathways and my own familiar routes. These trees were mine. This sidewalk
was mine. When the snow melted and the trees blos-
somed, the damp earth and the new leaves and the
spring water running in the gutters would be mine.

She turned on to a main street with cars moving on
it and walked a block and turned and walked two
more blocks until she reached the store. There had
been another store nearer to the old place. I had
never been in this particular store.

She went in the glass doors and through the turn-
stile. Then she hesitated: she did not know whether
to take a pushcart or a wire basket. She felt that the
pushcarts are easier, wire baskets are heavy to carry;
but I said she wouldn't be buying that much and
pushcarts get in the way and slow things up so she
finally took a basket.

I always have to watch how much she spends. She
would like to buy steak and mushrooms, of course,
and olives and pies and pork roasts. Her old habits
are hard to break. But I insist that she get things that

are cheap and nourishing. It is, after all, the middle of the month, and the government cheque will not come for some time. After the rent has been paid there is not a great quantity of money left for other things. I must remember to have her make out a change-of-address card. She dislikes wieners but I made her buy a package of six. They have a lot of protein for the money. She got bread, and butter (I draw the line at margarine) and a quart of milk and some packaged soups, they are nice on a cold day, and some tea and eggs and several small tins of baked beans. She wanted some ice cream but I told her to get a package of frozen peas instead.

The check-out girl was rude to her simply because some of the things got mixed up with those of the woman ahead. Also I suspect she would have tried to short-change if she had dared. I wonder if it is worth while walking the extra distance to the old store?

She carried the parcel back easily enough and put the milk and the eggs and the frozen peas into the refrigerator, which is in the ground-floor hallway. The refrigerator has a peculiar odour. Perhaps the landlord should be told to clean it. She then went upstairs and got some water from the bathroom and made herself a cup of coffee on the one-burner hotplate (the coffee came in the suitcase along with the sugar and the salt and the pepper) and ate some bread and butter. While she was eating, someone went into the bathroom; not the old man this time, but a woman. She must talk to herself; at any rate I distinguished two voices, one high and querulous, the other an urgent whisper: most curious. The walls are thin but I could not quite hear what she was saying.

When the footsteps had gone out she took the cup and spoon into the bathroom and washed them in the basin. Then she lay down and had a nap. I felt she deserved it after all the walking she had done. It was suppertime when she woke up. She opened one of the cans of beans. When the cheque comes she must buy a new can-opener.

After I finish this I will do a little reading in the Bible (the lighting in this room is better than I would have expected) and then she will go to bed. Note: tomorrow she must take a bath.

Wednesday

This appears to be a daily occurrence. At nine o'clock exactly I was again awakened by the old man limping into the bathroom. He has a most rending cough. It sounds as though he is vomiting. Perhaps it would be possible for her to change the position of the bed so that her head is farther away from the wall. But when I consider the size and shape of the room I can see that there is only one place for it. Really it is annoying. Somehow when she coughs herself it is quite different from listening to someone else cough. If he keeps on coughing like that he will soon cough up everything inside him. I suppose I should feel sorry. Again this morning he stayed in the bathroom for half an hour.

Later, when she had got up and put on the clothes, she went downstairs to get the milk from the refrigerator. The old man had arranged the letters on the hall table: one letter in each corner of the table, and one in the centre. I must remember to have her fill out a change-of-address card.

Several times during the morning the woman with the two voices came into the bathroom. She seemed to be emptying pails or saucepans of water into the basin. Again I could hear the high voice and the harsh whisper. Talking to oneself is a bad habit. When she went in to wash the cup and plate after lunch, she found a potato peeling caught in the drain.

Later in the afternoon I told her that she must take a bath. She would like to have avoided it because the bathroom tends to be chilly, but I keep telling her that cleanliness and good health necessarily go together. She locked the door and I had her kneel beside the bathtub so that I could inspect it thoroughly.

I found a small hair, and some lint around the drain.

At the old place there was only one other person who used the same bathroom, a working girl who used to wash her stockings and leave them on the towel-rack. There is something repugnant about sharing the bathroom with other people. She always feels that the toilet seat is warmer than it ought to be, and I must say that I find even the thought of brushing one's teeth in the same basin used by total strangers disagreeable. I told her that someday soon she would have a bathroom of her own again, but I think she did not believe me. I must have her get a fresh bottle of antiseptic: the present one is almost empty.

The water was hot and she had a pleasant bath, though it was not as leisurely as it might have been. There were anxious footsteps walking outside the door, several times. It would certainly help if the landlord would install another bathroom; perhaps there is space for one in the basement.

Of course I had her clean the bathtub thoroughly after using it. The landlord has provided a sponge for this purpose, as well as a can of cleanser, which indicates that he, at least, has the right idea. Today also she washed out the underwear and hung it over the electric heater to dry.

Thursday

This morning it rained, which, I can see from the window, has melted the snow in the backyard considerably. If it continues warm she will have to start keeping the butter in the refrigerator; thus far the cupboard has been quite cool enough for it.

The old man is becoming intolerable. I am beginning to sense a certain aggressiveness about his activities in the bathroom. I feel that he does not want her in this house: he is trying to make her leave. This time he gargled, making a most repulsive sound. He must be discouraged; he must be made to understand that I cannot put up with it for long. She needs her sleep and must have peace. I am sure it would be possible for him to do that sort of thing in his own room, out of earshot.

I had her leave a note for the landlord about the smell in the refrigerator, but by suppertime, although the note was gone from the table, the refrigerator had still not been cleaned. Some people are quite difficult.

The woman with two voices continues to be active. Today she had a bath. I am beginning to think that she is actually two people, there was such a lot of splashing in the tub; but I can distinguish only one set of footsteps going in and coming out. The whispering voice becomes more violent, almost hysterical. The other voice remains formless.

The food supply is running low. Today she finished the frozen peas and the milk. Soon she will have to go to the store again, but I hope that it will be on a day when it is not raining. The overshoes are none too solid, and I agree with her that wet feet are unpleasant as well as being bad for the health.

Friday

She passed the old man on the stairs today. After his nine o'clock ritual, an even nastier one than usual this morning, he had the gall to smile, as though he is not even aware that I live next to the bathroom (although he must have heard her walking down the hall). There was something malevolent beneath the innocence of his smile. I told her not to smile back: she frowned and closed her mouth more tightly. He must not be encouraged to think that he can continue to get away with it.

Today I found a piece of cooked macaroni stuck in the drain. That is the doing of the woman with two voices. Perhaps she is a foreigner. Whatever she is, she is obviously not a neat person.

Saturday

Today she went to the store again, before lunch. I thought she could do without the scarf, as the sun was out. The streets are almost clear of snow now but there will doubtless be another storm before spring. As she walked I thought about the old man. Clearly something must be done soon. I cannot relay a message through the landlord: he is evidently untrustworthy. The refrigerator still has not been cleaned. If she begins to keep the butter in the refrigerator I know it will pick up the smell. The windowsill may be cool enough.

She bought more milk and another package of wieners, and a tin of tunafish for variety (although the latter was quite expensive). She bought also a quarter of a pound of cheese and a package of brown rice. One must regulate one's vitamins. When the cheque comes she will be able to get some oranges. This time she went through a different checkout counter and there was no trouble.

I thought that it would not do to talk to him in person. He would only take offence, or pretend that he did not know she was being awakened, or that no one had any right to question what he did in the bathroom. He will have some evasive answer and will continue to behave in the same way every morning. I kept thinking about the time: he is always so punctual. I wonder what would happen if his pattern were to be interrupted? Everyone else in the house seems to regard the half hour between nine and nine-thirty as his; at least, no one is ever in the bathroom just before nine. Certainly it would let him know that I know, and that it will be difficult for him to continue. He will not be allowed to drive her out.

When she was going up the steps I thought I saw him looking out from behind the Venetian blind in the front window. Is he trying to keep track of her movements?

This afternoon I decided that I had to know about
the woman with two voices. She went into the bathroom about mid-afternoon, and there were loud
splashing noises. I strained, trying to tell the separate
voices apart, but they seemed to overlap. I told her
that she had to wait behind the door and open it
quickly as soon as she heard the key being turned in
the bathroom lock. She managed to time it just right.
I was able to confront the woman as she was coming
out. I know now that there are two women. The one
that whispers is an old lady, very thin, with small
dark eyes that are like holes in her head. She was
wrapped in a blanket and was being carried by the
other woman; her legs and her crooked bare feet
dangled from the blanket. When she saw me she
nodded and grinned. The other woman is heavy set
and muscular, with a round vacuous face. She stood
in the doorway and stared until the old woman said
something to her in a sharp whisper and prodded her
with a twisted hand. Then she turned and carried the
old woman down the hall, plodding on her thick feet,
replying in a high whine that had no words in it at all.
The old woman's head looked over her shoulder,
grinning, until they disappeared around the corner of
the hall.

I told her to close the door. She was upset so I let
her lie down for a short rest. I will never allow her to
live like that.

After supper I thought about the old man again. I
had her sit up later than usual so that I could listen
for the clock of the church on the corner strike the
hour. I set the alarm exactly.

Sunday

The alarm went off at twenty minutes to nine. I
had allowed for the usual five to ten minutes that it
takes to urge her out of bed. She put on the dressing
gown and the slippers that I had her leave on the
chair, ready, the night before, and shut the window

and collected the things together: soap, toothbrush, bath towel, nail brush, Notebook, antiseptic bottle, room key, and the clock. At ten minutes to nine she went out of the room, locking the door, and went into the bathroom and turned the key carefully in the lock. She cleaned the bathtub and disinfected it and ran the bathwater till the tub was quite full. I thought how pleasant it was that the sound of running water drowned out all the noises from the rest of the house. It is a true luxury to make noises that the outside people have to listen to while being unable to hear any that they may make in return. I thought, this bathroom is mine now. It is my territory; I can go into it and out of it whenever I please. It is the only place where I am safe.

She placed the clock and the Notebook on the floor and lay back in the warm water. I told her not to be disturbed.

At nine o'clock exactly I heard his limping steps coming down the hall; she smiled. The footsteps paused outside the door, shuffled hesitantly, then began to pace back and forth. The clock ticked. I told her to make some splashing noises. At twenty minutes past nine the footsteps began to jig up and down impatiently outside. Then he knocked on the door. I told her not to say anything; she put her hand over her mouth to keep from laughing out loud.

The knocking increased to a pounding. He was hammering on the door with both fists. "Let me in," he shouted, pleading. His voice was frantic. I pictured his thin legs in the striped pyjamas, and the bathrobe and the maroon slippers.

At nine-thirty the pounding stopped. He made a choking noise, an inarticulate sound of rage and despair, and the footsteps limped away down the hall. Urgently, almost running. She smiled and swirled some of the water over her stomach. She keeps her figure remarkably well.

The footsteps went down two or three stairs; then there was a crash and a thumping sound and a wail of pain that faded into silence. I could hear other doors being opened.

She made a movement to get out of the bathtub but I told her to stay where she was. She lay in the bathtub, staring at her pink toes floating on the surface of the water, while I listened. I knew the bathroom door was securely locked.

For the time being I have won.

The Man from Mars

o   o   o

A long time ago Christine was walking through the park. She was still wearing her tennis dress; she hadn't had time to shower and change, and her hair was held back with an elastic band. Her chunky reddish face, exposed with no softening fringe, looked like a Russian peasant's, but without the elastic band the hair got in her eyes. The afternoon was too hot for April; the indoor courts had been steaming, her skin felt poached.

The sun had brought the old men out from wherever they spent the winter: she had read a story recently about one who lived for three years in a manhole. They sat weedishly on the benches or lay on the grass with their heads on squares of used newspaper. As she passed, their wrinkled toadstool faces drifted towards her, drawn by the movement of her body, then floated away again, uninterested.

The squirrels were out, too, foraging; two or three of them moved towards her in darts and pauses, eyes fixed on her expectantly, mouths with the ratlike receding chins open to show the yellowed front teeth. Christine walked faster, she had nothing to give them.

People shouldn't feed them, she thought; it makes them anxious and they get mangy.

Halfway across the park she stopped to take off her cardigan. As she bent over to pick up her tennis racquet again someone touched her on her freshly bared arm. Christine seldom screamed; she straightened up suddenly, gripping the handle of her racquet. It was not one of the old men, however; it was a dark-haired boy of twelve or so.

"Excuse me," he said, "I search for Economics Building. Is it there?" He motioned towards the west.

Christine looked at him more closely. She had been mistaken: he was not young, just short. He came a little above her shoulder, but then, she was above the average height; "statuesque," her mother called it when she was straining. He was also what was referred to in their family as "a person from another culture": oriental without a doubt, though perhaps not Chinese. Christine judged he must be a foreign student and gave him her official welcoming smile. In high school she had been president of the United Nations Club; that year her school had been picked to represent the Egyptian delegation at the Mock Assembly. It had been an unpopular assignment—nobody wanted to be the Arabs—but she had seen it through. She had made rather a good speech about the Palestinian refugees.

"Yes," she said, "that's it over there. The one with the flat roof. See it?"

The man had been smiling nervously at her the whole time. He was wearing glasses with transparent plastic rims, through which his eyes bulged up at her as though through a goldfish bowl. He had not followed where she was pointing. Instead he thrust towards her a small pad of green paper and a ballpoint pen.

"You make map," he said.

Christine set down her tennis racquet and drew a careful map. "We are here," she said, pronouncing distinctly. "You go this way. The building is here." She indicated the route with a dotted line and an X. The man leaned close to her, watching the progress of the map attentively; he smelled of cooked cauliflower and an unfamiliar brand of hair grease. When she had finished Christine handed the paper and pen back to him with a terminal smile.

"Wait," the man said. He tore the piece of paper with the map off the pad, folded it carefully and put it in his jacket pocket; the jacket sleeves came down over his wrists and had threads at the edges. He began to write something; she noticed with a slight feeling of revulsion that his nails and the ends of his fingers were so badly bitten they seemed almost deformed. Several of his fingers were blue from the leaky ballpoint.

"Here is my name," he said, holding the pad out to her.

Christine read an odd assemblage of cs, ys and ns, neatly printed in block letters. "Thank you," she said.

"You now write *your* name," he said, extending the pen.

Christine hesitated. If this had been a person from her own culture she would have thought he was trying to pick her up. But then, people from her own culture never tried to pick her up; she was too big. The only one who had made the attempt was the Moroccan waiter at the beer parlour where they sometimes went after meetings, and he had been direct. He had just intercepted her on the way to the Ladies' Room and asked and she said no; that had been that. This man was not a waiter though, but a student; she didn't want to offend him. In his culture, whatever it was, this exchange of names on pieces of paper was probably a formal politeness, like saying thank you. She took the pen from him.

"That is a very pleasant name," he said. He folded the paper and placed it in his jacket pocket with the map.

Christine felt she had done her duty. "Well, goodbye," she said. "It was nice to have met you." She bent for her tennis racquet but he had already stooped and retrieved it and was holding it with both hands in front of him, like a captured banner.

"I carry this for you."

"Oh no, please. Don't bother, I am in a hurry," she said, articulating clearly. Deprived of her tennis racquet she felt weaponless. He started to saunter along the path; he was not nervous at all now, he seemed completely at ease.

"*Vous parlez français?*" he asked conversationally.

"*Oui, un petit peu,*" she said. "Not very well." How am I going to get my racquet away from him without being rude? she was wondering.

"*Mais vous avez un bel accent.*" His eyes goggled at her through the glasses: was he being flirtatious? She was well aware that her accent was wretched.

"Look," she said, for the first time letting her impatience show, "I really have to go. Give me my racquet, please."

He quickened his pace but gave no sign of returning the racquet. "Where you are going?"

"Home," she said. "My house."

"I go with you now," he said hopefully.

"*No,*" she said: she would have to be firm with him. She made a lunge and got a grip on her racquet; after a brief tug of war it came free.

"Goodbye," she said, turning away from his puzzled face and setting off at what she hoped was a discouraging jog-trot. It was like walking away from a growling dog: you shouldn't let on you were frightened. Why should she be frightened anyway? He was only half her size and she had the tennis racquet, there was nothing he could do to her.

Although she did not look back she could tell he was still following. Let there be a streetcar, she thought, and there was one, but it was far down the line, stuck behind a red light. He appeared at her side, breathing audibly, a moment after she reached the stop. She gazed ahead, rigid.

"You are my friend," he said tentatively.

Christine relented: he hadn't been trying to pick her up after all, he was a stranger, he just wanted to meet some of the local people; in his place she would have wanted the same thing.

"Yes," she said, doling him out a smile.

"That is good," he said. "My country is very far."

Christine couldn't think of an apt reply. "That's interesting," she said. "*Très interessant.*" The street-car was coming at last; she opened her purse and got out a ticket.

"I go with you now," he said. His hand clamped on her arm above the elbow.

"You . . . stay . . . *here,*" Christine said, resisting the impulse to shout but pausing between each word as though for a deaf person. She detached his hand—his hold was quite feeble and could not compete with her tennis biceps—and leapt off the curb and up the streetcar steps, hearing with relief the doors grind shut behind her. Inside the car and a block away she permitted herself a glance out a side window. He was standing where she had left him; he seemed to be writing something on his little pad of paper.

When she reached home she had only time for a snack, and even then she was almost late for the Debating Society. The topic was, "Resolved: That War Is Obsolete." Her team took the affirmative and won.

Christine came out of her last examination feeling depressed. It was not the exam that depressed her but the fact that it was the last one: it meant the end of the school year. She dropped into the coffee shop as usual, then went home early because there didn't seem to be anything else to do.

"Is that you, dear?" her mother called from the living-room. She must have heard the front door close. Christine went in and flopped on the sofa, disturbing the neat pattern of cushions.

"How was your exam, dear?" her mother asked.

"Fine," said Christine flatly. It had been fine; she

had passed. She was not a brilliant student, she knew that, but she was conscientious. Her professors always wrote things like "A serious attempt" and "Well thought out but perhaps lacking in *élan*" on her term papers; they gave her BS, the occasional B+. She was taking Political Science and Economics, and hoped for a job with the Government after she graduated; with her father's connections she had a good chance.

"That's nice."

Christine felt, resentfully, that her mother had only a hazy idea of what an exam was. She was arranging gladioli in a vase; she had rubber gloves on to protect her hands as she always did when engaged in what she called "housework." As far as Christine could tell her housework consisted of arranging flowers in vases: daffodils and tulips and hyacinths through gladioli, irises and roses, all the way to asters and mums. Sometimes she cooked, elegantly and with chafing-dishes, but she thought of it as a hobby. The girl did everything else. Christine thought it faintly sinful to have a girl. The only ones available now were either foreign or pregnant; their expressions usually suggested they were being taken advantage of somehow. But her mother asked what they would do otherwise; they'd either have to go into a Home or stay in their own countries, and Christine had to agree this was probably true. It was hard, anyway, to argue with her mother. She was so delicate, so preserved-looking, a harsh breath would scratch the finish.

"An interesting young man phoned today," her mother said. She had finished the gladioli and was taking off her rubber gloves. "He asked to speak with you and when I said you weren't in we had quite a little chat. You didn't tell me about him, dear." She put on the glasses which she wore on a decorative chain around her neck, a signal that she was in her modern, intelligent mood rather than her old-fashioned whimsical one.

"Did he leave his name?" Christine asked. She knew

a lot of young men but they didn't often call her; they
conducted their business with her in the coffee shop
or after meetings.

"He's a person from another culture. He said he
would call back later."

Christine had to think a moment. She was vaguely
acquainted with several people from other cultures,
Britain mostly; they belonged to the Debating Society.

"He's studying Philosophy in Montreal," her mother
prompted. "He sounded French."

Christine began to remember the man in the park.
"I don't think he's French, exactly," she said.

Her mother had taken off her glasses again and was
poking absent-mindedly at a bent gladiolus. "Well, he
sounded French." She meditated, flowery sceptre in
hand. "I think it would be nice if you had him to tea."

Christine's mother did her best. She had two other
daughters, both of whom took after her. They were
beautiful; one was well married already and the
other would clearly have no trouble. Her friends consoled her about Christine by saying, "She's not fat,
she's just big-boned, it's the father's side," and "Christine is so healthy." Her other daughters had never
gotten involved in activities when they were at school,
but since Christine could not possibly ever be beautiful even if she took off weight, it was just as well
she was so athletic and political, it was a good thing
she had interests. Christine's mother tried to encourage her interests whenever possible. Christine
could tell when she was making an extra effort, there
was a reproachful edge to her voice.

She knew her mother expected enthusiasm but she
could not supply it. "I don't know, I'll have to see,"
she said dubiously.

"You look tired, darling," said her mother. "Perhaps
you'd like a glass of milk."

Christine was in the bathtub when the phone rang.
She was not prone to fantasy but when she was in the
bathtub she often pretended she was a dolphin, a

game left over from one of the girls who used to
bathe her when she was small. Her mother was being
bell-voiced and gracious in the hall; then there was a
tap at the door.

"It's that nice young French student, Christine,"
her mother said.

"Tell him I'm in the bathtub," Christine said, louder than necessary. "He isn't French."

She could hear her mother frowning. "That
wouldn't be very polite, Christine. I don't think he'd
understand."

"Oh, all right," Christine said. She heaved herself
out of the bathtub, swathed her pink bulk in a towel
and splattered to the phone.

"Hello," she said gruffly. At a distance he was not
pathetic, he was a nuisance. She could not imagine
how he had tracked her down: most likely he went
through the phone book, calling all the numbers with
her last name until he hit on the right one.

"It is your friend."

"I know," she said. "How are you?"

"I am very fine." There was a long pause, during
which Christine had a vicious urge to say, "Well, goodbye then," and hang up; but she was aware of her
mother poised figurine-like in her bedroom doorway.
Then he said, "I hope you also are very fine."

"Yes," said Christine. She wasn't going to partici-
pate.

"I come to tea," he said.

This took Christine by surprise. "You do?"

"Your pleasant mother ask me. I come Thursday,
four o'clock."

"Oh," Christine said, ungraciously.

"See you then," he said, with the conscious pride
of one who has mastered a difficult idiom.

Christine set down the phone and went along the
hall. Her mother was in her study, sitting innocently
at her writing desk.

"Did you ask him to tea on Thursday?"

"Not exactly, dear," her mother said. "I did mention he might come round to tea *some*time, though."

"Well, he's coming Thursday. Four o'clock."

"What's wrong with that?" her mother said serenely. "I think it's a very nice gesture for us to make. I do think you might try to be a little more co-operative." She was pleased with herself.

"Since you invited him," said Christine, "you can bloody well stick around and help me entertain him. I don't want to be left making nice gestures all by myself."

"Christine, *dear*," her mother said, above being shocked. "You ought to put on your dressing gown, you'll catch a chill."

After sulking for an hour Christine tried to think of the tea as a cross between an examination and an executive meeting: not enjoyable, certainly, but to be got through as tactfully as possible. And it *was* a nice gesture. When the cakes her mother had ordered arrived from *The Patisserie* on Thursday morning she began to feel slightly festive; she even resolved to put on a dress, a good one, instead of a skirt and blouse. After all, she had nothing against him, except the memory of the way he had grabbed her tennis racquet and then her arm. She suppressed a quick impossible vision of herself pursued around the living-room, fending him off with thrown sofa cushions and vases of gladioli; nevertheless she told the girl they would have tea in the garden. It would be a treat for him, and there was more space outdoors.

She had suspected her mother would dodge the tea, would contrive to be going out just as he was arriving: that way she could size him up and then leave them alone together. She had done things like that to Christine before; the excuse this time was the Symphony Committee. Sure enough, her mother carefully mislaid her gloves and located them with a faked murmur of joy when the doorbell rang. Christine relished for weeks afterwards the image of her mother's dropped jaw and flawless recovery when he was introduced: he wasn't quite the foreign potentate her optimistic, veil-fragile mind had concocted.

He was prepared for celebration. He had slicked on so much hair cream that his head seemed to be covered with a tight black patent-leather cap, and he had cut the threads off his jacket sleeves. His orange tie was overpoweringly splendid. Christine noticed, however, as he shook her mother's suddenly-braced white glove that the ballpoint ink on his fingers was indelible. His face had broken out, possibly in anticipation of the delights in store for him; he had a tiny camera slung over his shoulder and was smoking an exotic-smelling cigarette.

Christine led him through the cool flowery softly-padded livingroom and out by the French doors into the garden. "You sit here," she said. "I will have the girl bring tea."

This girl was from the West Indies. Christine's parents had been enraptured with her when they were down at Christmas and had brought her back with them. Since that time she had become pregnant, but Christine's mother had not dismissed her. She said she was slightly disappointed but what could you expect, and she didn't see any real difference between a girl who was pregnant before you hired her and one who got that way afterwards. She prided herself on her tolerance; also there was a scarcity of girls. Strangely enough, the girl became progressively less easy to get along with. Either she did not share Christine's mother's view of her own generosity, or she felt she had gotten away with something and was therefore free to indulge in contempt. At first Christine had tried to treat her as an equal. "Don't call me 'Miss Christine,'" she had said with an imitation of light, comradely laughter. "What you want me to call you then?" the girl had said, scowling. They had begun to have brief, surly arguments in the kitchen, which Christine decided were like the arguments between one servant and another. Her moth-

er's attitude towards each of them was similar; they
were not altogether satisfactory but they would have
to do.

The cakes, glossy with icing, were set out on a plate
and the teapot was standing ready; on the counter
the electric kettle boiled. Christine headed for it, but
the girl, till then sitting with her elbows on the kitch-
en table and watching her expressionlessly, made a
dash and intercepted her. Christine waited until she
had poured the water into the pot. Then, "I'll carry
it out, Elvira," she said. She had just decided she
didn't want the girl to see her visitor's orange tie; already, she knew, her position in the girl's eyes had
suffered because no one had yet attempted to get *her*
pregnant.

"What you think they pay me for, Miss Christine?"
the girl said insolently. She swung towards the garden with the tray; Christine trailed her, feeling lump-
ish and awkward. The girl was at least as big as she
was but in a different way.

"Thank you, Elvira," Christine said when the tray
was in place. The girl departed without a word, casting
a disdainful backward glance at the frayed jacket
sleeves, the stained fingers. Christine was now determined to be especially kind to him.

"You are very rich," he said.

"No," Christine protested, shaking her head, "we're
not." She had never thought of her family as rich; it
was one of her father's sayings that nobody made any
money with the Government.

"Yes," he repeated, "you are very rich." He sat
back in his lawn chair, gazing about him as though
dazed.

Christine set his cup of tea in front of him. She
wasn't in the habit of paying much attention to the
house or the garden; they were nothing special, far
from being the largest on the street; other people took
care of them. But now she looked where he was
looking, seeing it all as though from a different
height: the long expanses, the border flowers blazing

in the early-summer sunlight, the flagged patio and walks, the high walls and the silence.

He came back to her face, sighing a little. "My English is not good," he said, "but I improve."

"You do," Christine said, nodding encouragement.

He took sips of his tea, quickly and tenderly as though afraid of injuring the cup. "I like to stay here."

Christine passed him the cakes. He took only one, making a slight face as he ate it; but he had several more cups of tea while she finished the cakes. She managed to find out from him that he had come over on a church fellowship—she could not decode the denomination—and was studying Philosophy or Theology, or possibly both. She was feeling well-disposed towards him: he had behaved himself, he had caused her no inconvenience.

The teapot was at last empty. He sat up straight in his chair, as though alerted by a soundless gong. "You look this way, please," he said. Christine saw that he had placed his miniature camera on the stone sundial her mother had shipped back from England two years before. He wanted to take her picture. She was flattered, and settled herself to pose, smiling evenly.

He took off his glasses and laid them beside his plate. For a moment she saw his myopic, unprotected eyes turned towards her, with something tremulous and confiding in them she wanted to close herself off from knowing about. Then he went over and did something to the camera, his back to her. The next instant he was crouched beside her, his arm around her waist as far as it could reach, his other hand covering her own hands which she had folded in her lap, his cheek jammed up against hers. She was too startled to move. The camera clicked.

He stood up at once and replaced his glasses, which glittered now with a sad triumph. "Thank you, Miss," he said to her. "I go now." He slung the camera back over his shoulder, keeping his hand on it as though to hold the lid on and prevent escape. "I send to my family; they will like."

He was out the gate and gone before Christine had recovered; then she laughed. She had been afraid he would attack her, she could admit it now, and he had; but not in the usual way. He had raped, *rapeo, rapere, rapui, to seize and carry off*, not herself but her celluloid image, and incidently that of the silver tea service, which glinted mockingly at her as the girl bore it away, carrying it regally, the insignia, the official jewels. Christine spent the summer as she had for the past three years: she was the sailing instructress at an expensive all-girls camp near Algonquin Park. She had been a camper there, everything was familiar to her; she sailed almost better than she played tennis.

The second week she got a letter from him, postmarked Montreal and forwarded from her home address. It was printed in block letters on a piece of the green paper, two or three sentences. It began, "I hope you are well," then described the weather in monosyllables and ended, "I am fine." It was signed, "Your friend." Each week she got another of these letters, more or less identical. In one of them a colour print was enclosed: himself, slightly crosseyed and grinning hilariously, even more spindly than she remembered him against her billowing draperies, flowers exploding around them like firecrackers, one of his hands an equivocal blur in her lap, the other out of sight; on her own face, astonishment and outrage, as though he was sticking her in the behind with his hidden thumb.

She answered the first letter, but after that the seniors were in training for the races. At the end of the summer, packing to go home, she threw all the letters away.

When she had been back for several weeks she received another of the green letters. This time there was a return address printed at the top which Christine noted with foreboding was in her own city. Every day she waited for the phone to ring; she was so certain his first attempt at contact would be a disembodied voice that when he came upon her abruptly in mid-campus she was unprepared.

"How are you?"

His smile was the same, but everything else about him had deteriorated. He was, if possible, thinner; his jacket sleeves had sprouted a lush new crop of threads, as though to conceal hands now so badly bitten they appeared to have been gnawed by rodents. His hair fell over his eyes, uncut, ungreased; his eyes in the hollowed face, a delicate triangle of skin stretched on bone, jumped behind his glasses like hooked fish. He had the end of a cigarette in the corner of his mouth, and as they walked he lit a new one from it.

"I'm fine," Christine said. She was thinking, I'm not going to get involved again, enough is enough, I've done my bit for internationalism. "How are you?"

"I live here now," he said. "Maybe I study Economics."

"That's nice." He didn't sound as though he was enrolled anywhere.

"I come to see you."

Christine didn't know whether he meant he had left Montreal in order to be near her or just wanted to visit her at her house as he had done in the spring; either way she refused to be implicated. They were outside the Political Science building. "I have a class here," she said. "Goodbye." She was being callous, she realized that, but a quick chop was more merciful in the long run, that was what her beautiful sisters used to say.

Afterwards she decided it had been stupid of her to let him find out where her class was. Though a timetable was posted in each of the colleges: all he had to do was look her up and record her every probable movement in block letters on his green notepad. After that day he never left her alone.

Initially he waited outside the lecture rooms for her to come out. She said hello to him curtly at first

and kept on going, but this didn't work; he followed her at a distance, smiling his changeless smile.
Then she stopped speaking altogether and pretended
to ignore him, but it made no difference, he followed
her anyway. The fact that she was in some way
afraid of him—or was it just embarrassment?—
seemed only to encourage him. Her friends started to
notice, asking her who he was and why he was tag-
ging along behind her; she could hardly answer
because she hardly knew.

As the weekdays passed and he showed no signs of
letting up, she began to jog-trot between classes, finally to run. He was tireless, and had an amazing
wind for one who smoked so heavily: he would speed
along behind her, keeping the distance between them
the same, as though he were a pull-toy attached to
her by a string. She was aware of the ridiculous spectacle they must make, galloping across campus, something out of a cartoon short, a lumbering elephant
stampeded by a smiling, emaciated mouse, both of
them locked in the classic pattern of comic pursuit
and flight; but she found that to race made her less
nervous than to walk sedately, the skin on the back of
her neck crawling with the feel of his eyes on it. At
least she could use her muscles. She worked out rou-
tines, escapes: she would dash in the front door of
the Ladies' Room in the coffee shop and out the
back door, and he would lose the trail, until he discovered the other entrance. She would try to shake him
by detours through baffling archways and corridors,
but he seemed as familiar with the architectural
mazes as she was herself. As a last refuge she could
head for the women's dormitory and watch from safety as he was skidded to a halt by the receptionist's
austere voice: men were not allowed past the entrance.

Lunch became difficult. She would be sitting, usually with other members of the Debating Society, just
digging nicely into a sandwich, when he would appear suddenly as though he'd come up through an

unseen manhole. She then had the choice of barging
out through the crowded cafeteria, sandwich half-
eaten, or finishing her lunch with him standing behind her chair, everyone at the table acutely aware
of him, the conversation stilting and dwindling. Her
friends learned to spot him from a distance; they
posted lookouts. "Here he comes," they would whisper, helping her collect her belongings for the sprint
they knew would follow.

Several times she got tired of running and turned to
confront him. "What do you want?" she would ask,
glowering belligerently down at him, almost clench-
ing her fists; she felt like shaking him, hitting him.

"I wish to talk with you."

"Well, here I am," she would say. "What do you
want to talk about?"

But he would say nothing; he would stand in front
of her, shifting his feet, smiling perhaps apologetical-
ly (though she could never pinpoint the exact tone
of that smile, chewed lips stretched apart over the
nicotine-yellowed teeth, rising at the corners, flesh
held stiffly in place for an invisible photographer),
his eyes jerking from one part of her face to another
as though he saw her in fragments.

Annoying and tedious though it was, his pursuit of
her had an odd result: mysterious in itself, it ren-
dered her equally mysterious. No one had ever found
Christine mysterious before. To her parents she was a
beefy heavyweight, a plodder, lacking in flair, ordinary as bread. To her sisters she was the plain one,
treated with an indulgence they did not give to
each other: they did not fear her as a rival. To her
male friends she was the one who could be relied on.
She was helpful and a hard worker, always good for a
game of tennis with the athletes among them. They
invited her along to drink beer with them so they
could get into the cleaner, more desirable Ladies and
Escorts side of the beer parlour, taking it for granted
she would buy her share of the rounds. In moments
of stress they confided to her their problems with

women. There was nothing devious about her and
nothing interesting.

Christine had always agreed with these estimates
of herself. In childhood she had identified with the
false bride or the ugly sister; whenever a story had
begun, "Once there was a maiden as beautiful as she
was good," she had known it wasn't her. That was
just how it was, but it wasn't so bad. Her parents never expected her to be a brilliant social success and
weren't overly disappointed when she wasn't. She was
spared the manoeuvring and anxiety she witnessed
among others her age, and she even had a kind of
special position among men: she was an exception,
she fitted none of the categories they commonly used
when talking about girls; she wasn't a cock-teaser,
a cold fish, an easy lay or a snarky bitch; she was an
honorary person. She had grown to share their contempt for most women.

Now, however, there was something about her that
could not be explained. A man was chasing her, a
peculiar sort of man, granted, but still a man, and he
was without doubt attracted to her, he couldn't leave
her alone. Other men examined her more closely
than they ever had, appraising her, trying to find out
what it was those twitching bespectacled eyes saw in
her. They started to ask her out, though they returned
from these excursions with their curiosity unsatisfied,
the secret of her charm still intact. Her opaque
dumpling face, her solid bear-shaped body became
for them parts of a riddle no one could solve. Christine sensed this. In the bathtub she no longer imagined she was a dolphin; instead she imagined she
was an elusive water-nixie, or sometimes, in moments
of audacity, Marilyn Monroe. The daily chase was
becoming a habit; she even looked forward to it. In
addition to its other benefits she was losing weight.

All these weeks he had never phoned her or turned
up at the house. He must have decided however that
his tactics were not having the desired result, or perhaps he sensed she was becoming bored. The phone

began to ring in the early morning or late at night
when he could be sure she would be there. Sometimes
he would simply breathe (she could recognize, or
thought she could, the quality of his breathing), in
which case she would hang up. Occasionally he would
say again that he wanted to talk to her, but even
when she gave him lots of time nothing else would
follow. Then he extended his range: she would see
him on her streetcar, smiling at her silently from a
seat never closer than three away; she could feel him
tracking her down her own street, though when she
would break her resolve to pay no attention and
would glance back he would be invisible or in the act
of hiding behind a tree or hedge.

Among crowds of people and in daylight she had
not really been afraid of him; she was stronger than
he was and he had made no recent attempt to touch
her. But the days were growing shorter and colder,
it was almost November, often she was arriving home
in twilight or a darkness broken only by the feeble
orange streetlamps. She brooded over the possibility
of razors, knives, guns; by acquiring a weapon he
could quickly turn the odds against her. She avoided
wearing scarves, remembering the newspaper stories
about girls who had been strangled by them. Putting
on her nylons in the morning gave her a funny feeling. Her body seemed to have diminished, to have
become smaller than his.

Was he deranged, was he a sex maniac? He seemed
so harmless, yet it was that kind who often went
berserk in the end. She pictured those ragged fingers
at her throat, tearing at her clothes, though she could
not think of herself as screaming. Parked cars, the
shrubberies near her house, the driveways on either
side of it, changed as she passed them from unno-
ticed background to sinister shadowed foreground,
every detail distinct and harsh: they were places a
man might crouch, leap out from. Yet every time she
saw him in the clear light of morning or afternoon
(for he still continued his old methods of pursuit), his

aging jacket and jittery eyes convinced her that it was she herself who was the tormentor, the persecutor. She was in some sense responsible; from the folds and crevices of the body she had treated for so long as a reliable machine was emanating, against her will, some potent invisible odour, like a dog's in heat or a female moth's, that made him unable to stop following her.

Her mother, who had been too preoccupied with the unavoidable fall entertaining to pay much attention to the number of phone calls Christine was getting or to the hired girl's complaints of a man who hung up without speaking, announced that she was flying down to New York for the weekend; her father decided to go too. Christine panicked: she saw herself in the bathtub with her throat slit, the blood drooling out of her neck and running in a little spiral down the drain (for by this time time she believed he could walk through walls, could be everywhere at once). The girl would do nothing to help; she might even stand in the bathroom door with her arms folded, watching. Christine arranged to spend the weekend at her married sister's.

When she arrived back Sunday evening she found the girl close to hysterics. She said that on Saturday she had gone to pull the curtains across the French doors at dusk and had found a strangely contorted face, a man's face, pressed against the glass, staring at her from the garden. She claimed she had fainted and had almost had her baby a month too early right there on the livingroom carpet. Then she had called the police. He was gone by the time they got there but she had recognized him from the afternoon of the tea; she had informed them he was a friend of Christine's.

They called Monday evening to investigate, two of them. They were very polite, they knew who Christine's father was. Her father greeted them heartily; her mother hovered in the background, fidgeting with her porcelain hands, letting them see how frail and

worried she was. She didn't like having them in the
livingroom but they were necessary.

Christine had to admit he'd been following her
around. She was relieved he'd been discovered, relieved also that she hadn't been the one to tell, though
if he'd been a citizen of the country she would have
called the police a long time ago. She insisted he was
not dangerous, he had never hurt her.

"That kind don't hurt you," one of the policemen
said. "They just kill you. You're lucky you aren't
dead."

"Nut cases," the other one said.

Her mother volunteered that the thing about people from another culture was that you could never
tell whether they were insane or not because their
ways were so different. The policeman agreed with
her, deferential but also condescending, as though
she was a royal halfwit who had to be humoured.

"You know where he lives?" the first policeman
asked. Christine had long ago torn up the letter with
his address on it; she shook her head.

"We'll have to pick him up tomorrow then," he
said. "Think you can keep him talking outside your
class if he's waiting for you?"

After questioning her they held a murmured conversation with her father in the front hall. The girl,
clearing away the coffee cups, said if they didn't lock
him up she was leaving, she wasn't going to be scared
half out of her skin like that again.

Next day when Christine came out of her Modern
History lecture he was there, right on schedule. He
seemed puzzled when she did not begin to run. She
approached him, her heart thumping with treachery
and the prospect of freedom. Her body was back to
its usual size; she felt herself a giantess, self-con-
trolled, invulnerable.

"How are you?" she asked, smiling brightly.

He looked at her with distrust.

"How have you been?" she ventured again. His own

perennial smile faded; he took a step back from her.

"This the one?" said the policeman, popping out from behind a notice board like a Keystone Cop and laying a competent hand on the worn jacket shoulder. The other policeman lounged in the background; force would not be required.

"Don't *do* anything to him," she pleaded as they took him away. They nodded and grinned, respectful, scornful. He seemed to know perfectly well who they were and what they wanted.

The first policeman phoned that evening to make his report. Her father talked with him, jovial and managing. She herself was now out of the picture; she had been protected, her function was over.

"What did they *do* to him?" she asked anxiously as he came back into the livingroom. She was not sure what went on in police stations.

"They didn't do anything to him," he said, amused by her concern. "They could have booked him for Watching and Besetting, they wanted to know if I'd like to press charges. But it's not worth a court case: he's got a visa that says he's only allowed in the country as long as he studies in Montreal, so I told them to just ship him down there. If he turns up here again they'll deport him. They went around to his rooming house, his rent's two weeks overdue; the landlady said she was on the point of kicking him out. He seems happy enough to be getting his back rent paid and a free train ticket to Montreal." He paused. "They couldn't get anything out of him though."

"*Out* of him?" Christine asked.

"They tried to find out why he was doing it; following you, I mean." Her father's eyes swept her as though it was a riddle to him also. "They said when they asked him about that he just clammed up. Pretended he didn't understand English. He understood well enough, but he wasn't answering."

Christine thought this would be the end, but some-

how between his arrest and the departure of the
train he managed to elude his escort long enough for
one more phone call.

"I see you again," he said. He didn't wait for her to
hang up.

Now that he was no longer an embarrassing present reality, he could be talked about, he could become an amusing story. In fact, he was the only
amusing story Christine had to tell, and telling it pre-
served both for herself and for others the aura of her
strange allure. Her friends and the men who continued to ask her out speculated about his motives. One
suggested he had wanted to marry her so he could
remain in the country; another said that oriental men
were fond of well-built women: "It's your Rubens
quality."

Christine thought about him a lot. She had not
been attracted to him, rather the reverse, but as an
idea only he was a romantic figure, the one man who
had found her irresistible; though she often wondered, inspecting her unchanged pink face and hefty
body in her full-length mirror, just what it was about
her that had done it. She avoided whenever it was
proposed the theory of his insanity: it was only that
there was more than one way of being sane.

But a new acquaintance, hearing the story for the
first time, had a different explanation. "So he got
you, too," he said, laughing. "That has to be the
same guy who was hanging around our day camp a
year ago this summer. He followed all the girls like
that. A short guy, Japanese or something, glasses, smiling all the time."

"Maybe it was another one," Christine said.

"There couldn't be two of them, everything fits.
This was a pretty weird guy."

"What . . . *kind* of girls did he follow?" Christine
asked.

"Oh, just anyone who happened to be around. But
if they paid any attention to him at first, if they were

nice to him or anything, he was unshakeable. He was a bit of a pest, but harmless."

Christine ceased to tell her amusing story. She had been one among many, then. She went back to playing tennis, she had been neglecting her game.

A few months later the policeman who had been in charge of the case telephoned her again.

"Like you to know, Miss, that fellow you were having the trouble with was sent back to his own country. Deported."

"What for?" Christine asked. "Did he try to come back here?" Maybe she had been special after all, maybe he had dared everything for her.

"Nothing like it," the policeman said. "He was up to the same tricks in Montreal but he really picked the wrong woman this time—a Mother Superior of a convent. They don't stand for things like that in Quebec—had him out of here before he knew what happened. I guess he'll be better off in his own place."

"How old was she?" Christine asked, after a silence.

"Oh, around sixty, I guess."

"Thank you very much for letting me know," Christine said in her best official manner. "It's such a relief." She wondered if the policeman had called to make fun of her.

She was almost crying when she put down the phone. What *had* he wanted from her then? A Mother Superior. Did she really look sixty, did she look like a mother? What did convents mean? Comfort, charity? Refuge? Was it that something had happened to him, some intolerable strain just from being in this country; her tennis dress and exposed legs too much for him, flesh and money seemingly available everywhere but withheld from him wherever he turned, the nun the symbol of some final distortion, the robe and veil reminiscent to his near-sighted eyes of the women of his homeland, the ones he was able to understand? But he was back in his own country, remote from her as another planet; she would never know.

He hadn't forgotten her though. In the spring she got a postcard with a foreign stamp and the familiar block-letter writing. On the front was a picture of a temple. He was fine, he hoped she was fine also, he was her friend. A month later another print of the picture he had taken in the garden arrived, in a sealed manila envelope otherwise empty.

Christine's aura of mystery soon faded; anyway, she herself no longer believed in it. Life became again what she had always expected. She graduated with mediocre grades and went into the Department of Health and Welfare; she did a good job, and was seldom discriminated against for being a woman because nobody thought of her as one. She could afford a pleasant-sized apartment, though she did not put much energy into decorating it. She played less and less tennis; what had been muscle with a light coating of fat turned gradually into fat with a thin substratum of muscle. She began to get headaches.

As the years were used up and the war began to fill the newspapers and magazines, she realized which eastern country he had actually been from. She had known the name but it hadn't registered at the time, it was such a minor place; she could never keep them separate in her mind.

But though she tried, she couldn't remember the name of the city, and the postcard was long gone— had he been from the North or the South, was he near the battle zone or safely far from it? Obsessively she bought magazines and pored over the available photographs, dead villagers, soldiers on the march, colour blowups of frightened or angry faces, spies being executed; she studied maps, she watched the late-night newscasts, the distant country and terrain becoming almost more familiar to her than her own. Once or twice she thought she could recognize him but it was no use, they all looked like him.

Finally she had to stop looking at the pictures. It bothered her too much, it was bad for her; she was beginning to have nightmares in which he was coming through the French doors of her mother's house in his shabby jacket, carrying a packsack and a rifle and a huge bouquet of richly coloured flowers. He was smiling in the same way but with blood streaked over his face, partly blotting out the features. She gave her television set away and took to reading nineteenth-century novels instead; Trollope and Galsworthy were her favourites. When, despite herself, she would think about him, she would tell herself that he had been crafty and agile-minded enough to survive, more or less, in her country, so surely he would be able to do it in his own, where he knew the language. She could not see him in the army, on either side; he wasn't the type; and to her knowledge he had not believed in any particular ideology. He would be something nondescript, something in the background, like herself. Perhaps he had become an interpreter.

Polarities

o   o   o

Gentle and just pleasure
It is, being human, to have won from space
This unchill, habitable interior. . . .
—MARGARET AVISON, "New Year's Poem"

He hadn't seen her around for a week, which was unusual: he asked her if she'd been sick.

"No," she said, "working." She always spoke of what she had been doing with organizational, almost military briskness. She had a little packsack in which she carried around her books and notebooks. To Morrison, whose mind shambled from one thing to another, picking up, fingering, setting down, she was a small model of the kind of efficiency he ought to be displaying more of. Perhaps that was why he had never wanted to touch her: he liked women who were not necessarily more stupid but lazier than himself. Sloth aroused him: a girl's unwashed dishes were an invitation to laxity and indulgence.

She marched beside him along the corridor and down the stairs, her short clipped steps syncopating with his own lank strides. As they descended, the smell of straw, droppings and formaldehyde grew stronger: a colony of overflow experimental mice from the science building lived in the cellar. When he saw that she was leaving the building too and probably going home, he offered her a lift.

"Only if you're heading that way anyway." Louise didn't accept favours, she had made that clear from the start. When he'd asked her if she wanted to take in a film with him she said, "Only if you let me pay for my own ticket." If she had been taller he might have found this threatening.

It was colder, the weak red sun almost down, the snow purpling and creaky. She jumped up and down beside the car till he got the plug-in engine heater untangled and the door opened, her head coming out of the enormous second-hand fur coat she wore like a gopher's out of its burrow. He had seen a lot of gophers on the drive across, many of them dead; one he had killed himself, an accident, it had dived practically under the car wheels. The car itself hadn't held up either: by the time he'd made it to the outskirts—though later he realized that this was in fact the city—a fender had come off and the ignition was failing. He'd had to junk it, and had decided stoically to do without a car until he found he couldn't.

He swung the car onto the driveway that led from the university. It bumped as though crossing a metal-plated bridge: the tires were angular from the cold, the motor sluggish. He should take the car for long drives more often; it was getting stale. Louise was talking more than she normally did; she was excited about something. Two of her students had been giving her a hassle, but she told them they didn't have to come to class. "It's your heads, not mine." She knew she had won, they would shape up, they would contribute. Morrison was not up on the theories of group dynamics. He liked the old way: you taught the subject and forgot about them as people. It disconcerted him when they slouched into his office and mumbled at him, fidgeting and self-conscious, about their fathers

or their love lives. He didn't tell them about his father or his love life and he wished they would ob-
serve the same reticence, though they seemed to
think they had to do it in order to get extensions on
their term papers. At the beginning of the year one of
his students had wanted the class to sit in a circle
but luckily the rest of them preferred straight lines.

"It's right here," she said; he had been driving past
it. He crunched the car to a halt, fender against the
rockbank, snowbank. Here they did not take the snow
away; they spread sand on it, layer by layer as it fell,
confident there would be no thaw.

"It's finished; you can come in and see it," she said,
suggesting but really demanding.

"What's finished?" he asked. He hadn't been paying attention.

"I told you. My place, my apartment, that's what
I've been working on."

The house was one of the featureless two-storey
boxes thrown up by the streetful in the years after
the war when there was a housing boom and ma-
terials were scarce. It was stuccoed with a greyish
gravel Morrison found spiritually depleting. There
were a few older houses, but they were quickly being
torn down by developers; soon the city would have no
visible past at all. Everything else was highrises, or
worse, low barrack-shaped multiple housing units,
cheaply tacked together. Sometimes the rows of flimsy buildings—snow on their roofs, rootless white faces
peering suspiciously out through their windows, kids'
toys scattered like trash on the walks—reminded him
of old photographs he had seen of mining camps.
They were the houses of people who did not expect
to be living in them for long.

Her apartment was in the basement. As they went
around to the back and down the stairs, avoiding on
the landing a newspaper spread with the overshoes
and boots of the family living upstairs, Morrison remembered vividly and with a recurrence of panic

his own search for a place, a roof, a container, his trudges from address to address, his tours of clammy, bin-like cellars hastily done up by the owners in vinyl tile and sheets of cheap panelling to take advantage of the student inflow and the housing squeeze. He'd known he would never survive a winter buried like that or closed in one of the glass-sided cardboard-carton apartment buildings. Were there no real ones, mellowed, interesting, possible? Finally he had come upon an available second storey; the house was pink gravel instead of grey, the filth was daunting and the landlady querulous, but he had taken it immediately just to be able to open a window and look out.

He had not known what to expect of Louise's room. He had never visualized her as living anywhere, even though he had collected her and dropped her off outside the house a number of times.

"I finished the bookshelves yesterday," she said, waving at a wall-length structure of varnished boards and cement blocks. "Sit down, I'll make you some cocoa." She went into the kitchen, still with her fur coat on, and Morrison sat down in the leatherette swivel armchair. He swivelled, surveying, comparing it with the kind of interior he thought of himself as inhabiting but never got around to assembling.

She had obviously put a lot of energy into it, but the result was less like a room than like several rooms, pieces of which had been cut out and pasted onto one another. He could not decide what created this effect: it was the same unity in diversity he had found in the motels on the way across, the modernish furniture, the conventional framed northern landscapes on the walls. But her table was ersatz Victorian and the prints Picasso. The bed was concealed behind a partly drawn dyed burlap curtain at the end of the room, but visible on the bedside rug were two light blue fuzzy slippers that startled, almost shocked him: they were so unlike her.

Louise brought the cocoa and sat down opposite

him on the floor. They talked as usual about the city: they were both still looking for things to do, a quest based on their shared eastern assumption that cities ought to be entertaining. It was this rather than mutual attraction which led them to spend as much time together as they did; most of the others were married or had been here too long and had given up.

The films changed slowly; the one theatre, with its outdated popular comedies, they had sneered at. They had gone to the opera together when it had come, though: local chorus and imported stars—*Lucia*, it had been, and really quite well done, considering. At intermission Morrison had glanced around at the silent, chunky audience in the lobby, some of the women still in early-sixties pointed-toe spike heels, and murmured to Louise that it was like tourist brochures from Russia.

One Sunday before the snow came they had gone for an impromptu drive; at her suggestion they had aimed for the zoo twenty miles from the city. After they made it through the oil derricks there had been trees; not the right kind of trees—he had felt, as he had on the way across, that the land was keeping itself apart from him, not letting him in, there had to be more to it than this repetitive, non-committal drabness—but still trees; and the zoo once they reached it was spacious, the animals kept in enclosures large enough for them to run in and even hide in if they wanted to.

Louise had been there before—how, since she had no car, he didn't ask—and showed him around. "They choose animals that can survive the winter," she said. "It's open all year. They don't even know they're in a zoo." She pointed out the artificial mountain made of cement blocks for the mountain goats to climb on. Morrison didn't as a rule like any animal bigger and wilder than a cat, but these kept far enough away to be tolerable. That day she had told him a little about herself, a departure: mostly she talked about her work. She had travelled in Europe, she told him, and had spent a year studying in England.

"What are you doing here?" he had asked.

She shrugged. "They gave me money; nobody else would."

Essentially it was his reason too. It wasn't the draft; he was really over-age, though here they kept wanting to think he was a dodger, it made his presence more acceptable to them. The job market had been tight back in the States and also, when he tried later, in what they called here the East. But in all fairness it hadn't been only the money or the dismalness of the situation back home. He had wanted something else, some adventure; he felt he might learn something new. He had thought the city would be near the mountains. But except for the raw gully through which the brownish river curved, it was flat.

"I don't want you to think of it as typical," Louise was saying. "You ought to see Montreal."

"Are *you* typical?" he asked.

She laughed. "None of us is typical, or do we all look alike to you? I'm not typical, I'm all-inclusive."

She let her fur coat fall down from around her shoulders as she said this, and he wondered again whether he was expected to make a move, to approach her. He ought to approach someone or something; he was beginning to feel isolated inside his clothes and skin. His students were out of the question. Besides, they were so thick, so impermeable; the girls, even the more slender ones, made him think of slabs of substance white and congealed, like lard. And the other single women on staff were much older than he was: in them Louise's briskness had degenerated into a pinpointing, impaling quality.

There must be a place where he could meet someone, some nice loosely structured girl with ungroomed, seedy breasts, more thing than idea, slovenly and gratuitous. They existed, he was familiar with them from what he had begun to think of as his previous life, but he had not kept in touch with any of them. They had

all been good at first but even the sloppiest had in
time come to require something from him he thought
he was not yet ready to give: they wanted him to be
in love with them, an exertion of the mind too strenuous for him to undertake. His mind, he felt, was
needed for other things, though he wasn't quite sure
what they were. He was tasting, exploring: goals
would come later.

Louise wasn't at all like them; she would never
lend him her body for nothing, even temporarily,
though she had the fur spread out around her now
like a rug and had raised one corduroy-trousered
knee, letting him see in profile the taut bulge of her
somewhat muscular thigh. She probably went skiing
and ice skating. He imagined his long body locked in
that athletic, chilly grip, his eyes darkened by fur.
Not yet, he thought, raising his half-full cocoa cup
between them. I can do without, I don't need it yet.

It was the weekend and Morrison was painting his
apartment as he habitually did on weekends; he had
been at it off and on since he moved in.

"You'll have to have it painted, of course," he'd
said smoothly to the landlady when inspecting it, but
he had already shown himself too eager and she'd out-
foxed him. "Well, I don't know, there's another boy
wants it says he'll paint it himself. . . ." So of course
Morrison had to say he would too. This was the third
coat.

Morrison's vision of wall-painting had been drawn
from the paint ads—spot-free housewives gliding it
on, one-handed and smiling—but it wasn't easy. The
paint got on the floor, on the furniture, in his hair.
Before he could even begin he had to cart out the ac-
cumulated discards of several generations of previous
tenants: baby clothes, old snapshots, an inner tube,
heaps of empty liquor bottles, and (intriguingly) a
silk parachute. Messiness interested him only in wom-
en; he could not live surrounded by it himself.

One wall of the livingroom had been pink, one green, one orange and one black. He was painting them white. The last tenants, a group of Nigerian students, had left weird magic-looking murals on the walls: a sort of swamp, in black on the orange wall, and an upright shape, in pink on the green wall, was either a very poorly done Christ Child or—could it be?—an erect penis with a halo around it. Morrison painted these two walls first, but it made him uneasy to know the pictures were still there underneath the paint. Sometimes as he rollered his way around the room he wondered what the Nigerians had thought the first time it hit forty below.

The landlady seemed to prefer foreign students, probably because they were afraid to complain: she had been aggrieved when Morrison had demanded a real lock for his door. The cellar was a warren of cubbyholes; he was not sure yet exactly who lived in them. Soon after he had moved in a Korean had appeared at his door, hopefully smiling. He wanted to talk about income tax.

"I'm sorry," Morrison had said, "some other time, okay? I have a lot of work to do." He was nice enough, no doubt, but Morrison didn't want to get involved with someone he didn't know; and he did have work to do. He felt picayune about it later when he discovered the Korean had a wife and child down in his cubbyhole with him; often in the fall they had put fishes out to dry, stringing them on the clotheslines where they twirled in the wind like plastic gas-station decorations.

He was doing the ceiling, craning his neck, with the latex oozing down the handle of the roller onto his arm, when the buzzer went. He almost hoped it was the Korean, he seldom saw anyone on the weekends. But it was Louise.

"Hi," he said, surprised.

"I just thought I'd drop in," she said. "I don't use the phone any more."

"I'm painting," he said, partly as an excuse: he wasn't sure he wanted her in the house. What would she demand from him?

"Can I help?" she asked, as though it was a big treat.

"Actually I was about to stop for the day," he lied. He knew she would be better at it than he was.

He made tea in the kitchen and she sat at the table and watched him.

"I came to talk about Blake," she said. "I have to do a paper." Unlike him she was only a Graduate Assistant, she was taking a course.

"What aspect?" Morrison asked, not interested. Blake wasn't his field. He didn't mind the earlier lyrics but the prophecies bored him and the extravagant letters in which Blake called his friends angels of light and vilified his enemies he found in bad taste.

"We each have to analyze one poem in *Songs of Experience*. I'm supposed to do the 'Nurse's Song.' But they don't know what's going on in that course, he doesn't know what's going on. I've been trying to get through to them but they're all doing the one-up thing, they don't know what's happening. They sit there and pull each other's papers apart, I mean, they don't know what poetry's supposed to be *for*." She wasn't drinking her tea.

"When's it due?" he asked, keeping on neutral ground.

"Next week. But I'm not going to do it, not the way *they* want. I'm giving them one of my own poems. That says it all. I mean, if they have to read one right there in the class they'll get what Blake was trying to do with *cadences*. I'm getting it xeroxed." She hesitated, less sure of herself. "Do you think that'll be all right?"

Morrison wondered what he would do if one of his own students tried such a ploy. He hadn't thought of Louise as the poetry-writing type. "Have you checked with the professor about it?"

"I try to talk to him," she said. "I try to *help* him but I can't get *through* to him. If they don't get what I mean though I'll know they're all phonies and I can just walk out." She was twisting her cup on the table top, her lips were trembling.

Morrison felt his loyalties were being divided; also he didn't want her to cry, that would involve dangerous comforting pats, even an arm around her shoulder. He tried to shut out an involuntary quick image of himself on top of her in the middle of the kitchen floor, getting white latex all over her fur. *Not today*, his mind commanded, pleaded.

As if in answer the reverberations of an organ boomed from beneath their feet, accompanied by a high quavering voice: *Rock of a-ges, cleft for me . . . Let me HIIIDE myself. . . .* Louise took it as a signal. "I have to go," she said. She got up and went out as abruptly as she had come, thanking him perfunctorily for the tea she hadn't drunk.

The organ was a Hammond, owned by the woman downstairs, a native. When her husband and nubile child were home she shouted at them. The rest of the time she ran the vacuum cleaner or picked out hymn tunes and old favourites on the organ with two fingers, singing to herself. The organ was to Morrison the most annoying. At first he tried to ignore it; then he put on opera records, attempting to drown it out. Finally he recorded it with his tape recorder. When the noise got too aggravating he would aim the speakers down the hot air register and run the tape through as loudly as possible. It gave him a sense of participation, of control.

He did this now, admiring the way the tape clashed with what she was currently playing: "Whispering Hope" with an overlay of "Annie Laurie"; "The Last Rose of Summer" counterpointing "Come to the Church in the Wildwood." He was surprised at how much he was able to hate her: he had only seen her once, looking balefully out at him from between her hideous flowered drapes as he wallowed through the snow on his way to the garage. Her husband was supposed to keep the walk shovelled but didn't.

Louise came back the next day before Morrison was up. He was awake but he could tell by the chill in the room—his breath was visible—and by the faint smell of oil that something had gone wrong with the furnace again. It was less trouble to stay in bed, at least till the sun was well risen, than to get up and try the various ways of keeping warm.

When the buzzer went he pulled a blanket around himself and stumbled to the door.

"I thought of something," Louise said tragically. She was in the door before he could fend her off.

"I'm afraid it's cold in here," he said.

"I had to come over and tell you. I don't use the phone any more. You should have yours taken out."

She stomped the snow from her boots while Morrison retreated into the livingroom. There was a thick crust of frost on the insides of the windows; he lit the gas fireplace. Louise stalked impatiently around the uncarpeted floor.

"You aren't listening," she said. He looked out obediently at her from his blanket. "What I thought of is this: *The city has no right to be here.* I mean, why is it? No city should be here, this far north: it isn't even on a lake or an important river, even. Why is it here?" She clasped her hands, gazing at him as though everything depended on his answer.

Morrison, standing on one bare foot, reflected that he had often since his arrival asked himself the same question. "It started as a trading post," he said, shivering.

"But it doesn't *look* like one. It doesn't look like anything, it doesn't *have* anything, it could be anywhere. Why is it *here?*" She implored; she even clutched a corner of his blanket.

Morrison shied away. "Look," he said, "do you mind if I get some clothes on?"

"Which room are they in?" she asked suspiciously.

"The bedroom," he said.

"That's all right. That room's all right," she said.

Contrary to his fear she made no attempt to follow him in. When he was dressed he returned to find her sitting on the floor with a piece of paper. "We have to complete the circle," she said. "We need the others."

"What others?" He decided she was overtired, she had been working too hard: she had deep red blotches around her eyes and the rest of her face was pale green.

"I'll draw you a diagram of it," she said. But instead she sat on the floor, jabbing at the paper with the pencil point. "I wanted to work out my own system," she said plaintively, "but they wouldn't let me." A tear slid down her cheek.

"Maybe you need to talk to someone," Morrison said, over-casually.

She raised her head. "But I'm talking to you. Oh," she said, reverting to her office voice, "you mean a shrink. I saw one earlier. He said I was very sane and a genius. He took a reading of my head: he said the patterns in my brain are the same as Julius Caesar's, only his were military and mine are creative." She started jabbing with the pencil again.

"I'll make you a peanut butter sandwich," Morrison said, offering the only thing he himself wanted right then. It did not occur to him until months later when he was remembering it to ask himself how anyone could have known about the patterns in Julius Caesar's brain. At the moment he was wondering whether Louise might not in fact be a genius. He felt helpless because of his own inability to respond; she would think him as obtuse as the others, whoever they were.

At first she did not want him to go into the kitchen: she knew the telephone was in there. But he promised not to use it. When he came out again with a piece

of bread on which he had spread with difficulty the
gelid peanut butter, she was curled inside her coat
in front of the fire, sleeping. He laid the bread gently
beside her as if leaving crumbs on a stump for unseen
animals. Then he changed his mind, retrieved it, took
it on tiptoe into the kitchen and ate it himself. He
turned on the oven, opened the oven door, wrapped
himself in a blanket from the bedroom and read Mar-
vell.

She slept for nearly three hours; he didn't hear her
get up. She appeared in the kitchen doorway, looking
much better, though a greyish-green pallor still lingered around her mouth and eyes.

"That was just what I needed," she said in her
old brisk voice. "Now I must be off; I have lots of work
to do." Morrison took his feet off the stove and saw her
to the door.

"Don't fall," he called after her cheerfully as she
went down the steep wooden steps, her feet hidden
under the rim of her coat. The steps were icy, he
didn't keep them cleared properly. His landlady was
afraid someone would slip on them and sue her.

At the bottom Louise turned and waved at him.
The air was thickening with ice fog, frozen water
particles held in suspension; if you ran a horse in it,
they'd told him, the ice pierced its lungs and it bled
to death. But they hadn't told him that till after he'd
trotted to the university in it one morning when the
car wouldn't start and complained aloud in the coffee
room about the sharp pains in his chest.

He watched her out of sight around the corner of
the house. Then he went back to the livingroom
with a sense of recapturing lost territory. Her pencil
and the paper she had used, covered with dots and
slashing marks, an undeciphered code, were still by
the fireplace. He started to crumple the paper up,
but instead folded it carefully and put it on the
mantelpiece where he kept his unanswered letters.
After that he paced the apartment, conscious of his

own work awaiting him but feeling as though he had nothing to do.

Half an hour later she was back again; he discovered he had been expecting her. Her face was mournful, all its lines led downwards as though tiny hands were pulling at the jawline skin.

"Oh, you have to come out," she said, pleading. "You have to come out, there's too much fog."

"Why don't you come in?" Morrison said. That would be easier to handle. Maybe she'd been into something, if that was all it was he could wait it out. He'd been cautious himself; it was a small place and the local pusher was likely to be one of your own students; also he had no desire to reduce his mind to oatmeal mush.

"No," she said, "I can't go through this door any more. It's wrong. You have to come out." Her face became crafty, as though she was planning. "It will do you good to get out for a walk," she said reasonably.

She was right, he didn't get enough exercise. He pulled on his heavy boots and went to find his coat.

As they creaked and slid along the street Louise was pleased with herself, triumphant; she walked slightly ahead of him as if determined to keep the lead. The ice fog surrounded them, deadened their voices, it was crystallizing like a growth of spruce needles on the telephone wires and the branches of the few trees which he could not help thinking of as stunted, though to the natives, he supposed, they must represent the normal size for trees. He took care not to breathe too deeply. A flock of grosbeaks whirred and shrilled up ahead, picking the last few red berries from a mountain ash.

"I'm glad it isn't sunny," Louise said. "The sun was burning out the cells in my brain, but I feel a lot better now."

Morrison glanced at the sky. The sun was up there

somewhere, marked by a pale spot in the otherwise
evenly spread grey. He checked an impulse to shield
his eyes and thereby protect his brain cells: he realized it was an attempt to suppress the undesired
knowledge that Louise was disturbed or, out with it,
she was crazy.

"Living here isn't so bad," Louise said, skipping
girlishly on the hard-packed snow. "You just have to
have inner resources. I'm glad I have them; I think I
have more than you, Morrison. I have more than most
people. That's what I said to myself when I moved
here."

"Where are we going?" Morrison asked when they
had accomplished several blocks. She had taken him
west, along a street he was not familiar with, or was
it the fog?

"To find the others, of course," she said, glancing
back at him contemptuously. "We have to complete
the circle."

Morrison followed without protest; he was relieved
there would soon be others.

She stopped in front of a medium-tall highrise.
"They're inside," she said. Morrison went towards the
front door, but she tugged at his arm.

"You can't go in that door," she said. "It's facing
the wrong way. It's the wrong door."

"What's the matter with it?" Morrison asked. It
might be the wrong door (and the longer he looked
at it, plate glass and shining evilly, the more he saw
what she meant), but it was the only one.

"It faces east," she said. "Don't you know? The city
is polarized north and south; the river splits it in two;
the poles are the gas plant and the power plant.
Haven't you ever noticed the bridge joins them
together? That's how the current gets across. We
have to keep the poles in our brains lined up with
the poles of the city, that's what Blake's poetry is all
about. You can't break the current."

"Then how do we get in?" he said. She sat down

in the snow; he was afraid again she was going to cry.

"Listen," he said hastily, "I'll go in the door sideways and bring them out; that way I won't break the current. You won't have to go through the door at all. Who are they?" he asked as an afterthought.

When he recognized the name he was elated: she wasn't insane after all, the people were real, she had a purpose and a plan. This was probably just an elaborate way of arranging to see her friends.

They were the Jamiesons. Dave was one of those with whom Morrison had exchanged pleasantries in the hallways but nothing further. His wife had a recent baby. Morrison found them in their Saturday shirts and jeans. He tried to explain what he wanted, which was difficult because he wasn't sure. Finally he said he needed help. Only Dave could come, the wife had to stay behind with the baby.

"I hardly know Louise, you know," Dave volunteered in the elevator.

"Neither do I," said Morrison.

Louise was waiting behind a short fir tree on the front lawn. She came out when she saw them. "Where's the baby?" she said. "We need the baby to complete the circle. We *need* the baby. Don't you know the country will split apart without it?" She stamped her foot at them angrily.

"We can come back for it," Morrison said, which pacified her. She said there were only two others they had to collect; she explained that they needed people from both sides of the river. Dave Jamieson suggested they take his car, but Louise was now off cars: they were as bad as telephones, they had no fixed directions. She wanted to walk. At last they persuaded her onto the bus, pointing out that it ran north and south. She had to make certain first that it went over the right bridge, the one near the gas plant.

The other couple Louise had named lived in an apartment overlooking the river. She seemed to have picked them not because they were special friends but because from their livingroom, which she had been in once, both the gas plant and the power plant were visible. The apartment door faced south; Louise entered the building with no hesitation.

Morrison was not overjoyed with Louise's choice. This couple was foremost among the local anti-Americans: he had to endure Paul's bitter sallies almost daily in the coffee room, while Leota at staff parties had a way of running on in his presence about the wicked Americans and then turning to him and saying, mouth but not eyes gushing, "Oh, but I forgot—*you're* an American." He had found the best defence was to agree. "You Yanks are coming up and taking all our jobs," Paul would say, and Morrison would nod affably. "That's right, you shouldn't let it happen. I wonder why you hired me?" Leota would start in about how the Americans were buying up all the industry, and Morrison would say, "Yes, it's a shame. Why are you selling it to us?" He saw their point, of course, but he wasn't Procter and Gamble. What did they want him to do? What were they doing themselves, come to think of it? But Paul had once broken down after too many beers in the Faculty Club and confided that Leota had been thin when he married her but now she was fat. Morrison held the memory of that confession as a kind of hostage.

He had to admit though that on this occasion Paul was much more efficient than he himself was capable of being. Paul saw at once what it had taken Morrison hours, perhaps weeks, to see: that something was wrong with Louise. Leota decoyed her into the kitchen with a glass of milk while Paul conspired singlehandedly in the livingroom.

"She's crazy as a coot. We've got to get her to the loony bin. We'll pretend to go along with her, this circle business, and when we get her downstairs we'll grab her and stuff her into my car. How long has this been going on?"

Morrison didn't like the sound of the words "grab" and "stuff." "She won't go in cars," he said.

"Hell," said Paul, "I'm not walking in this bloody weather. Besides, it's miles. We'll use force if necessary." He thrust a quick beer at each of them, and when he judged they ought to have finished they all went into the kitchen and Paul carefully told Louise that it was time to go.

"Where?" Louise asked. She scanned their faces: she could tell they were up to something. Morrison felt guilt seeping into his eyes and turned his head away.

"To get the baby," Paul said. "Then we can form the circle."

Louise looked at him strangely. "What baby? What circle?" she said testing him.

"*You* know," Paul said persuasively. After a moment she put down her glass of milk, still almost full, and said she was ready.

At the car she balked. "Not in there," she said, planting her feet. "I'm not going in there." When Paul gripped her arm and said, soothingly and menacingly, "Now be a good girl," she broke away from him and ran down the street, stumbling and sliding. Morrison didn't have the heart to run after her; already he felt like a traitor. He watched stupidly while Dave and Paul chased after her, catching her at last and half-carrying her back; they held her wriggling and kicking inside her fur coat as though it was a sack. Their breath came out in white spurts.

"Open the back door, Morrison," Paul said, sergeant-like, giving him a scornful glance as though he was good for nothing else. Morrison obeyed and Louise was thrust in, Dave holding her more or less by the scruff of the neck and Paul picking up her feet. She did not resist as much as Morrison expected. He got in on one side of her; Dave was on the other. Leota, who had waddled down belatedly, had reached the front seat; once they were in motion she turned around and made false, cheering-up noises at Louise.

"Where are they taking me?" Louise whispered to

Morrison. "It's to the hospital, isn't it?" She was almost hopeful, perhaps she had been depending on them to do this. She snuggled close to Morrison, rubbing her thigh against his; he tried not to move away.

As they reached the outskirts she whispered to him again. "This is silly, Morrison. They're being silly, aren't they? When we get to the next stoplight, open the door on your side and we'll jump out and run away. We'll go to my place."

Morrison smiled wanly at her, but he was almost inclined to try it. Although he knew he couldn't do anything to help her and did not want the responsibility anyway, he also didn't want his mind burdened with whatever was going to happen to her next. He felt like someone appointed to a firing squad: it was not his choice, it was his duty, no one could blame him.

There was less ice fog now. The day was turning greyer, bluer: they were moving east, away from the sun. The mental clinic was outside the city, reached by a curving, expressionless driveway. The buildings were the same assemblage of disparate once-recent styles as those at the university: the same jarring fragmentation of space, the same dismal failure at modishness. Government institutions, Morrison thought; they were probably done by the same architect.

Louise was calm as they went to the reception entrance. Inside was a glass-fronted cublicle, decorated with rudimentary Christmas bells cut from red and green construction paper. Louise stood quietly, listening with an amused, tolerant smile, while Paul talked with the receptionist; but when a young intern appeared she said, "I must apologize for my friends; they've been drinking and they're trying to play a practical joke on me."

The intern frowned enquiringly. Paul blustered, relating Louise's theories of the circle and the poles. She denied everything and told the intern he should call the police; a joke was a joke but this was a misuse of public property.

Paul appealed to Morrison: he was her closest friend. "Well," Morrison hedged, "she *was* acting a little strange, but maybe not enough to. . . ." His eyes trailed off to the imitation-modern interior, the corridors leading off into god knew where. Along one of the corridors a listless figure shuffled.

Louise was carrying it off so well, she was so cool, she had the intern almost convinced; but when she saw she was winning she lost her grip. Giving Paul a playful shove on the chest, she said, "We don't need *your* kind here. *You* won't get into the circle." She turned to the intern and said gravely, "Now I have to go. My work is very important, you know. I'm preventing the civil war."

After she had been registered, her few valuables taken from her and locked in the safe ("So they won't be stolen by the patients," the receptionist said), her house keys delivered to Morrison at her request, she disappeared down one of the corridors between two interns. She was not crying, nor did she say goodbye to any of them, though she gave Morrison a dignified, freezing nod. "I expect you to bring my notebook to me," she said with a pronounced English accent. "The black one, I need it. You'll find it on my desk. And I'll need some underwear. Leota can bring that."

Morrison, shamed and remorseful, promised he would visit.

When they got back to the city they dropped Dave Jamieson off at his place; then the three of them had pizza and cokes together. Paul and Leota were friendlier than usual: they wanted to find out more. They leaned across the table, questioning, avid, prying; they were enjoying it. This, he realized, was for them the kind of entertainment the city could best afford.

Afterwards they all went to Louise's cellar to gather up for her those shreds of her life she had asked them to allow her. Leota found the underwear (surprisingly frilly, most of it purple and black) after an indecently long search through Louise's bureau drawers; he and

Paul tried to decide which of the black notebooks on her desk she would want. There were eight or nine of them; Paul opened a few and read excerpts at random, though Morrison protested weakly. References to the poles and the circle dated back several months; before he had known her, Morrison thought.

In her notebooks Louise had been working out her private system, in aphorisms and short poems which were thoroughly sane in themselves but which taken together were not; though, Morrison reflected, the only difference is that she's taken as real what the rest of us pretend is only metaphorical. Between the aphorisms were little sketches like wiring diagrams, quotations from the English poets, and long detailed analyses of her acquaintances at the university.

"Here's you, Morrison," Paul said with a relishing chuckle. " 'Morrison is not a complete person. He needs to be completed, he refuses to admit his body is part of his mind. He can be in the circle possibly, but only if he will surrender his role as a fragment and show himself willing to merge with the greater whole.' Boy, she must've been nutty for months."

They were violating her, entering her privacy against her will. "Put that away," Morrison said, more sharply than he ordinarily dared speak to Paul. "We'll take the half-empty notebook, that must be the one she meant."

There were a dozen or so library books scattered around the room, some overdue: geology and history for the most part, and one volume of Blake. Leota volunteered to take them back.

As he was about to slip the catch on the inside lock Morrison glanced once more around the room. He could see now where it got its air of pastiche: the bookcase was a copy of the one in Paul's livingroom, the prints and the table were almost identical with those at the Jamiesons'. Other details stirred dim images of objects half-noted in the various houses, at the various but nearly identical get-acquainted parties.

Poor Louise had been trying to construct herself out of the other people she had met. Only from himself had she taken nothing; thinking of his chill interior, embryonic and blighted, he realized it had nothing for her to take.

He kept his promise and went to see her. His first visit was made with Paul and Leota, but he sensed their resentment: they seemed to think their country-woman should be permitted to go mad without witness or participation by any Yanks. After that he drove out by himself in his own car.

On the second visit Louise initially seemed better. They met in a cramped cubicle furnished with two chairs; Louise sat on the edge of hers, her hands folded in her lap, her face polite, withholding. Her English accent was still noticeable, though hard r's surfaced in it from time to time. She was having a good rest, she said; the food was all right and she had met some nice people but she was eager to get back to her work; she worried about who was looking after her students.

"I guess I said some pretty crazy things to you," she smiled.

"Well . . ." Morrison stalled. He was pleased by this sign of her recovery.

"I had it all wrong. I thought I could put the country together by joining the two halves of the city into a circle, using the magnetic currents." She gave a small disparaging laugh, then dropped her voice. "What I hadn't figured out though was that the currents don't flow north and south, like the bridge. They flow east and west, like the river. And I didn't *need* to form the circle out of a bunch of incomplete segments. I didn't even need the baby. I mean," she said in a serious whisper, dropping her accent completely, "I *am* the circle. I have the poles within myself. What I have to do is keep myself in one piece, it *depends* on me."

At the desk he tried to find out what was officially wrong with Louise but they would not tell him anything; it wasn't the policy.

On his next visit she spoke to him almost the whole time in what to his untrained ear sounded like perfectly fluent French. Her mother was a French Protestant, she told him, her father an English Catholic. *"Je peux vous dire tout ceci,"* she said, *"parce que vous êtes americain.* You are outside it." To Morrison this explained a lot; but the next time she claimed to be the daughter of an Italian opera singer and a Nazi general. "Though I also have some Jewish blood," she added hastily. She was tense and kept standing up and sitting down again, crossing and recrossing her legs; she would not look at Morrison directly but addressed her staccato remarks to the centre of his chest.

After this Morrison stayed away for a couple of weeks. He did not think his visits were doing either of them any good, and he had papers to mark. He occupied himself once more with the painting of his apartment and the organ music of the woman downstairs; he shovelled his steps and put salt on them to melt the ice. His landlady, uneasy because she had still not supplied him with a lock, unexpectedly had him to tea, and the tacky plastic grotesqueries of her interior decoration fueled his reveries for a while. The one good thing in her bogus ranch-style bungalow had been an egg, blown and painted in the Ukrainian manner, but she had dismissed it as ordinary, asking him to admire instead a cake of soap stuck with artificial flowers to resemble a flowerpot; she had got the idea out of a magazine. The Korean came up one evening to ask him about life insurance.

But the thought of Louise out there in the windswept institution grounds with nothing and no one she knew bothered him in twinges, like a mental neuralgia, goading him finally into the section of the city that passed for downtown: he would buy her a gift. He selected a small box of water-colour paints: she ought to have something to do. He was intending to mail it, but sooner than he expected he found himself again on the wide deserted entrance driveway.

They met once more in the visitors' cubicle. He was alarmed by the change in her: she had put on weight, her muscles had slackened, her breasts drooped. Instead of sitting rigidly as she had done before, she sprawled in the chair, legs apart, arms hanging; her hair was dull and practically uncombed. She was wearing a short skirt and purple stockings, in one of which there was a run. Trying not to stare at this run and at the white, loose thigh flesh it revealed, Morrison had the first unmistakably physical stirrings of response he had ever felt towards her.

"They have me on a different drug," she said. "The other one was having the wrong effect. I was allergic to it." She mentioned that someone had stolen her hairbrush, but when he offered to bring her another one she said it didn't matter. She had lost interest in the circle and her elaborate system and did not seem to want to talk much. What little she said was about the hospital itself: she was trying to help the doctors, they didn't know how to treat the patients but they wouldn't listen to her. Most of those inside were getting worse rather than better; many had to stay there because no one would take the responsibility of looking after them, even if they were drugged into manageability. They were poor, without relations; the hospital would not let them go away by themselves. She told him about one girl from further north who thought she was a cariboo.

She hardly glanced at the water-colour paints, though she thanked him sluggishly. Her eyes, normally wide and vivacious, were puffed shut nearly to slits and her skin appeared to have darkened. She reminded him of someone, though it took him several minutes to remember: it was an Indian woman he had seen early in the fall while he was still searching for a place to have a civilized drink. She had been sitting outside a cheap hotel with her legs apart, taking off her clothes and chanting, "Come on boys, what're you waiting for, come on boys, what're you waiting for." Around her a group of self-conscious, sniggering men had gathered. Morrison, against his will and appalled at her, the men, and himself, had joined them. She was naked to the waist when the police got there.

When he rose to say goodbye Louise asked him, as if it was a matter of purely academic interest, whether he thought she would ever get out.

On his way out to the car it struck him that he loved her. The thought filled him like a goal, a destiny. He would rescue her somehow; he could pretend she was his cousin or sister; he would keep her hidden in the apartment with all his dangerous implements, razors, knives, nailfiles, locked away; he would feed her, give her the right drugs, comb her hair. At night she would be there in the sub-zero bedroom for him to sink into as into a swamp, warm and obliterating.

This picture at first elated, then horrified him. He saw that it was only the hopeless, mad Louise he wanted, the one devoid of any purpose or defence. A sane one, one that could judge him, he would never be able to handle. So this was his dream girl then, his ideal woman found at last: a disintegration, mind returning to its component shards of matter, a defeated formless creature on which he could inflict himself like shovel on earth, axe on forest, use without being used, know without being known. Louise's notebook entry, written when she had surely been saner than she was now, had been right about him. Yet in self-defence he reasoned that his desire for her was not altogether evil: it was in part a desire to be reunited with his own body, which he felt less and less that he actually occupied.

Oppressed by himself and by the building, the prison he had just left, he turned when he reached the main road away from the city instead of towards it:

he would take his car for a run. He drove through the clenched landscape, recalling with pain the gentle drawl of the accommodating hills east and south, back in that settled land which was so far away it seemed not to exist. Here everything was tightlipped, ungiving, good for nothing and nothing.

He was halfway to the zoo before he knew he was going there. Louise had said it was kept open all winter.

Not much of the day was left when he reached the entrance: he would be driving back in darkness. He would have to make his visit short, he did not want to be caught inside when they locked the gates. He paid the admission fee to the scarfed and muffled figure in the booth, then took his car along the empty drives, glancing out the side window at the herds of llama, of yak, the enclosure of the Siberian tiger in which only the places a tiger might hide were to be seen.

At the buffalo field he stopped the car and got out. The buffalo were feeding near the wire fence, but at his approach they lifted their heads and glared at him, then snorted and rocked away from him through the haunch-deep snowdunes.

He plodded along the fence, not caring that the wind was up and chilling him through his heavy coat, the blood retreating from his toes. Thin sinister fingers of blown snow were creeping over the road; on the way back he would have to watch for drifts. He imagined the snow rising up, sweeping down in great curves, in waves over the city, each house a tiny centre of man-made warmth, fending it off. By the grace of the power plant and the gas plant: a bomb, a catastrophe to each and the houses would close like eyes. He thought of all the people he barely knew, how they would face it, chopping up their furniture for firewood until the cold overcame. How they were already facing it, the Koreans' fishes fluttering on the clothesline like defiant silver flags, the woman downstairs shrilling "Whispering Hope" off-key into the blizzard, Paul in the flimsy armour of his cheap nationalism, the landlady holding aloft torchlike her bar of soap stuck with artificial flowers. Poor Louise, he saw now what she had been trying desperately to do: the point of the circle, closed and self-sufficient, was not what it included but what it shut out. His own efforts to remain human, futile work and sterile love, what happened when it was all used up, what would he be left with? Black trees on a warm orange wall; and he had painted everything white. . . .

Dizzy with cold, he leaned against the fence, forehead on mittened hand. He was at the wolf pen. He remembered it from his trip with Louise. They had stood there for some time waiting for the wolves to come over to them but they had kept to the far side. Three of them were near the fence now though, lying in its shelter. An old couple, a man and a woman in nearly identical grey coats, were standing near the wolves. He had not noticed them earlier, no cars had passed him, they must have walked from the parking lot. The eyes of the wolves were yellowish grey: they looked out through the bars at him, alert, neutral.

"Are they timber wolves?" Morrison said to the old woman. Opening his mouth to speak, he was filled with a sudden chill rush of air.

The woman turned to him slowly: her face was a haze of wrinkles from which her eyes stared up at him, blue, glacial.

"You from around here?" she asked.

"No," Morrison said. Her head swung away; she continued to look through the fence at the wolves, nose to the wind, short white fur ruffled up on edge.

Morrison followed her fixed gaze: something was being told, something that had nothing to do with him, the thing you could learn only after the rest was finished with and discarded. His body was numb; he swayed. In the corner of his eye the old woman swelled, wavered, then seemed to disappear, and the land opened before him. It swept away to the north and he thought he could see the mountains, white-covered, their crests glittering in the falling sun, then forest upon forest, after that the barren tundra and the blank solid rivers, and beyond, so far that the endless night had already descended, the frozen sea.

Under Glass

o o o

I'm feeling better. For once the sky is out, there's a breeze, I'm walking through the ellipses and arranged vistas of the park, the trees come solidly up through the earth as though they belong there, nothing wavers. I have confidence in the grass and the distant buildings, they can take care of themselves, they don't need my attention on them to keep them together, my eyes holding them down.

The steam-covered mothers and shrill, hyperthyroid children of yesterday's trip to the zoo are far away, the traces they have left in me are faint as grease smudges and scratchings of twigs on window panes. That was a risk I shouldn't have taken, it would have been cleverer to have waited, but I managed it. I even made it through the Moonlight Pavilion, darkened tunnels full of screaming, the goggling rodents and shrunken foetal-headed primates deluded by the grey light into going about their lives, so publicly, behind the soundproof panels. I enjoy knowing I can do it without anyone to help.

I pass the 7-B greenhouse: it glitters, it beckons. Inside are the plants that look like stones, their fleshy lobed leaves knuckle-sized and mottled so that they blend perfectly with the pebbles. I was pleased at first to have discovered them. I think with a kind of horror at myself of the hours I've spent watching them, all of us keeping quite still. Today, however, the greenhouse has no attraction: I walk on two legs, I wear clothes.

In the street outside the station I go shopping. It feels new, my legs ripple as though I've just gotten out of a wheelchair. I buy little brown paper parcels and stow them away inside my serviceable black bag with handles on it like a doctor's. Bread and butter, grapes, greengages which he has probably never had before but we must all try different experiences. Before I zip the bag I rearrange the packages to safeguard the rose, encased in plastic wrap with stem swathed in wet toilet paper. Redundant. It's a gift though and I'm proud of myself for being able, we don't do much of that. I cut it in the garden, which isn't mine. I admire roses but I've never wanted to be one, maybe that's why I'm not worrying much about whether the stem hurts.

What part of a rose bush is the body? Last night I dreamed I had a baby which was the right size and colour. It's a healthy sign, maybe I'll be able to after all, the way other women are supposed to. Usually when I dream of babies they are scrawny as kittens, pale greenish and highly intelligent; they talk in polysyllables and I know they aren't mine but are creatures from another planet sent to take over the earth, or that they are dead. Sometimes they're covered with fur. But last night's was pink and reassuringly illiterate; it cried. He ought to find this promising, he wants to have sons. I've thought about it, I've even gone so far as to read a couple of books on exercises and what they call natural childbirth, though having a gourd or a tomato would surely be more pleasant and useful these days than having a baby, the world has no need of my genes. That's an excuse though.

I put the bag on my knees and keep hold of the handles. It's playing house, we both know I can't cook him anything till he gets his stove repaired, which somehow he postpones: still it's the first domestic thing I've ever done for him. He ought to approve, he's obliged to approve, he'll see it's getting better. I'm feeling so good I even look at other people in the train, their faces and clothes, noticing them, wondering about their lives. See how kind I am, what a cornucopia.

The cement stairway going down to his door smells of piss and antiseptic; I hold my breath as usual. I look in through the letter flap: he isn't up, so I let myself in with my key. His two-room flat is more untidy than last time but it's been worse. Today the dust and litter leave my skin alone. I set my black bag on the table and go through to the bedroom.

He's on the bed, asleep in a tangled net of blankets, on his back with his knees up. I'm always afraid to wake him: I remember the stories about men who kill in their sleep with their eyes open, thinking the woman is a burglar or an enemy soldier. You can't be convicted for it. I touch him on the leg and stand back, ready to run, but he wakes immediately and turns his head towards me.

"Hi," he says. "Jesus I'm hung over."

It's rude of him to be hung over when I've come all this way to see him. "I brought you a flower," I say, determined to be calm and cheerful.

I go out to the other room and unwind the rose from its toilet paper and look for something to put it in. There's a stack of never-used plates in his cupboard, the rest of the space is books and papers. I find a lone glass and fill it with water at the sink. Forks and knives, also unused, are rusting in the drainer. I list to myself the things he needs: a vase, more glasses, a dishtowel.

I carry the rose in to him and he sniffs at it dutifully and I set the glass beside the alarm clock on the improvised table, two chairs and a board. He would really like to go back to sleep, but he compromises by pulling me down beside him and involving me in the blankets. His head seeks the hollow between my shoulder and collarbone and he closes his eyes.

"I've missed you," he says. Why should he have missed me, I've only been gone five days. The last time wasn't good, I was nervous, the wallpaper was bothering me and the bright peel-off stick-on butter-flies on the cupboard, not his, prior to him. He kisses me: he does have a hangover, his mouth tastes of used wine, tobacco resin and urban decay. He doesn't want to make love, I can tell, I stroke his head un-derstandingly; he nuzzles. I think again of the Moon-light Pavilion, the Slow Loris creeping cautiously through its artificial world, water dishes and wither-ing branches, its eyes large with apprehension, its baby clutched to its fur.

"Want to have lunch?" he says. This is his way of telling me he's in no shape.

"I brought it. Or most of it anyway. I'll go round the corner and get the rest. It's healthier than those greasy hamburgers and chips."

"Great," he says, but he makes no move to get up.

"Have you been taking your vitamin pills?" They were my idea, I was afraid he'd get scurvy, eating the way he does. I always take them myself. I feel him nod ritualistically.

I can't see whether he's telling the truth. I turn over so I'm looking down at him. "Who were you drink-ing with? Did you go out after you moved the furni-ture?"

"The furniture was already moved when I got there. She couldn't call to tell me." That's true, he has no phone; our conversations take place in booths. "She wanted to go out and drink instead. I spilled chop suey all over myself," he says with self-pity.

I am supposed to commiserate. "Was it digested or undigested?" I ask.

"I hadn't touched a bite of it."

I'm surprised at her for being so obvious, but then

she's always seemed unsubtle, blunt and straightforward, captain of a women's basketball team, no, highschool gym teacher with whistle in mouth. An old friend. No nonsense. Mine had bloomers and skinny legs and made jokes about what she called The Cramps in a way that suggested we weren't supposed to have them. Trampolines, the body contorted, made to perform, the mind barking orders.

"She's been trying to seduce you for months," I say, smiling; the thought amuses me, she looks like a marmot. At this he tries to shrug, but I have him pinned, one arm across the neck. "Did she succeed?"

"By the time we got out of the bar the subway was closed."

I hadn't been serious, but this is suddenly a confession. I want to ignore it but I go on. "You mean she spent the night here?"

"As opposed to trying to get all the way back to her place," he says, "yes." It would be a reason like that. Logical as hell.

What do you think you are, the YWCA, I want to say, but instead I ask the obvious. "I suppose you slept with her." My voice is steady, I'm steady too, I won't let it tip me.

"It was her idea. I was drunk." He thinks both these things are good excuses.

"Why did you tell me?" If he hadn't told me and I'd found out I'd say, Why didn't you tell me; I know this while I'm asking it.

"You could have figured it out for yourself, the alarm's set for eight."

"What does that mean?" I say; I don't connect. I'm cold, I get up off the bed and move backwards towards the doorway.

I am sitting in a brand-new hamburger palace; across the table from me is a man eating a cheeseburger. Feeding places are the only chances I have to watch him: the rest of the time I'm looking at the blurs through taxi windows or tracing the unfamiliar wallpaper designs. The colour of his face matches the formica tabletops: off-white. At other tables are other men, also eating cheeseburgers and being watched by other women. We all have our coats on. The air shimmers with rock music and the smell of exhausted french fries. Though it is winter the room reminds me of a beach, even to the crumpled paper napkins and pop bottles discarded here and there and the slightly gritty texture of the cheeseburgers.

He pushes away his cole slaw.

"You should eat it," I say.

"No no; can't eat vegies," he says. The suppressed dietician in me notes that he is probably suffering from a vitamin A deficiency. I should have been a health inspector, or maybe an organic farmer.

"I'll trade you then," I say. "I'll eat your cole slaw if you'll finish my cheeseburger."

He thinks there's a catch somewhere but decides to risk it. The switch is made and we both examine our halves of the deal. Beyond the plate-glass window slush drifts from the night sky, inside though we are lighted, safe and warm, filtering music through our gills as though it's oxygen.

He finishes my cheeseburger and lights a cigarette. I'm annoyed with him for some reason, though I can't recall which. I thumb my card-file of nasty remarks, choose one: You make love like a cowboy raping a sheep. I've been waiting for the right time to say that, but maybe peace is more important.

Not for him; hunger satisfied, he turns back to an earlier argument. "You're trying to see how much shit I'll take, aren't you?" he says. "Stop treating me like a nine-year-old."

"There's one good way to keep me from treating you like one," I say. What I mean is that he should stop acting like one, but he doesn't bite. In fact he may not even have heard: the music is louder.

"Let's split," he says, and we get up. I check the cashier as we go out: cashiers fill me with dismay, I want them to be happy but they never are. This one is waterlogged and baggy, saturated with too much sound and too many french fries. She is apathetic rather than surly. Fight back, I tell her silently.

We hit the air and walk, not touching. I can't remember what he did but he won't get away with it. He's wearing a long khaki army surplus coat with brass buttons; it's handsome, but right now it only reminds me of my fear of doormen, bus drivers and postal officials, those who use their uniforms as excuses. I steer my course so he will have to go through all the puddles. If I can't win, I tell him, neither can you. I was saner then, I had defences.

"I never get up at eight. She had to go to work." He's conscious now that I'm not going to laugh with him over this one as I have over the others. "If you'd been here it wouldn't have happened," he says, trying to put it off on me.

I see it so clearly, in such an ordinary light, I know what he did, how he moved, what he said even, one warm body attracts another, it's how people behave and I want to be sick. More, I want to take my carefully selected brown paper parcels and shove them down his never-cleaned toilet, which I even—crown of idiocy—had thoughts of cleaning for him, poor thing, no one ever showed him how to do it. Where they belong. So this is what it would be like, me picking up his dirty socks and cigarette butts in my experienced way, woman's greatest joy, safely eight months pregnant so you can't get out of it now, grunting away at the natural childbirth exercises while he's off screwing whatever was propped against him when he hit the mystic number of drinks. A spiritual relationship with you, he said, and merely physical ones with the others. Shove that. What does he think I saw in him in the first place, his remarkable soul?

"I'm going out to do some shopping," I say. I'm too visible here, desert mice with their burrows running down the side of the glass, what an intrusion I thought at the time. "Do you want me to come back?"

This is the call to repentance, he nods without speaking, he really is unhappy but I don't have time to think about that, I have to get out where there are a lot more around me, camouflage. I'm careful not to slam the door, I cross to the market street and dig in among the crowd of shoppers.

It's a room, with bed, dressing table surmounted by mirror, night table plus lamp and telephone, linoleum-patterned drapes covering the windows which in their turn cover the night and a drop of ten stories to molten lights and metal parts, hall opening on bathroom which includes a sink and two taps, hot and cold, closed door. Outside the door is another hall and a line of similar closed doors. It is all correct, all in place though slightly dented around the edges. I've been trying to sleep in the bed, with no success. I'm going back and forth across the floor, raising from the carpet an airport smell of upholstery cleaner. Earlier there was a tray with steak rinds and shreds of old salad on it, but I set it out in the hall a long time ago.

From time to time I open the windows and the room is inundated with traffic noise as though it is part of a city-sized motor; then I close the windows and the room heats again, internal combustion engine. Sometimes I go into the bathroom and turn the taps on and off, taking drinks of water and sleeping pills, it gives me the illusion of action. I also look at my watch. It's early spring, there are no leaves and no snow; the days have too much sun, it shows the dust on everything, it hurts your eyes. Three hours ago he phoned to say he would be home in half an hour. He speaks of this room where we have never been before and will never be again as home, I suppose because I'm in it. I'm in it and I can't get out, he has the key, where would I go, it's a foreign city. I work out plans: I'll pack now, leave, he'll come back after being—where is he? He could have been in an accident, he's in the hospital, he's dying, no, he would never do it so neatly. The room will be empty. The room is empty now, I'm a place not a person. I'll go into the bathroom, lock the door, lie down in the tub

with my arms crossed in the lily position, eyes
weighted with invisible pennies. I'll wash down the
rest of the sleeping pills and be found draped over
something, the bureau, the telephone, in a coma.
Their breathing is always described in murder mysteries as 'stertorous,' I've never known what that
meant. He'll come in just as I'm about to fly out the
window into the solid hurricane below, my nightgown
spread out around me like a huge nylon kite. Hold on
to the string, it's tied to my head.

The mechanisms of the room continue their clicking
and gurgling, indifferent. I've turned all the knobs on
the heating unit but nothing happens, maybe I'm not
really here. He ought to be here, he has no right not
to be here, this machine is his creation. I get back
into the bed for the fifth or sixth time and try to concentrate on the shapes moving across my closed eyelids. Sun, dust, bright colours, headlights, a Persian
carpet. There are pictures now, ducks oddly enough,
a woman sitting in a chair, a lawn with a country
house, Grecian portico and all, clocks made of flowers,
a line of dancing cartoon mice, who put them there?
Whoever you are, get me out and I promise I'll never
never again. Next time it will be just from the neck
down, I'll leave his motivations alone.

It was so simple at first, you should have kept it
that way, it's the only thing you can handle. Cool it,
said the doctor, trying to communicate but coming
through like Fred MacMurray in a Walt Disney family picture, take pills. Maybe he's just asserting his
freedom, you're too possessive. He's escaping, you've
driven him to it, into the phone booth and out comes
Superstud. A self-propelling prick with a tiny brain
attached to it like a termite's, couple of drinks and
he'd stick it into anything. Like night-hunting snakes
it has infra-red sensors on the front end, in the dark it
strikes at anything warm. When the lights went on he
was fucking the hot air register.

That's unfair. What really annoys you is that she

got it last night and there wasn't any left for you. Why couldn't he have chosen some other time? He knew I'd be there this morning. He didn't choose it, it just happened. Why can't you see him as a confused human being with problems? Do I ever do anything else? Already I couldn't tell you whether he's my lover or my out-patient. You think you're so magic, you can cure anything. Can't you admit you've failed?

Maybe I'm not a confused human being with problems, maybe I'm something altogether different, an artichoke. . . . None of that.

Actually she's his type, they must have made it fine together, they're both athletic, maybe she keeps time with the whistle, *peep*! they're off. . . .

In a way I admire her, she gets through the days.

When I come back he's dressed and miserable. I move about the room in a parody of domesticity, savaging the bread into sandwiches with his one inadequate knife, sloshing water over the fruit. I open the Pepsi I've brought him.

"Do you have more than one glass?"

He shakes his head. "There's only the one."

I bring the soft-headed rose out of the bedroom, throw it into the clothes hamper he uses for trash, rinse out the glass and pour half of the warm Pepsi into it for myself. That's the nearest I can bring myself to physical anger. He starts to eat; I can't. I'm shivering; I get his coat down from the hook and wrap myself up in it.

"Don't look at me like that," he says.

"Like what?" I say.

I'm not allowed to be angry, he thinks it's unfair. In fact I'm not angry, I'm flipping through my images, trying to find one that will save me from speaking the unforgivable, the words that can't be recalled. Tortoises in cement cubicles, the otters in their green-scummed pool, they were eating, bones and the head of something, no, what about the foxes; they were barking, you couldn't hear them but you could see the insides of their mouths. The achidnas, waddling

through the sawdust like fat fur-coated madwomen,
that's no comfort. Back to the plants, the water-lily
house, and in Greenhouse 12, *Victoria Amazonica*
with her huge plate-shaped leaves six feet across and
her spiky blossom, floating in her pond, her har-
bour, doing nothing at all.

"Look," he says, "I can't stand these silences."

"Then say something."

"Whatever I say you'll think I'm sinister."

"I don't think you're sinister," I say, "I just think
you're thoughtless and stupid. Anyone clever would
wait until after he'd got the woman moved in with
him before starting on that." Part of him, I know,
doesn't want me to move in at all, the stove stays
broken. Hang on to your defences, I think; you'll be
sunk without them.

"I thought it was better to tell the truth right off."

I look at him; he's hurting all right, but I need
my mouthful of flesh, I need back some of that blood.
He's so unhappy though and it isn't his fault, it's just
the way he is, accept me, accept my nervous tics, and
he thinks that's all it is, a kind of involuntary muscle
spasm.

I want to tell him now what no one's ever taught
him, how two people who love each other behave,
how they avoid damaging each other, but I'm not sure
I know. The love of a good woman. But I don't feel
like a good woman right now. My skin is numb,
bloodless as a mushroom. It was wrong of me to think
I could ever accommodate; he's too human. "I'll walk
you to the subway." He can't cope with it, he doesn't
believe in talking it through, he wants me out of the
way. He won't come near me, touch me, doesn't he
know that's all he needs to do? He'll wait for me to
cool off, as he puts it. But if I go away like this I
won't be back.

Outside I put on my sunglasses, though the sun has
gone in. I walk severely, not looking at him, I can't
bear to. The outlines are slipping again, it's an effort
to press the sidewalk down, it billows under my feet

like a mattress. He really is going to take me to the subway and let me disappear without making any effort to stop me. I put my hand on his arm.

"Do you want to talk about it?"

"You just want out," he says, "and you're using this as an excuse."

"That's not true," I say. "If I'd wanted that excuse I could have used it before this." We turn off towards the small park where there is a statue on horseback with a lot of pigeons.

"You're making too much of it," he says. "You always exaggerate."

"Oh, I think I know more or less what happened. You had a few drinks and felt horny, that's all."

"Very perceptive of you," he says. He isn't being ironic, he thinks I've had a genuine though rare insight. He leans forward and takes off my sunglasses so he can see me.

"You can't hide behind those," he says.

The sun gets in and I squint; his face swells, darkens, a paper flower dropped in water. He spreads tendrils; I watch them creeping over my shoulder.

"I wish I didn't love you," I say.

He smiles, his hair scintillating in the parklight, his tie blossoming and receding, his face oriental, inscrutable as an eggplant. I grip the handles on my black bag, force him back to snapshot dimensions.

He kisses my fingers; he thinks we have all been cured. He believes in amnesia, he will never mention it again. It should hurt less each time.

I'm happier though as I go down the stairs to the ticket window. My hands function, exchanging round silver disks for oblong paper. That this can be done, that everyone knows what it means, there may be a chance. If we could do that: I would give him a pebble, a flower, he would understand, he would translate exactly. He would reply, he would give me. . . .

I ponder again his need for more glasses and consider buying him a large bath towel. Once on the train though, I find myself being moved gradually, station by station, back towards the 7-B greenhouse. Soon I will be there; inside are the plants that have taught themselves to look like stones. I think of them; they grow silently, hiding in dry soil, minor events, little zeros, containing nothing but themselves; no food value, to the eye soothing and round, then suddenly nowhere. I wonder how long it takes, how they do it.

The Grave of the Famous Poet

o o o

There are a couple of false alarms before we actually get there, towns we pass through that might be it but aren't, uninformative stores and houses edging the road, no signs. Even when we've arrived we aren't sure; we peer out, looking for a name, an advertisement. The bus pauses.

"This has to be it," I say. I have the map.

"Better ask the driver," he says, not believing me.

"Have I ever been wrong?" I say, but I ask the driver anyway. I'm right again and we get off.

We're in a constricted street of grey flat-fronted houses, their white lace curtains pulled closed, walls rising cliff-straight and lawnless from the narrow sidewalk. There are no other people; at least it isn't a tourist trap. I have to eat, we've been travelling all morning, but he wants to find a hotel first, he always needs a home base. Right in front of us there's a building labelled HOTEL. We hesitate outside it, patting down our hair, trying to look acceptable. When he finally grits up the steps with our suitcase the doors are locked. Maybe it's a pub.

Hoping there may be a place further along, we

walk down the hill, following the long stone wall, crossing the road when the sidewalk disappears at the corners. Cars pass us, driving fast as though on their way to somewhere else.

At the bottom of the hill near the beach there's a smattering of shops and a scarred, listing inn. Radio music and hilarious voices from inside.

"It seems local," I say, pleased.

"What does 'Inn' mean here?" he asks, but I don't know. He goes in to see; then he comes out, dispirited. I'm too tired to think up solutions; I'm scarcely noticing the castle on the hill behind us, the sea.

"No wonder he drank," he says.

"I'll ask," I say, aggrieved: it was his idea, he should do the finding. I try the general store. It's full of people, women mostly, with scarves on their heads and shopping baskets. They say there is no hotel; one woman says her mother has some rooms free though, and she gives me directions while the others gaze pityingly, I'm so obviously a tourist.

The house, when we find it, is eighteenth century and enormous, a summer residence when the town was fashionable. It offers Bed and Breakfast on a modest sign. We're glad to have something spelled out for us. The door is open, we go into the hall, and the woman emerges from the parlour as though startled; she has a forties bobby-soxer hairdo with curious frontal lobes, only it's grey. She's friendly to us, almost sprightly, and yes, she has a room for us. I ask, in a lowered voice, if she can tell us where the grave is.

"You can almost see it right from the window," she says, smiling—she knew we would ask that—and offers to lend us a book with a map in it of the points of interest, his house and all. She gets the book, scampers up the wide maroon-carpeted staircase to show us our room. It's vast, chill, high-ceilinged, with floral wallpaper and white-painted woodwork; instead of curtains the windows have inside shutters. There are three beds and numerous dressers and cupboards, crowded into the room as though in storage, a chunky bureau blocking the once-palatial fireplace. We say it will be fine.

"The grave is just up the hill, that way," she says, pointing through the window. We can see the tip of a church. "I'm sure you'll enjoy it."

I change into jeans and boots while he opens and closes the drawers on all the pieces of furniture, searching for ambushes or reading matter. He discovers nothing and we set out.

We ignore the church—he once said it was unremarkable—and head for the graveyard. It must rain a lot: ivy invades everything, and the graveyard is lush with uncut grass, succulent and light green. Feet have beaten animal-trail paths among the tombstones. The graves themselves are neatly tended, most of them have the grass clipped and fresh flowers in the tea-strainer-shaped flower holders. There are three old ladies in the graveyard now, sheaves of flowers in their arms, gladioli, chrysanthemums; they are moving among the graves, picking out the old flowers and distributing the new ones impartially, like stewardesses. They take us for granted, neither approaching nor avoiding us: we are strangers and as such part of this landscape.

We find the right grave easily enough; as the book says, it's the only one with a wooden cross instead of a stone. The cross has been recently painted and the grave is planted with a miniature formal-garden arrangement of moss roses and red begonias; the sweet alyssum intended for a border hasn't quite worked. I wonder who planned it, surely it wouldn't have been her. The old ladies have been here and have left a vase, yellowish glassware of the kind once found in cereal boxes, with orange dahlias and spikes of an unknown pink flower. We've brought nothing and have no ceremonies to perform; we muse for an acceptable length of time, then retreat to the scroll-worked bench up the hill and sit in the sun, listening to the cows in the field across the road and the mur-

mur of the ladies as they stoop and potter below us,
their print dresses fluttering in the easy wind.

"It's not such a bad place," I say.

"But dull," he answers.

We have whatever it was we came for, the rest of
the day is our own. After a while we leave the graveyard and stroll back down the main street, holding
hands absentmindedly, looking in the windows of the
few shops: an overpriced antique store, a handicrafts
place with pottery and Welsh weaving, a nondescript
store that sells everything, including girlie joke magazines and copies of his books. In the window, half-
hidden among souvenir cups, maps and faded pen-
nants, is a framed photograph of his face, three-quarters profile. We buy a couple of ice-cream bars; they
are ancient and soapy.

We reach the bottom of the winding hill and decide
to walk along to his house, which we can see, an in-
distinct white square separated from us by half a mile
of rough beach. It's his house all right, it was marked
on the map. At first we have no trouble; there's a wide
uneven pathway, broken asphalt, the remains or perhaps the beginning of a road. Above us at the edge of
the steep, leaf-covered cliff, what is left of the castle
totters down, slowly, one stone a year. For him, tur-
rets are irresistible. He finds a scrabbly trail, a children's entrance up sheer mud.

He goes up sideways, crabwise, digging footholds
with the sides of his boots. "Come on!" he shouts
down. I'm hesitant but I follow. At the top he reaches
his hand to me, but, perpendicular and with the earth
beside me, afraid of losing my balance, I avoid it
and scramble the last few feet, holding on to roots. In
wet weather it would be impossible.

He's ahead, eager to explore. The tunnel through
the undergrowth leads to a gap in the castle wall; I
follow his sounds, rustlings, the soft thud of his feet.
We're in the skeleton of a garden, the beds marked
by brick borders now grass-infested, a few rose bushes
still attempting to keep order in spite of the aphids,

nothing else paying any attention. I bend over a rose, ivory hearted, browning at the edges; I feel like a usurper. He's already out of sight again, hidden by an archway.

I catch up to him in the main courtyard. Everything is crumbling, stairways, ramparts, battlements; so much has fallen it's hard for us to get our bearings, translate this rubbish back into its earlier clear plan.

"That must have been the fireplace," I say, "and that's the main gate. We must have come round from the back." For some reason we speak in whispers; he tosses a fragment of stone and I tell him to be careful.

We go up the remnants of a stairway into the keep. It's almost totally dark; the floors are earth-covered. People must come here though, there's an old sack, an unidentifiable piece of clothing. We don't stay long inside: I'm afraid of getting lost, though it's not likely, and I would rather be able to see him. I don't like the thought of finding his hand suddenly on me unannounced. Besides, I don't trust the castle; I expect it to thunder down on us at the first loud laugh or false step. But we make it outside safely.

We pass beneath the gateway, its Norman curve still intact. Outside is another, larger courtyard, enclosed by the wall we have seen from outside and broken through; it has trees, recent trees not more than a hundred years old, dark-foliaged as etchings. Someone must come here to cut the grass: it's short, hair-textured. He lies down on it and draws me down beside him and we rest on our elbows, surveying. From the front the castle is more complete; you can see how it could once have been lived in by real people.

He lies down, closing his eyes, raising his hand to shade them from the sun. He's pale and I realize he must be tired too. I've been thinking of my own lack of energy as something he has caused and must therefore be immune from.

"I'd like to have a castle like that," he says. When he admires something he wants to own it. For an instant I pretend that he does have the castle, he's always been here, he has a coffin hidden in the crypt, if I'm not careful I'll be trapped and have to stay with him forever. If I'd had more sleep last night I'd be able to frighten myself this way but as it is I give up and lean back on the grass beside him, looking up at the trees as their branches move in the wind, every leaf sharpened to a glass-clear edge by my exhaustion.

I turn my head to watch him. In the last few days he's become not more familiar to me as he should have but more alien. Close up, he's a strange terrain, pores and hairs; but he isn't nearer, he's further away, like the moon when you've finally landed on it. I move back from him so I can see him better, he misinterprets, thinking I'm trying to get up, and stretches himself over me to prevent me. He kisses me, teeth digging into my lower lip; when it hurts too much I pull away. We lie side by side, both suffering from unrequited love.

This is an interval, a truce; it can't last, we both know it, there have been too many differences, of opinion we called it but it was more than that, the things that mean safety for him mean danger for me. We've talked too much or not enough: for what we have to say to each other there's no language, we've tried them all. I think of the old science-fiction movies, the creature from another galaxy finally encountered after so many years of signals and ordeals only to be destroyed because he can't make himself understood. Actually it's less a truce than a rest, those silent black-and-white comedians hitting each other until they fall down, then getting up after a pause to begin again. We love each other, that's true whatever it means, but we aren't good at it; for some it's a talent, for others only an addiction. I wonder if they ever came here while he was still alive.

Right now though there's neither love nor anger, no resentment, it's a suspension, of fear even, like waiting for the dentist. But I don't want him to die. I feel nothing but I concentrate, somebody's version of God, I will him to exist, right now on the vacant lawn of this castle whose name we don't know in this foreign town we're in only because dead people are more real to him than living ones. Despite the mistakes I want everything to stay the way it is; I want to hold it.

He sits up: he's heard voices. Two little girls, baskets over their arms as though for a picnic or a game, have come into the grounds and are walking towards the castle. They stare at us curiously and decide we are harmless. "Let's play in the tower," one calls and they run and disappear among the walls. For them the castle is ordinary as a backyard.

He gets up, brushing off bits of grass. We haven't visited the house yet but we still have time. We find our break in the wall, our pathway, and slide back down to sealevel. The sun has moved, the green closes behind us.

The house is further than it looked from the village. The semi-road gives out and we pick our way along the stoney beach. The tide is out; the huge bay stretches as far as we can see, a solid mud-flat except for the thin silty river that cuts along beside us. The dry part narrows and vanishes, we are stranded below the tide line, clambering over slippery masses of purplish-brown rock or squelching through the mud, thick as clotted cream. All around us is an odd percolating sound: it's the mud, drying in the sun. There are gulls too, and wind bending the unhealthy-coloured rushes by the bank.

"How the hell did he get back and forth?" he says. "Think of doing this drunk on a dark night."

"There must be a road further up," I say.

We reach the house at last. Like everything else here it has a wall; this one is to keep out the waves at high tide. The house itself is on stilts, jammed up against the cliff, painted stone with a spindly-railed two-decker porch. It hasn't been lived in for many years: one window is broken and the railings are beginning to go. The yard is weed-grown, but maybe it always was. I sit on the wall, dangling my legs, while he pokes around, examining the windows, the outhouse (which is open), the shed once used perhaps for a boat. I don't want to see any of it. Graves are safely covered and the castle so derelict it has the status of a tree or a stone, but the house is too recent, it is still partly living. If I looked in the window there would be a table with dishes not yet cleared away, or a fresh cigarette or a coat just taken off. Or maybe a broken plate: they used to have fights, apparently. She never comes back and I can see why. He wouldn't leave her alone.

He's testing the railing on the second-storey porch; he's going to pull himself up by it.

"Don't do that," I say wearily.

"Why not?" he says. "I want to see the other side."

"Because you'll fall and I don't want to have to scrape you off the rocks."

"Don't be like that," he says.

How did she manage? I turn my head away, I don't want to watch. It will be such an effort, the police, I'll have to explain what I was doing here, why he was climbing and fell. He should be more considerate. But for once he thinks better of it.

There is another road, we discover it eventually, along the beach and up an asphalt walk beside a neat inhabited cottage. Did they see us coming, are they wondering who we are? The road above is paved, it has a railing and a sign with the poet's name on it, wired to the fence.

"I'd like to steal that," he says.

We pause to view the house from above. There's an old lady in a garden-party hat and gloves, explaining things to an elderly couple. "He always kept to himself, he did," she is saying. "No one here ever got to know him really." She goes on to detail the prices that have been offered for the house: America wanted to buy it and ship it across the ocean, she says, but the town wouldn't let them.

We start back towards our room. Halfway along we sit down on a bench to scrape the mud from our boots; it clings like melted marshmallow. I lean back; I'm not sure I can make it to the house, whatever reserves my body has been drawing on are almost gone. My hearing is blurred and it's hard to breathe.

He bends over to kiss me. I don't want him to, I'm not calm now, I'm irritated, my skin prickles, I think of case histories, devoted wives who turn kleptomaniac two days a month, the mother who threw her baby out into the snow, it was in *Reader's Digest*, she had a hormone disturbance, love is all chemical. I want it to be over, this long abrasive competition for the role of victim; it used to matter that it should finish right, with grace, but not now. One of us should just get up from the bench, shake hands and leave, I don't care who is last, it would sidestep the recriminations, the totalling up of scores, the reclaiming of possessions, your key, my book. But it won't be that way, we'll have to work through it, boring and foreordained though it is. What keeps me is a passive curiosity, it's like an Elizabethan tragedy or a horror movie, I know which ones will be killed but not how. I take his hand and stroke the back of it gently, the fine hairs rasping my fingertips like sandpaper.

We'd been planning to change and have dinner, it's almost six, but back in the room I have only strength enough to pull off my boots, Then with my clothes still on I crawl into the enormous, creaking bed, cold as porridge and hammock-saggy. I float for an instant in the open sky on the backs of my eyelids, free fall, until sleep rushes up to meet me like the earth.

I wake up suddenly in total darkness. I remember where I am. He's beside me but he seems to be lying outside the blankets, furled in the bedspread. I get stealthily out of the bed, grope to the window and open one of the wooden shutters. It's almost as dark

outside, there are no streetlights, but by straining I
can read my watch; two o'clock. I've had my eight
hours and my body thinks it's time for breakfast. I
notice I still have my clothes on, take them off and
get back in bed, but my stomach won't let me sleep.
I hesitate, then decide it won't do him any harm and
turn on the bedside lamp. On the dresser there's a
crumpled paper bag; inside it is a Welsh cake, a soft
white biscuit with currants in it. I bought it yesterday
near the train station, asking in bakeries crammed
with English buns and French pastries, running
through the streets in a crazed search for local colour
that almost made us late for the bus. Actually I
bought two of them. I ate mine yesterday, this one is
his, but I don't care; I take it out of the bag and de-
vour it whole.

In the mirror I'm oddly swollen, as though I've been
drowned, my eyes are purple-circled, my hair stands
out from my head like a second-hand doll's, there's
a diagonal scar-like mark across my cheek where I've
been sleeping on my face. This is what it does to you.
I estimate the weeks, months, it will take me to re-
cuperate. Fresh air, good food and plenty of sun.

We have so little time and he just lies there, rolled
up like a rug, not even twitching. I think of waking
him, I want to make love, I want all there is because
there's not much left. I start to think what he will do
after I'm over and I can't stand that, maybe I should
kill him, that's a novel idea, how melodramatic; nevertheless I look around the room for a blunt instru-
ment; there's nothing but the bedside lamp, a
grotesque woodland nymph with metal tits and a
lightbulb coming out of her head. I could never kill
anyone with that. Instead I brush my teeth, wondering if he'll ever know how close he came to being murdered, resolving anyway never to plant flowers for
him, never to come back, and slide in among the
chilly furrows and craters of the bed. I intend to
watch the sun rise but I fall asleep by accident and
miss it.

Breakfast, when the time for it finally comes, is shabby, decorous, with mended linens and plentiful but dinted silver. We have it in an ornate, dilapidated room whose grandiose mantelpiece now supports only china spaniels and tinted family photos. We're brushed and combed, thoroughly dressed; we speak in subdued voices.

The food is the usual: tea and toast, fried eggs and bacon and the inevitable grilled tomato. It's served by a different woman, grey-haired also but with a corrugated perm and red lipstick. We unfold our map and plan the route back; it's Sunday and there won't be a bus to the nearest railway town till after one, we may have trouble getting out.

He doesn't like fried eggs and he's been given two of them. I eat one for him and tell him to hack the other one up so it will look nibbled at least, it's only polite. He is grateful to me, he knows I'm taking care of him, he puts his hand for a moment over mine, the one not holding the fork. We tell each other our dreams: his of men with armbands, later of me in a cage made of frail slat-like bones, mine of escaping in winter through a field.

I eat his grilled tomato as an afterthought and we leave.

Upstairs in our room we pack; or rather I pack, he lies on the bed.

"What're we going to do till the bus comes?" he says. Being up so early unsettles him.

"Go for a walk," I say.

"We went for a walk yesterday," he says.

I turn around and he's holding out his arms, he wants me to come and lie down beside him. I do and he gives me a perfunctory initial kiss and starts to undo my buttons. He's using only his left hand, the right one is underneath me. He's having trouble. I stand up and take off, reluctantly, the clothes I've so recently put on. It's time for sex; he missed out on it last night.

He reaches up and hauls me in among the tangled sheets. I tense; he throws himself on me with the utilitarian urgency of a man running to catch a train, but it's more than that, it's different, he's biting down on my mouth, this time he'll get blood if it kills him. I pull him into me, wanting him to be with me, but for the first time I feel it's just flesh, a body, a beautiful machine, an animated corpse, he isn't in it any more, I want him so much and he isn't here. The bedpsrings mourn beneath us.

"Sorry about that," he says.

"It's all right."

"No, shit, I really am sorry. I don't like it when that happens."

"It's all right," I say. I smooth his back, distancing him: he's back by the deserted house, back lying on the grass, back in the graveyard, standing in the sun looking down, thinking of his own death.

"We better get up," I say, "she might want to make up the room."

We're waiting for the bus. They lied to me in the general store, there is a hotel, I can see it now, it's just around the corner. We've had our quarrel, argument, fight, the one we were counting on. It was a routine one, a small one comparatively, its only importance the fact that it was the last. It carries the weight of all the other, larger things we said we forgave each other for but didn't. If there were separate buses we'd take them. As it is we wait together, standing a little apart.

We have over half an hour. "Let's go down to the beach," I say. "We can see the bus from there; it has to go the other way first." I cross the road and he follows me at a distance.

There's a wall; I climb it and sit down. The top is scattered with sharp flakes of broken stone, flint possibly, and bleached thumbnail-sized cockleshells, I know what they are because I saw them in the museum two days ago, and the occasional piece of broken glass. He leans against the wall near me, chewing on a cigarette. We say what we have to say in even, conversational voices, discussing how we'll get back, the available trains. I wasn't expecting it so soon.

After a while he looks at his watch, then walks away from me towards the sea, his boots crunching on the shells and pebbles. At the edge of the reed bank by the river he stops, back to me, one leg slightly bent. He holds his elbows, wrapped in his clothes as though in a cape, the storm breaks, his cape billows, thick leather boots sprout up his legs, a sword springs to attention in his hand. He throws his head back, courage, he'll meet them alone. Flash of lightning. Onward.

I wish I could do it so quickly. I sit calmed, frozen, not yet sure whether I've survived, the words we have hurled at each other lying spread in fragments around me, solidified. It's the pause during the end of the world; how does one behave? The man who said he'd continue to tend his garden, does that make sense to me? It would if it were only a small ending, my own. But we aren't more doomed than anything else, it's dead already, at any moment the bay will vaporize, the hills across will lift into the air, the space between will scroll itself up and vanish; in the graveyard the graves will open to show the dry puff-ball skulls, his wooden cross will flare like a match, his house collapse into itself, cardboard and lumber, no more language. He will stand revealed, history scaling away from him, the versions of him I made up and applied, stripped down to what he really is for a last instant before he flames up and goes out. Surely we should be holding each other, absolving, repenting, saying goodbye to each other, to everything because we will never find it again.

Above us the gulls wheel and ride, crying like drowning puppies or disconsolate angels. They have black rims around their eyes; they're a new kind, I've never seen any like that before. The tide is going out;

the fresh wet mud gleams in the sun, miles of it, a
level field of pure glass, pure gold. He stands outlined
against it; a dark shape, faceless, light catching the
edges of his hair.

I turn aside and look down at my hands. They are
covered with greyish dust: I've been digging among
the shells, gathering them together. I arrange them in
a border, a square, each white shell overlapping the
next. Inside I plant the flints, upright in tidy rows,
like teeth, like flowers.

Rape Fantasies

o   o   o

The way they're going on about it in the magazines you'd think it was just invented, and not only that but it's something terrific, like a vaccine for cancer. They put it in capital letters on the front cover, and inside they have these questionnaires like the ones they used to have about whether you were a good enough wife or an endomorph or an ectomorph, remember that? with the scoring upside down on page 73, and then these numbered do-it-yourself dealies, you know? RAPE, TEN THINGS TO DO ABOUT IT, like it was ten new hairdos or something. I mean, what's so new about it?

So at work they all have to talk about it because no matter what magazine you open, there it is, staring you right between the eyes, and they're beginning to have it on the television, too. Personally I'd prefer a June Allyson movie anytime but they don't make them any more and they don't even have them that much on the Late Show. For instance, day before yesterday, that would be Wednesday, thank god it's Friday as they say, we were sitting around in the women's lunch room—the *lunch* room, I mean you'd

think you could get some peace and quiet in there—
and Chrissy closes up the magazine she's been reading and says, "How about it, girls, do you have rape
fantasies?"

The four of us were having our game of bridge the
way we always do, and I had a bare twelve points
counting the singleton with not that much of a bid in
anything. So I said one club, hoping Sondra would remember about the one club convention, because the
time before when I used that she thought I really
meant clubs and she bid us up to three, and all I had
was four little ones with nothing higher than a six,
and we went down two and on top of that we were
vulnerable. She is not the world's best bridge player.
I mean, neither am I but there's a limit.

Darlene passed but the damage was done, Sondra's head went round like it was on ball bearings and
she said, "What fantasies?"

"Rape fantasies," Chrissy said. She's a receptionist
and she looks like one; she's pretty but cool as a cu-
cumber, like she's been painted all over with nail
polish, if you know what I mean. Varnished. "It says
here all women have rape fantasies."

"For Chrissake, I'm eating an egg sandwich," I
said, "and I bid one club and Darlene passed."

"You mean, like some guy jumping you in an alley
or something," Sondra said. She was eating her lunch,
we all eat our lunches during the game, and she bit into a piece of that celery she always brings and started
to chew away on it with this thoughtful expression in
her eyes and I knew we might as well pack it in as
far as the game was concerned.

"Yeah, sort of like that," Chrissy said. She was
blushing a little, you could see it even under her
makeup.

"I don't think you should go out alone at night,"
Darlene said, "you put yourself in a position," and I
may have been mistaken but she was looking at me.
She's the oldest, she's forty-one though you wouldn't
know it and neither does she, but I looked it up in

the employees' file. I like to guess a person's age and then look it up to see if I'm right. I let myself have an extra pack of cigarettes if I am, though I'm trying to cut down. I figure it's harmless as long as you don't tell. I mean, not everyone has access to that file, it's more or less confidential. But it's all right if I tell you, I don't expect you'll ever meet her, though you never know, it's a small world. Anyway.

"For *heaven's* sake, it's only *Toronto*," Greta said. She worked in Detroit for three years and she never lets you forget it, it's like she thinks she's a war hero or something, we should all admire her just for the fact that she's still walking this earth, though she was really living in Windsor the whole time, she just worked in Detroit. Which for me doesn't really count. It's where you sleep, right?

"Well, do you?" Chrissy said. She was obviously trying to tell us about hers but she wasn't about to go first, she's cautious, that one.

"I certainly don't," Darlene said, and she wrinkled up her nose, like this, and I had to laugh. "I think it's disgusting." She's divorced, I read that in the file too, she never talks about it. It must've been years ago anyway. She got up and went over to the coffee machine and turned her back on us as though she wasn't going to have anything more to do with it.

"Well," Greta said. I could see it was going to be between her and Chrissy. They're both blondes, I don't mean that in a bitchy way but they do try to outdress each other. Greta would like to get out of Filing, she'd like to be a receptionist too so she could meet more people. You don't meet much of anyone in Filing except other people in Filing. Me, I don't mind it so much, I have outside interests.

"Well," Greta said, "I sometimes think about, you know my apartment? It's got this little balcony, I like to sit out there in the summer and I have a few plants out there. I never bother that much about locking the door to the balcony, it's one of those sliding glass ones, I'm on the eighteenth floor for heaven's sake, I've got a good view of the lake and the CN Tower and all. But I'm sitting around one night in my housecoat, watching TV with my shoes off, you know how you do, and I see this guy's feet, coming down past the window, and the next thing you know he's standing on the balcony, he's let himself down by a rope with a hook on the end of it from the floor above, that's the nineteenth, and before I can even get up off the chesterfield he's inside the apartment. He's all dressed in black with black gloves on"—I knew right away what show she got the black gloves off because I saw the same one—"and then he, well, you know."

"You know what?" Chrissy said, but Greta said, "And afterwards he tells me that he goes all over the outside of the apartment building like that, from one floor to another, with his rope and his hook . . . and then he goes out to the balcony and tosses his rope, and he climbs up it and disappears."

"Just like Tarzan," I said, but nobody laughed.

"Is that all?" Chrissy said. "Don't you ever think about, well, I think about being in the bathtub, with no clothes on . . ."

"So who takes a bath in their clothes?" I said, you have to admit it's stupid when you come to think of it, but she just went on, ". . . with lots of bubbles, what I use is Vitabath, it's more expensive but it's so relaxing, and my hair pinned up, and the door opens and this fellow's standing there. . . ."

"How'd he get in?" Greta said.

"Oh, I don't know, through a window or something. Well, I can't very well get out of the bathtub, the bathroom's too small and besides he's blocking the doorway, so I just *lie* there, and he starts to very slowly take his own clothes off, and then he gets into the bathtub with me."

"Don't you scream or anything?" said Darlene. She'd come back with her cup of coffee, she was getting really interested. "I'd scream like bloody murder."

"Who'd hear me?" Chrissy said. "Besides, all the articles say it's better not to resist, that way you don't get hurt."

"Anyway you might get bubbles up your nose," I said, "from the deep breathing," and I swear all four of them looked at me like I was in bad taste, like I'd insulted the Virgin Mary or something. I mean, I don't see what's wrong with a little joke now and then. Life's too short, right?

"Listen," I said, "those aren't *rape* fantasies. I mean, you aren't getting *raped*, it's just some guy you haven't met formally who happens to be more attractive than Derek Cummins"—he's the Assistant Manager, he wears elevator shoes or at any rate they have these thick soles and he has this funny way of talking, we call him Derek Duck—"and you have a good time. Rape is when they've got a knife or something and you don't want to."

"So what about you, Estelle," Chrissy said, she was miffed because I laughed at her fantasy, she thought I was putting her down. Sondra was miffed too, by this time she'd finished her celery and she wanted to tell about hers, but she hadn't got in fast enough.

"All right, let me tell you one," I said. "I'm walking down this dark street at night and this fellow comes up and grabs my arm. Now it so happens that I have a plastic lemon in my purse, you know how it always says you should carry a plastic lemon in your purse? I don't really do it, I tried it once but the darn thing leaked all over my chequebook, but in this fantasy I have one, and I say to him, 'You're intending to rape me, right?' and he nods, so I open my purse to get the plastic lemon, and I can't find it! My purse is full of all this junk, Kleenex and cigarettes and my change purse and my lipstick and my driver's licence, you know the kind of stuff; so I ask him to hold out his hands, like this, and I pile all this junk into them and down at the bottom there's the plastic lemon, and I can't get the top off. So I hand it to him and he's very obliging, he twists the top off and hands it back to me, and I squirt him in the eye."

I hope you don't think that's too vicious. Come to think of it, it is a bit mean, especially when he was so polite and all.

"*That's* your rape fantasy?" Chrissy says. "I don't believe it."

"She's a card," Darlene says, she and I are the ones that've been here the longest and she never will forget the time I got drunk at the office party and insisted I was going to dance under the table instead of on top of it, I did a sort of Cossack number but then I hit my head on the bottom of the table—actually it was a desk—when I went to get up, and I knocked myself out cold. She's decided that's the mark of an original mind and she tells everyone new about it and I'm not sure that's fair. Though I did do it.

"I'm being totally honest," I say. I always am and they know it. There's no point in being anything else, is the way I look at it, and sooner or later the truth will out so you might as well not waste the time, right? "You should hear the one about the Easy-Off Oven Cleaner."

But that was the end of the lunch hour, with one bridge game shot to hell, and the next day we spent most of the time arguing over whether to start a new game or play out the hands we had left over from the day before, so Sondra never did get a chance to tell about her rape fantasy.

It started me thinking though, about my own rape fantasies. Maybe I'm abnormal or something, I mean I have fantasies about handsome strangers coming in through the window too, like Mr. Clean, I wish one would, please god somebody without flat feet and big sweat marks on his shirt, and over five feet five, believe me being tall is a handicap though it's getting better, tall guys are starting to like someone whose nose reaches higher than their belly button. But if you're being totally honest you can't count those as rape fantasies. In a real rape fantasy, what you should feel is this anxiety, like when you think about

your apartment building catching on fire and whether
you should use the elevator or the stairs or maybe just
stick your head under a wet towel, and you try to remember everything you've read about what to do but
you can't decide.

For instance, I'm walking along this dark street at
night and this short, ugly fellow comes up and grabs
my arm, and not only is he ugly, you know, with a sort
of puffy nothing face, like those fellows you have to
talk to in the bank when your account's overdrawn—
of course I don't mean they're all like that—but he's
absolutely covered in pimples. So he gets me pinned
against the wall, he's short but he's heavy, and he
starts to undo himself and the zipper gets stuck. I
mean, one of the most significant moments in a girl's
life, it's almost like getting married or having a baby
or something, and he sticks the zipper.

So I say, kind of disgusted, "Oh for Chrissake," and
he starts to cry. He tells me he's never been able to
get anything right in his entire life, and this is the
last straw, he's going to go jump off a bridge.

"Look," I say, I feel so sorry for him, in my rape
fantasies I always end up feeling sorry for the guy, I
mean there has to be something *wrong* with them, if
it was Clint Eastwood it'd be different but worse
luck it never is. I was the kind of little girl who
buried dead robins, know what I mean? It used to
drive my mother nuts, she didn't like me touching
them, because of the germs I guess. So I say, "Listen,
I know how you feel. You really should do something
about those pimples, if you got rid of them you'd be
quite good looking, honest; then you wouldn't have to
go around doing stuff like this. I had them myself
once," I say, to comfort him, but in fact I did, and it
ends up I give him the name of my old dermatologist,
the one I had in high school, that was back in
Leamington, except I used to go to St. Catharines for
the dermatologist. I'm telling you, I was really lonely
when I first came here; I thought it was going to be

such a big adventure and all, but it's a lot harder to meet people in a city. But I guess it's different for a guy.

Or I'm lying in bed with this terrible cold, my face is all swollen up, my eyes are red and my nose is dripping like a leaky tap, and this fellow comes in through the window and *he* has a terrible cold too, it's a new kind of flu that's been going around. So he says, "I'b goig do rabe you"—I hope you don't mind me holding my nose like this but that's the way I imagine it—and he lets out this terrific sneeze, which slows him down a bit, also I'm no object of beauty myself, you'd have to be some kind of pervert to want to rape someone with a cold like mine, it'd be like raping a bottle of LePages mucilage the way my nose is running. He's looking wildly around the room, and I realize it's because he doesn't have a piece of Kleenex! "Id's ride here," I say, and I pass him the Kleenex, god knows why he even bothered to get out of bed, you'd think if you were going to go around climbing in windows you'd wait till you were healthier, right? I mean, that takes a certain amount of energy. So I ask him why doesn't he let me fix him a NeoCitran and scotch, that's what I always take, you still have the cold but you don't feel it, so I do and we end up watching the Late Show together. I mean, they aren't all sex maniacs, the rest of the time they must lead a normal life. I figure they enjoy watching the Late Show just like anybody else.

I do have a scarier one though . . . where the fellow says he's hearing angel voices that're telling him he's got to kill me, you know, you read about things like that all the time in the papers. In this one I'm not in the apartment where I live now, I'm back in my mother's house in Leamington and the fellow's been hiding in the cellar, he grabs my arm when I go downstairs to get a jar of jam and he's got hold of the axe too, out of the garage, that one is really scary. I mean, what do you say to a nut like that?

So I start to shake but after a minute I get control

of myself and I say, is he sure the angel voices have got the right person, because I hear the same angel voices and they've been telling me for some time that I'm going to give birth to the reincarnation of St. Anne who in turn has the Virgin Mary and right after that comes Jesus Christ and the end of the world, and he wouldn't want to interfere with that, would he? So he gets confused and listens some more, and then he asks for a sign and I show him my vaccination mark, you can see it's sort of an odd-shaped one, it got infected because I scratched the top off, and that does it, he apologizes and climbs out the coal chute again, which is how he got in in the first place, and I say to myself there's some advantage in having been brought up a Catholic even though I haven't been to church since they changed the service into English, it just isn't the same, you might as well be a Protestant. I must write to Mother and tell her to nail up that coal chute, it always has bothered me. Funny, I couldn't tell you at all what this man looks like but I know exactly what kind of shoes he's wearing, because that's the last I see of him, his shoes going up the coal chute, and they're the old-fashioned kind that lace up the ankles, even though he's a young fellow. That's strange, isn't it?

Let me tell you though I really sweat until I see him safely out of there and I go upstairs right away and make myself a cup of tea. I don't think about that one much. My mother always said you shouldn't dwell on unpleasant things and I generally agree with that, I mean, dwelling on them doesn't make them go away. Though not dwelling on them doesn't make them go away either, when you come to think of it.

Sometimes I have these short ones where the fellow grabs my arm but I'm really a Kung-Fu expert, can you believe it, in real life I'm sure it would just be a conk on the head and that's that, like getting your tonsils out, you'd wake up and it would be all over except for the sore places, and you'd be lucky if your neck wasn't broken or something, I could never even hit the

volleyball in gym and a volleyball is fairly large, you
know?—and I just go *zap* with my fingers into his
eyes and that's it, he falls over, or I flip him against
a wall or something. But I could never really stick my
fingers in anyone's eyes, could you? It would feel like
hot jello and I don't even like cold jello, just thinking
about it gives me the creeps. I feel a bit guilty about
that one, I mean how would you like walking around
knowing someone's been blinded for life because of
you?

But maybe it's different for a guy.

The most touching one I have is when the fellow
grabs my arm and I say, sad and kind of dignified,
"You'd be raping a corpse." That pulls him up short
and I explain that I've just found out I have leukaemia
and the doctors have only given me a few months to
live. That's why I'm out pacing the streets alone at
night, I need to think, you know, come to terms with
myself. I don't really have leukaemia but in the fantasy I do, I guess I chose that particular disease because a girl in my grade four class died of it, the
whole class sent her flowers when she was in the hospital. I didn't understand then that she was going to
die and I wanted to have leukaemia too so I could get
flowers. Kids are funny, aren't they? Well, it turns out
that he has leukaemia himself, and *he* only has a few
months to live, that's why he's going around raping
people, he's very bitter because he's so young and
his life is being taken from him before he's really lived
it. So we walk along gently under the street lights, it's
spring and sort of misty, and we end up going for
coffee, we're happy we've found the only other person
in the world who can understand what we're going
through, it's almost like fate, and after a while we just
sort of look at each other and our hands touch, and
he comes back with me and moves into my apartment
and we spend our last months together before we die,
we just sort of don't wake up in the morning, though
I've never decided which one of us gets to die first.
If it's him I have to go on and fantasize about the

funeral, if it's me I don't have to worry about that, so it just about depends on how tired I am at the time. You may not believe this but sometimes I even start crying. I cry at the ends of movies, even the ones that aren't all that sad, so I guess it's the same thing. My mother's like that too.

The funny thing about these fantasies is that the man is always someone I don't know, and the statistics in the magazines, well, most of them anyway, they say it's often someone you do know, at least a little bit, like your boss or something—I mean, it wouldn't be *my* boss, he's over sixty and I'm sure he couldn't rape his way out of a paper bag, poor old thing, but it might be someone like Derek Duck, in his elevator shoes, perish the thought—or someone you just met, who invites you up for a drink, it's getting so you can hardly be sociable any more, and how are you supposed to meet people if you can't trust them even that basic amount? You can't spend your whole life in the Filing Department or cooped up in your own apartment with all the doors and windows locked and the shades down. I'm not what you would call a drinker but I like to go out now and then for a drink or two in a nice place, even if I am by myself, I'm with Women's Lib on that even though I can't agree with a lot of the other things they say. Like here for instance, the waiters all know me and if anyone, you know, bothers me. . . . I don't know why I'm telling you all this, except I think it helps you get to know a person, especially at first, hearing some of the things they think about. At work they call me the office worry wart, but it isn't so much like worrying, it's more like figuring out what you should do in an emergency, like I said before.

Anyway, another thing about it is that there's a lot of conversation, in fact I spend most of my time, in the fantasy that is, wondering what I'm going to say and what he's going to say, I think it would be better if you could get a conversation going. Like, how could a fellow do that to a person he's just had a long conversation with, once you let them know you're human, you have a life too, I don't see how they could go ahead with it, right? I mean, I know it happens but I just don't understand it, that's the part I really don't understand.

Hair Jewellery

○ ○ ○

There must be some approach to this, a method, a technique, that's the word I want, it kills germs. Some technique then, a way of thinking about it that would be bloodless and therefore painless; devotion recollected in tranquillity. I try to conjure up an image of myself at that time, also one of you, but it's like conjuring the dead. How do I know I'm not inventing both of us, and if I'm not inventing then it really is like conjuring the dead, a dangerous game. Why should I disturb those sleepers, sleepwalkers, as they make their automaton rounds through the streets where we once lived, fading from year to year, their voices thinning to the sound of a thumb drawn across a wet window: an insect squeak, transparent as glass, no words. You can never tell with the dead whether it is they who wish to return or the living who want them to. The usual explanation is that they have something to tell us. I'm not sure I believe it; in this case it's more likely that I have something to tell them.

Be careful, I want to write. *There is a future*, God's hand on the temple wall, clear and unavoidable in the new snow, just in front of them where they are walking—I see it as December—along the brick sidewalk in Boston, city of rotting dignities, she in her wavering high heels, getting her feet wet from sheer vanity. Boots were ugly then, heavy shapeless rubber like rhinoceros paws, flight boots they called them, or furred at the tops like old ladies' or bedroom slippers, with stringy bows; or there were those plastic wedge-shaped rainboots, they would yellow quickly and become encrusted with dirt on the inside, they looked like buried teeth.

That's my technique, I resurrect myself through clothes. In fact it's impossible for me to remember what I did, what happened to me, unless I can remember what I was wearing, and every time I discard a sweater or a dress I am discarding a part of my life. I shed identities like a snake, leaving them pale and shrivelled behind me, a trail of them, and if I want any memories at all I have to collect, one by one, those cotton and wool fragments, piece them together, achieving at last a patchwork self, no defence anyway against the cold. I concentrate, and this particular lost soul rises miasmic from the Crippled Civilians' Clothing Donation Box in the Loblaws parking lot in downtown Toronto, where I finally ditched that coat.

The coat was long and black. It was good quality—good quality mattered then, and the women's magazines had articles about basic wardrobes and correct pressing and how to get spots out of camel's hair—but it was far too big for me, the sleeves came to my knuckles, the hem to the tops of my plastic rainboots, which did not fit either. When I bought it I meant to alter it, but I never did. Most of my clothes were the same, they were all too big, perhaps I believed that if my clothes were large and shapeless, if they formed a sort of tent around me, I would be less visible. But the reverse was true; I must have been more noticeable than most as I billowed along the streets in my black wool shroud, my head swathed in, was it a plaid angora scarf, also good quality; at any rate, my head swathed.

I bought these clothes, when I bought clothes at all—for you must remember that, like you, I was poor, which accounts for at least some of our desperation—in Filene's Basement, where good quality clothes that failed to sell at the more genteel levels were disposed of at slashed prices. You often had to try them on in the aisles as there were few dressing rooms, and the cellar, for it was a cellar, low-ceilinged, dimly lit, dank with the smell of anxious armpits and harassed feet, was filled on bargain days with struggling women in slips and bras, stuffing themselves into torn and soiled designer originals to the sound of heavy breathing and a hundred sticking zippers. It is customary to laugh at bargain-hunting women, at their voraciousness, their hysteria, but Filene's Basement was, in its own way, tragic. No one went there who did not aspire to a shape-change, a transformation, a new life; but the things never did quite fit.

Under the black coat I wear a heavy tweed skirt, grey in colour, and a brown sweater with only one not very noticeable hole, valued by me because it was your cigarette that burned it. Under the sweater I have a slip (too long), a brassiere (too small), some panties with little pink roses on them, also from Filene's Basement, only twenty-five cents, five for a dollar, and a pair of nylon stockings held up by a garter belt which, being too large, is travelling around my waist, causing the seams at the backs of my legs to spiral like barbers' poles. I am lugging a suitcase which is far too heavy—no one carried packsacks then except at summer camp—as it contains another set of my weighty, oversized clothes as well as six nineteenth-century Gothic novels and a sheaf of clean paper. On the other side, counterbalancing the suitcase, are my portable typewriter and my Filene's Basement handbag, gargantuan, bottomless as the tomb. It is February, the wind whips the black coat

out behind me, my plastic rainboots skid on the ice
of the sidewalk, in a passing store window I see a
woman thick and red-faced and bundled. I am hope-
lessly in love and I am going to the train station to
escape.

If I had been richer it would have been the airport.
I would have gone to California, Algiers, somewhere
oily and alien and above all warm. As it was, I had
just enough money for a return ticket and three days
in Salem, the only other place both accessible and not-
able being Walden Pond, which was not much good in
winter. I had already justified the trip to myself: it
would be more educational to go to Salem than to
Algiers, for I was supposed to be "doing work" on
Nathaniel Hawthorne. "Doing work," they called it;
they still call it that. I would be able to soak up
atmosphere; perhaps from this experience, to which I
did not look forward, the academic paper required
for my survival as a scholar would emerge, like a
stunted dandelion from a crack in the sidewalk. Those
dismal streets, that Puritanical melancholy combined
with the sodden February seawinds would be like a
plunge into cold water, shocking into action my criti-
cal faculties, my talent for word-chopping and the
construction of plausible footnotes which had assured
so far the trickle of scholarship money on which I
subsisted. For the past two months these abilities had
been paralyzed by unrequited love. I thought that
several days away from you would give me time to
think things over. In my subsequent experience, this
does no good at all.

Unrequited love was, at that period of my life, the
only kind I seemed to be capable of feeling. This
caused me much pain, but in retrospect I see it had
advantages. It provided all the emotional jolts of the
other kind without any of the risks, it did not interfere
with my life, which, although meagre, was mine and
predictable, and it involved no decisions. In the world
of stark physical reality it might call for the removal of
my ill-fitting garments (in the dark or the bathroom, if

possible: no woman wants a man to see her safety pins), but it left undisturbed their metaphysical counterparts. At that time I believed in metaphysics. My Platonic version of myself resembled an Egyptian mummy, a mysteriously wrapped object that might or might not fall into dust if uncovered. But unrequited love demanded no stripteases.

If, as had happened several times, my love was requited, if it became a question of the future, of making a decision that would lead inevitably to the sound of one's beloved shaving with an electric razor while one scraped congealed egg from his breakfast plate, I was filled with panic. My academic researches had made me familiar with the moment at which one's closest friend and most trusted companion grows fangs or turns into a bat; this moment was expected, and held few terrors for me. Far more disconcerting was that other moment, when the scales would fall from my eyes and my current lover would be revealed not as a demigod or a monster, impersonal and irresistible, but as a human being. What Psyche saw with the candle was not a god with wings but a pigeon-chested youth with pimples, and that's why it took her so long to win her way back to true love. It is easier to love a daemon than a man, though less heroic.

You were, of course, the perfect object. No banal shadow of lawnmowers and bungalows lurked in your melancholy eyes, opaque as black marble, recondite as urns, you coughed like Roderick Usher, you were, in your own eyes and therefore in mine, doomed and restless as Dracula. Why is it that dolefulness and a sense of futility are so irresistible to young women? I watch this syndrome among my students: those febrile young men who sprawl on the carpets which this institution of higher learning has so thoughtfully provided for them, grubby and slack as hookworm victims, each with some girl in tow who buys cigarettes and coffee for him and who receives in turn his outpourings of spleen, his condemnations of the world and his mockery of her in particular, of the way she

dresses, of the recreation room and two television sets
owned by her parents, who may be in fact identical
to his, of her friends, of what she reads, of how she
thinks. Why do they put up with it? Perhaps it makes
them feel, by contrast, healthful and life-giving; or
perhaps these men are their mirrors, reflecting the
misery and chaos they contain but are afraid to ac-
knowledge.

Our case was different only in externals; the desperation, I'm sure, was identical. I had ended up in
academia because I did not want to be a secretary, or,
to put it another way, because I did not want always
to have to buy my good-quality clothes in Filene's
Basement; you, because you did not want to be
drafted, and at that time the university dodge still
worked. We were both from small, unimportant cities,
whose Rotary Club denizens, unaware of our actual
condition, believed that their minute bursaries were
helping us to pursue arcane but glamorous careers
which would in some vague way reflect credit on the
community. But neither of us wanted to be professional scholars, and the real ones, some of whom had
brushcuts and efficient briefcases and looked like
junior executives of shoe companies, filled us with
dismay. Instead of "doing work" we would spend our
time drinking draft beer in the cheapest of the local
German restaurants, ridiculing the pomposity of our
seminars and the intellectual mannerisms of our fellow students. Or we would wander through the stacks
of the library, searching for recondite titles no one
could possibly have heard of so we could drop them
into the next literary debate in that reverential tone
soon mastered by every future departmental chair-
man, and watch the ripples of dismay spread through
the eyes of our fellow inmates. Sometimes we would
sneak into the Music Department, co-opt a vacant
piano and sing maudlin Victorian favourites or bouncy
choruses from Gilbert and Sullivan, or a plaintive bal-
lad by Edward Lear from which we had been compelled, earlier in the year, to extract the Freudian

symbols. I associate it with a certain brown corduroy skirt which I had made myself, the hem of which was stapled in several places because I had not had the moral energy to sew it.

> On the coast of Coromandel,
> Where the early pumpkins blow
> In the middle of the woods
> Lived the Yonghy-Bonghy-Bo ...

> Two old chairs, and half a candle
> One old jug without a handle,
> These were all his worldly goods
> In the middle of the woods ...

The mutilated candle and the broken jug had caused much snide merriment at the seminar, but for us they held a compelling pathos. The state of affairs in Coromandel, its squalor and hopelessness, seemed too apt a comment on our own.

Our problem, I thought, was that neither the world around us nor the future stretching before us contained any image of what we might conceivably become. We were stranded in the present as in a stalled, otherwise empty subway train, and in this isolation we clutched morosely at each other's shadows. That at any rate was my analysis as I lugged my suitcase through the icy twilight towards the only hotel in Salem that was open, or so the conductor had told me. I have trouble seeing this, but I think the railroad station was condensed and dark, lit by a muddy orange light like the subway stations in Boston, and it too had the smell of weak disinfectant unsuccessfully applied to a layer of dried urine so old as to be almost respectable. It did not remind me of Puritans or witches or even of overstuffed shipbuilders, but of undernourished millworkers with lung trouble, a later generation.

The hotel, too, smelt of decay and better days. It was being repainted, and the painters' canvas cloths and stepladders almost blocked the corridors. The hotel was open only because of the renovations; otherwise, said the desk clerk, who seemed also to be the bellboy, the manager, and possibly the owner, he would have shut it down and gone to Florida. "People only come here in the summer," he said, "to see the House of the Seven Gables and that." He resented my being there at all, and more especially for refusing to give a satisfactory explanation. I told him I had come to look at the tombstones but he did not believe this. As he hauled my suitcase and my typewriter towards the windswept cupboard in which he was about to deposit me, he kept looking back over my shoulder as though there ought to have been a man behind me. Illicit sex, he knew, was the only conceivable reason for Salem in February. He was right, of course.

The bed was narrow and hard as a mortuary slab, and I soon discovered that although there was a brisk seabreeze blowing through the closed window, the management was aware of it and had compensated; each fresh onslaught of central heating was announced by the sound of hammers and leaden gongs from the radiator.

Between my fits of sleep I thought about you, rehearsing our future, which I knew would be brief. Of course we would sleep together, though this topic had not yet been discussed. In those days, as you recall, it had to be discussed first, and so far we had not progressed beyond a few furtive outdoor gropings and one moment when, under a full moon on one of those deserted brick streets, you had put your hand on my throat and announced that you were the Boston Strangler; a joke which, for one with my literary predilections, amounted to a seduction. But though sex was a necessary and even a desirable ritual, I dwelt less on it than on our parting, which I visualized as sad, tender, inevitable and final. I rehearsed it in every conceivable location: doorways, ferry boat docks, train, plane and subway stations, park benches. We would not say much, we would look at each other, we would *know* (though precisely what we would know I wasn't sure); then you would turn a corner and be lost forever. I would be wearing a trenchcoat, not yet purchased, though I had seen the kind of thing I wanted in Filene's Basement the previous autumn. The park bench scene—I set it in spring, to provide a contrast to the mood—was so affecting that I cried, though since I had a horror of being overheard, even in an empty hotel, I timed it to coincide with the radiator. Futility is so attractive to the young, and I had not yet exhausted its possibilities.

By the next morning I was tired of brooding and snivelling. I decided to seek out the main derelict graveyard, which might provide me with a quaint seventeenth-century tombstone epitaph suitable for my Hawthorne paper. In the hall the workmen were hammering and painting; as I walked down the corridor they stared after me like frogs in a pond. The desk clerk grudgingly relinquished a Chamber of Commerce tourist brochure, which had a map and a short list of the points of interest.

There was no one in the streets outside, and very few cars. The houses, filmed with soot, their paint peeled by the salty air, seemed deserted, though in several of the front windows behind the greying lace curtains I could see the shadowy outline of a face. The sky was grey and furrowed, like the inside of a mattress, and there was a high wind blowing. I skidded over the sidewalks in my slippery boots, the wind pushing my black coat like a sail, making good progress until I turned a corner and the wind was no longer behind me. Soon after that I gave up the graveyard idea.

Instead I turned into a small restaurant; I had not yet had breakfast—the hotel had been surly about it —and I wanted to eat and to consider what to do next. I ordered an egg sandwich and a glass of milk and studied the brochure. The waitress and the proprietor, who were the only other people in the room, retreated to the far end and stood with folded arms, watching me suspiciously while I ate as though expecting me to leap up and perform some act of necromancy with the butter knife. Meanwhile, the House of the Seven Gables was closed for the winter. It had nothing to do with Hawthorne anyway; it was just an old house that had avoided being torn down, and which people now paid money to see because it had been given the name of a novel. No genuine author's sweat on the banisters. I think this was the moment at which I started to become cynical about literature.

The only other point of interest, according to the Chamber of Commerce, was the library. Unlike everything else it was open in February, and was apparently world-famous for its collection of genealogies. The last thing I wanted was a visit to the library, but returning to the hotel with its noise and chemical smells was pointless, and I couldn't stay in the restaurant all day.

The library was empty, except for a middle-aged man in a felt hat who was looking doggedly at the rows of genealogies, palpably killing time. An official woman with a bun and a scowl was sitting behind a blunt desk doing crossword puzzles. The library served also as a museum of sorts. There were several ship's figureheads, maidens with rigid eyes, wooden men, ornate fish and lions, their gilt worn thin; and, displayed in glass cases, a collection of Victorian hair jewellery; brooches and rings, each with a crystal front protecting a design of woven hair; flowers, initials, wreaths or weeping willows. The more elaborate ones had hair of different colours. Though originally they must have shone, the strands by now had aged to the texture of something you find under a chair cushion. It struck me that Donne had been wrong about the circlet of bright hair about the bone. A hand-lettered card explained that many of these pieces were memorial jewellery, intended for distribution to the mourners at funerals.

"The funeral ones," I said to the woman at the
desk. "I mean, how did they . . . did they cut the
hair off before or after?"

She looked up from her puzzle. She did not understand at all what I was talking about.

"Before or after the person died," I said. If it was
before, it seemed to me a callous thing to do. If after,
how did they have time to weave all those willow
trees before the funeral? And why would they want to?
I could not imagine wearing at my throat one of those
heavy brooches, like a metal pillow, stuffed with the
gradually dimming tresses of one I loved. It would be
like a dried hand. It would be like a noose.

"I'm sure I don't know," she said with distaste. "This
is a travelling exhibition."

The man in the felt hat was lying in wait for me
outside the door. He asked me to join him for a drink.
He must have been staying at the hotel.

"No, thank you," I said, adding, "I'm with someone." I said this to mollify him—women always feel
compelled to mollify men by whom they are declining
to be picked up—but as I said it I realized I had come
here not to get away from you, as I had thought, but
to be with you, more completely than your actual
presence would allow. In the flesh your irony was im-
penetrable, but alone I could wallow uninterrupted in
romantic doom. I've never understood why people
consider youth a time of freedom and joy. It's probably because they have forgotten their own. Surrounded now by the doleful young, I can only feel
grateful for having escaped, hopefully forever (for I
no longer believe in reincarnation), from the intolerable bondage of being twenty-one.

I had told you I was going away for three days, but
undiluted fantasy was too much for me. Salem was a
vacuum and you were expanding to fill it. I knew
whose hair that was in the massive black and gold
memento mori in the second row of brooches, I knew
who I had heard in the vacant hotel room to the left

of mine, breathing almost inaudibly between the spasms of the radiator. Luckily there was an afternoon train; I took it, and fled back to the present.

I called you from the Boston train station. You accepted my early return with your usual fatalism, expressing neither glee nor surprise. You were supposed to be doing work on ambiguity in Tennyson's "Locksley Hall," which, you informed me, was clearly out of the question. Ambiguity was big in those days. We went for a walk instead. It was milder and the snow was turning to mush; we ended up at the Charles River, where we rolled snowballs and pitched them into the water. After that we constructed a damp statue of Queen Victoria, complete with jutting bosom, monumental bustle and hooked nose, then demolished it with snowballs and chunks of ice, sniggering at intervals with what I then thought was liberated abandon but now recognize as hysteria.

And then, and then. What did I have on? My coat, of course, and a different skirt, a sickly greenish plaid; the same sweater with the burnt hole in it. We slithered together through the partially frozen slush beside the river, holding each other's chilly hands. It was evening and getting colder. From time to time we stopped, to jump up and down and kiss each other, in order to keep warm. On the oily surface of the Charles were reflected, like bright mirages, the towers and belfries from which the spring examination hopeless ones would later hurl themselves, as they did every year; in its sludgey depths floated the literary suicides, Faulkner's among them, encrusted with crystalline words and glittering like eyes; but we were reckless, we sang in mockery of them, a ragged duet:

Two old chairs, and a half a candle,
One old jug without a handle. . . .

For once you were laughing. I renounced my carefully constructed script, the ending I had planned for us. The future opened like a wide-screen vista, promising and dangerous, any direction was possible. I felt as if I was walking along the edge of a high bridge. It seemed to us—at least it seemed to me—that we were actually happy.

When the cold was finally too much for us and you had begun to sneeze, we went to one of the cheap restaurants where, it was rumoured, you could live for nothing by eating the free packets of ketchup, relish and sugar and drinking the cream out of the cream-jugs when no one was looking. There we debated the advisability of sleeping together, the pros and cons and, quite soon after that, the ways and means. It was not done lightly, especially by female graduate students, who were supposed to be like nuns, dedicated and unfleshly. Not that in those monastic surroundings they had much chance to be anything else, as the male ones mostly went to the opera together in little groups and had sherry parties to which they invited only each other. We both lived in residence; we both had cellmates who were always in the room, biting their nails and composing bibliographies. Neither of us had a car, and we were sure the local hotels would reject us. It would have to be somewhere else. We settled on New York at Easter Break.

The day before the trip I went to Filene's Basement and bought, after some deliberation, a red nylon baby-doll nightgown, only one size too big and with a shoulder strap that could easily be sewed back on. I lingered over a mauve one with Carmen-like flounces, but I could wear only one at a time and the money would be needed for other things. On Good Friday I took the bus down to New York. You had left several days earlier, but I had stayed to finish an overdue essay on Mrs. Radcliffe's *The Italian*. You yourself had three overdue papers by that time, but you no longer seemed to care. You had been spending a lot of time taking showers, which had annoyed your roommate; you had also been suffering from extended nightmares, which features, as I recall, elephants, alli-

gators and other large animals rolling down hills in
wheelchairs, and people being nailed to crosses and
incinerated. I viewed these as evidence of your sen-
sitivity.

The plan was that you would stay at the apartment
of an old friend from your hometown, while I was to
get a single hotel room. This would defeat suspicion,
we hoped; also it would be less expensive.

At that time I had never been to New York and I
was not prepared for it. At first it made me dizzy. I
stood in the Port Authority in my long black coat,
with my heavy suitcase and my bottomless purse,
looking for a phone booth. The crowd was like a
political demonstration, though at that time I had
never seen a real one. Women jostled each other and
spat insults as if they were slogans, hauling grumpy
children in their wake; there was a lineup of seedy
old men on the benches, and the floor was dotted
with gum, candy wrappers and cigarette stubs. I'm
not sure but I think there were pinball machines; can
that be possible? I wished now that I had asked you
to meet the bus, but such dependencies were not part
of our understanding.

As I headed for what I guessed was the exit, a
black man grabbed hold of my suitcase and began to
pull. He had a fresh cut on his forehead from which
the blood was running, and his eyes were filled with
such desperation that I almost let go. He was not
trying to steal my suitcase, I realized after a minute;
he just wanted to carry it to a taxi for me.

"No thank you," I said. "No money."

He glanced with scorn at my coat—it was, after all,
good quality—and did not let go. I pulled harder
and he gave up. He shouted something after me that
I didn't understand; those words had not yet become
common currency.

I knew the address of the hotel, but I didn't know
how to get there. I began to walk. The sun was out
and I was sweating, from fright as well as heat. I

found a telephone booth: the phone had been eviscerated and was a tangle of wires. The next one was intact, but when I called you there was no answer. This was strange, as I'd told you what time I was arriving.

I leaned against the side of the phone booth, making an effort not to panic. New York had been designed like a barred window, so by looking at the street signs and counting, I should be able to deduce the location of the hotel. I did not want to ask anyone: the expressions of blank despair or active malice made me nervous, and I had passed several people who were talking out loud to themselves. New York, like Salem, appeared to be falling to pieces. A rich person might have seen it as potential urban renewal, but the buildings with chunks missing, the holes in the sidewalks, did not reassure me.

I set out to drag my suitcase to the hotel, stopping at every phone booth to dial your number. In one of these I left your copy of *The Education of Henry Adams*, by mistake. It was just as well, as it was the only thing of yours I had; it would have been unlucky to have kept it.

The hotel clerk was nearly as suspicious of me as the one in Salem had been. I had ascribed the distrust of me there to small-town xenophobia, but it occurred to me now for the first time that it might be the way I was dressed. With my cuffs down to my knuckles, I did not look like someone with a credit card.

I sat in my room, which was really very much like the one in Salem, wondering what had happened to you, where you were. I phoned every half hour. There was not much I could do while waiting. I unpacked the red nightgown with the broken strap, only to find I'd forgotten the needle and thread with which I'd intended to repair it; I didn't even have a safety pin. I wanted to take a bath, but the handle of my door kept turning, and although I had fastened the chain I did not want to take the chance. I even kept my coat on. I began to think that you had given me the wrong number, or, worse, that you were something I had invented.

Finally at about seven o'clock someone answered the phone at your end. It was a woman. When I asked for you she laughed, not pleasantly.

"Hey, Voice of Doom," I heard her say. "Some chick wants you." When you came on your voice was even more remote than usual.

"Where were you?" I said, trying not to sound like a nagging wife. "I've been trying to get hold of you since two-thirty."

"It's my friend," you said. "She swallowed a bottle of sleeping pills this morning. I had to walk her around a lot."

"Oh," I said. I'd had the impression that the friend was male. "Couldn't you have taken her to a hospital or something?"

"You don't take people to hospitals here unless you really have to."

"Why did she do it?" I asked.

"Who knows?" you said, in the voice of someone annoyed at being involved, however peripherally. "To pass the time, I guess." In the background the woman said something that sounded like "You shit."

The soles of my feet turned cold, my legs went numb. I had realized suddenly that she was not just an old friend, as you had told me. She had been a lover, she was still a lover, she was serious, she had taken the pills because she found out I was arriving that day and she was trying to stop you; yet all this time you were calmly writing down the room number, the phone number, that I was just as calmly giving you. We arranged to meet the next day. I spent the night lying on the bed with my coat on.

Of course you failed to arrive, and by that time I had thought twice about phoning. You did not even return to Boston. In May I got a cryptic note from you on a postcard with a picture of the Atlantic City boardwalk on the front:

I ran off to join the Navy but they wouldn't have me, they didn't think Ancient Greek was a good enough qualification. I got a job in a hash joint by lying about my literacy. It's better than jumping off the bell tower. Give my regards to Coromandel. Ever yours, Bo.

As usual, I couldn't decide whether or not you were sneering.

Of course I mourned; not so much for your departure, as that had been, I now saw, a foregone conclusion, but for its suddenness. I had been deprived of that last necessary scene, the park bench, the light spring wind, the trenchcoat (which I was destined never to buy), your vanishing figure. Even after I realized that our future would have contained neither the dreaded bungalow and electric razor nor those vague, happy possibilities I had once imagined, but, inevitable as a rhymed couplet, an emptied bottle of sleeping pills whose effects you might not have helped me walk off, I continued to mourn.

Because you had not left in the proper way it seemed as though you had never left at all. You hung around, like a miasma or the smell of mice, waiting to deflate my attempts at optimism—for out of sheer fright I soon began to make them—with your own jaundiced view of my behaviour. As if you were my darker twin or an adept in sinister telepathy I could sense on every occasion what your opinion would be. When I became engaged (seven months later, to an architect who designed, and continues to design, apartment buildings), you let me know you had expected other things of me. The actual wedding, and yes, I had all the trimmings including a white gown, filled you with scorn. I could see you in your dingy room, surrounded by empty sardine tins and lint-covered socks, living on nothing but your derision and your refusal to sell out, as I was so palpably doing. (To what? To whom? Unlike later generations, we were never able to pinpoint the enemy.)

My two children did not impress you, nor did the
academic position which I subsequently achieved. I
have become, in a minor way, an authority on women
domestic novelists of the nineteenth century. I discovered after my marriage that I really had more in
common with them than I did with Gothic romances;
I suppose this insight into my true character signifies
maturity, a word you despise. The most prominent of
my subjects is Mrs. Gaskell, but you may have heard
of Mrs. J.H. Riddell as well; she wrote also under the
pen name of F.G. Trafford. I gave quite a creditable
paper on her *George Geith of Fen Court*, which was
later published in a reputable journal. Needless to say
I have tenure, as my department, averse to women
for many years, has recently been under some pres-
sure to justify its hiring policies. I am a token, as you
never tire of pointing out. I dress well, too, as befits a
token. The drab, defiantly woollen wardrobe you may
remember vanished little by little into the bins of the
Salvation Army as I grew richer, and was replaced by
a moderately chic collection of pantsuits and brisk
dresses. My male colleagues think of me as efficient
and rather cold. I no longer have casual affairs, as I
hate mementoes that cannot be thrown away. My
coats no longer flap, and when I attend academic
conferences nobody stares.

It was at one of these, the big one, the central flesh
market and hiring fair, that I saw you last. Curiously
enough, it was held in New York that year. I was
giving a paper on Amelia Edwards and other female
journalists of the period. When I saw your name on
the agenda I thought it must be someone else. But it
was you, all right, and you spent the entire session
discussing whether or not John Keats had had syphilis.
You had done a considerable amount of research on
the medical uses of mercury in the early part of the
century, and your last paragraph was a masterpiece of
inconclusion. You had gained weight, in fact you
looked healthy, you looked as if you played golf.

Though I watched in vain for a sardonic smile: your delivery was deadpan.

Afterwards I went up to congratulate you. You were surprised to see me; you had never thought of me, you said, ending up quite like this, and your possibly dismayed gaze took in my salon haircut, my trim-fitting red jumpsuit, my jaunty boots. You yourself were married, with three children, and you hastily showed me wallet snapshots, holding them out like protective talismans. I matched them with my own. Neither of us suggested having a drink. We wished each other well; we were both disappointed. You had wanted me, I saw now, to die young of consumption or some equally operatic disease. Underneath it all you too were a romantic.

That should have been that, and I can't understand why it isn't. It is absolutely true that I love my husband and children. In addition to attending faculty meetings, where I crotchet afghan squares during discussions of increments and curriculae, I cook them nourishing meals, arrange birthday parties and make my own bread and pickles, most of the time. My husband admires my achievements and is supportive, as they say, during my depressions, which become rarer. I have a rich and rewarding sex life, and I can already hear you ridiculing the adjectives, but it is rich and rewarding in spite of you. And you have done no better than I have.

But when I returned from the conference to the house where I live, which is not a bungalow but a two-storey colonial and in which, ever since I moved in, you have occupied the cellar, you were not gone. I expected you to have been dispelled, exorcised: you had become real, you had a wife and three snapshots, and banality is after all the magic antidote for unrequited love. But it was not enough. There you were, in your accustomed place, over by the shelf to the right of the cellar stairs where I keep the preserves, standing dusty and stuffed like Jeremy Bentham in his glass case, looking at me not with your former scorn, it's true, but with reproach, as if I had let it happen, as if it was my fault. Surely you don't want it back, that misery, those decaying buildings, that seductive despair and emptiness, that fear? Surely you don't want to be stuck on that slushy Boston street forever. You should have been more careful. I try to tell you it would have ended badly, it was not the way you remember, you are deceiving yourself, but you refuse to be consoled. *Goodbye,* I tell you, waiting for your glance, pensive, regretful. You are supposed to turn and walk away, past the steamer trunks, around the corner into the laundry room, and vanish behind the twinset washer-dryer; but you do not move.

When It Happens

o o o

Mrs. Burridge is putting up green tomato pickles. There are twelve quarts in each lot with a bit left over, and that is the end of the jars. At the store they tell her there's a strike on at the factory where they get made. She doesn't know anything about that but you can't buy them anywhere, and even before this they were double what they were last year; she considers herself lucky she had those in the cellar. She has a lot of green tomatoes because she heard on the weather last night there was going to be a killer frost, so she put on her parka and her work gloves and took the lantern out to the garden in the pitch dark and picked off all the ones she could see, over three bushels. She can lift the full baskets herself but she asked Frank to carry them in for her; he grumbles, but he likes it when she asks. In the morning the news said the growers had been hit and that would shoot the price up, not that the growers would get any of it themselves, everyone knows it's the stores that make the money.

She feels richer than she did yesterday, but on the other hand there isn't that much you can do with green tomatoes. The pickles hardly made a dint in them, and Frank has said, as he does every year, that they will never eat twenty-four quarts of green tomato pickle with just the two of them and the children gone. Except when they come to visit and eat me out of house and home, Mrs. Burridge adds silently. The truth is she has always made two batches and the children never liked it anyway, it was Frank ate them all and she knows perfectly well he'll do it again, without even noticing. He likes it on bread and cheese when he's watching the hockey games, during every commercial he goes out to the kitchen and makes himself another slice, even if he's just had a big meal, leaving a trail of crumbs and bits of pickle from the counter across the floor and over the front room rug to his big chair. It used to annoy Mrs. Burridge, especially the crumbs, but now she watches him with a kind of sadness; she once thought their life together would go on forever but she has come to realize this is not the case.

She doesn't even feel like teasing him about his spare tire any more, though she does it all the same because he would miss it if she stopped. "There you go," she says, in the angular, prodding, metallic voice she cannot change because everyone expects it from her, if she spoke any other way they would think she was ill, "you keep on muching away like that and it'll be easy for me to get you out of bed in the mornings, I'll just give you a push and you'll roll all the way down the stairs like a barrel." And he answers in his methodical voice, pretending to be lazy even though he isn't, "You need a little fun in life," as though his pickles and cheese are slightly disreputable, almost like an orgy. Every year he tells her she's made too much but there would be a fuss all right if he went down to the cellar one day and there wasn't any left.

Mrs. Burridge has made her own pickles since 1952, which was the first year she had the garden. She remembers it especially because her daughter Sarah was on the way and she had trouble bending down to do the weeding. When she herself was growing up everyone did their own pickles, and their own canning and preserving too. But after the war most women gave it up, there was more money then and it was easier to buy things at the store. Mrs. Burridge never gave it up, though most of her friends thought she was wasting her time, and now she is glad she didn't, it kept her in practice while the others were having to learn all over again. Though with the sugar going up the way it is, she can't understand how long anyone is going to be able to afford even the homemade things.

On paper Frank is making more money than he ever has; yet they seem to have less to spend. They could always sell the farm, she supposes, to people from the city who would use it as a weekend place; they could get what seems like a very high price, several of the farms south of them have gone that way. But Mrs. Burridge does not have much faith in money; also it is a waste of the land, and this is her home, she has it arranged the way she wants it.

When the second batch is on and simmering she goes to the back door, opens it, and stands with her arms folded across her stomach, looking out. She catches herself doing this four or five times a day now and she doesn't quite know why. There isn't much to see, just the barn and the back field with the row of dead elms Frank keeps saying he's going to cut down, and the top of Clarke's place sticking over the hill. She isn't sure what she is looking for but she has the odd idea she may see something burning, smoke coming up from the horizon, a column of it or perhaps more than one column, off to the south. This is such a peculiar thought for her to have that she hasn't told it to any one else. Yesterday Frank saw her standing at the back door and asked her about it at dinner; anything he wants to talk to her about he saves up till dinner, even if he thinks about it in the morning. He wondered why she was at the back door, doing nothing at all for over ten minutes, and Mrs.

Burridge told him a lie, which made her very uneasy.
She said she heard a strange dog barking, which
wasn't a good story because their own dogs were
right there and they didn't notice a thing. But Frank
let it pass; perhaps he thinks she is getting funny in
her old age and doesn't want to call attention to it,
which would be like him. He'll track mud all over
her nice shiny kitchen floor but he'd hate to hurt
anyone's feelings. Mrs. Burridge decides, a little wist-
fully, that despite his pig-headedness he is a kind and
likable man, and for her this is like renouncing a
cherished and unquestionable belief, such as the flat-
ness of the earth. He has made her angry so many
times.

When the pickles are cool she labels them as she
always does with the name and the date and carries
them down the cellar stairs. The cellar is the old kind,
with stone walls and a dirt floor. Mrs. Burridge likes
to have everything neat—she still irons her sheets—
so she had Frank build her some shelves right after
they were married. The pickles go on one side, jams
and jellies on the other, and the quarts of preserves
along the bottom. It used to make her feel safe to
have all that food in the cellar; she would think to
herself, well, if there's a snowstorm or anything and
we're cut off, it won't be so bad. It doesn't make her
feel safe any more. Instead she thinks that if she
has to leave suddenly she won't be able to take any
of the jars with her, they'd be too heavy to carry.

She comes back up the stairs after the last trip. It's
not as easy as it used to be, her knee still bothers
her as it has ever since she fell six years ago, she
tripped on the second-last step. She's asked Frank a
million times to fix the stairs but he hasn't done it,
that's what she means by pig-headed. If she asks him
more than twice to do something he calls it nagging,
and maybe it is, but who's going to do it if he won't?
The cold vacant hole at the back of this question is
too much for her.

She has to stop herself from going to the back door

again. Instead she goes to the back window and looks
out, she can see almost the same things anyway.
Frank is going towards the barn, carrying something,
it looks like a wrench. The way he walks, slower than
he used to, bent forward a little—from the back he's
like an old man, how many years has he been walking
that way?—makes her think, *He can't protect me.*
She doesn't think this on purpose, it simply occurs
to her, and it isn't only him, it's all of them, they've
lost the power, you can tell by the way they walk.
They are all waiting, just as Mrs. Burridge is, for
whatever it is to happen. Whether they realize it or
not. Lately when she's gone to the Dominion Store in
town she has seen a look on the faces of the women
there—she knows most of them, she wouldn't be mistaken—an anxious, closed look, as if they are frightened of something but won't talk about it. They're
wondering what they will do, perhaps they think
there's nothing they can do. This air of helplessness
exasperates Mrs. Burridge, who has always been practical.

For weeks she has wanted to go to Frank and ask
him to teach her how to use the gun. In fact he has
two guns, a shotgun and a twenty-two rifle; he used
to like going after a few ducks in the fall, and of
course there are the groundhogs, they have to be shot
because of the holes they make in the fields Frank
drives over on the tractor five or six times a year. A
lot of men get injured by overturning tractors. But she
can't ask him because she can't explain to him why
she needs to know, and if she doesn't explain
he will only tease. "Anyone can shoot a gun," he'll say,
"all you have to do is pull the trigger . . . oh, you
mean you want to hit something, well now, that's
different, who you planning to kill?" Perhaps he won't
say that; perhaps this is only the way he talked twenty years ago, before she stopped taking an interest in
things outside the house. But Mrs. Burridge will
never know because she will never ask. She doesn't
have the heart to say to him, *Maybe you'll be dead.*

Maybe you'll go off somewhere when it happens, maybe there will be a war. She can remember the last war.

Nothing has changed outside the window, so she turns away and sits down at the kitchen table to make out her shopping list. Tomorrow is their day for going into town. She tries to plan the day so she can sit down at intervals; otherwise her feet start swelling up. That began with Sarah and got worse with the other two children and it's never really gone away. All her life, ever since she got married, she has made lists of things that have to be bought, sewed, planted, cooked, stored; she already has her list made for next Christmas, all the names and the gift she will buy for each, and the list of what she needs for Christmas dinner. But she can't seem to get interested in it, it's too far away. She can't believe in a distant future that is orderly like the past, she no longer seems to have the energy; it's as if she is saving it up for when she will have to use it.

She is even having trouble with the shopping list. Instead of concentrating on the paper—she writes on the backs of the used-up days off the page-a-day calendar Frank gives her every New Year's—she is gazing around the kitchen, looking at all the things she will have to leave behind when she goes. That will be the hardest part. Her mother's china, her silver, even though it is an old-fashioned pattern and the silver is wearing off, the egg timer in the shape of a chicken Sarah gave her when she was twelve, the ceramic salt-and-pepper shakers, green horses with perforated heads, that one of the other children brought back from the Ex. She thinks of walking up the stairs, the sheets folded in the chest, the towels stacked neatly on the shelves, the beds made, the quilt that was her grandmother's, it makes her want to cry. On her bureau, the wedding picture, herself in a shiny satin gown (the satin was a mistake, it emphasized her hips), Frank in the suit he has not worn since except to funerals, his hair cut too short on the sides and a surprising tuft at the top, like a woodpecker's. The children when they were babies. She thinks of her girls now and hopes they will not have babies; it is no longer the right time for it.

Mrs. Burridge wishes someone would be more precise, so she could make better plans. Everyone knows something is going to happen, you can tell by reading the newspapers and watching the television, but nobody is sure what it will be, nobody can be exact. She has her own ideas about it though. At first it will simply become quieter. She will have an odd feeling that something is wrong but it will be a few days before she is able to pin it down. Then she will notice that the planes are no longer flying over on their way to the Malton Airport, and that the noise from the highway two miles away, which is quite distinct when the leaves are off the trees, has almost disappeared. The television will be non-committal about it; in fact, the television, which right now is filled with bad news, of strikes, shortages, famines, layoffs and price increases, will become sweet-tempered and placating, and long intervals of classical music will appear on the radio. About this time Mrs. Burridge will realize that the news is being censored as it was during the war.

Mrs. Burridge is not positive about what will happen next; that is, she knows what will happen but she is not positive about the order. She expects it will be the gas and oil: the oil delivery man will simply not turn up at his usual time, and one morning the corner filling station will be closed. Just that, no explanations, because of course they—she does not know who "they" are, but she has always believed in their existence—they do not want people to panic. They are trying to keep things looking normal, possibly they have already started on this program and that is in fact why things still do look normal. Luckily she and Frank have the diesel fuel tank in the shed, it is three-quarters full, and they don't use the filling station anyway, they have their own gas pump. She has Frank bring in the old wood stove, the one they

stored under the barn when they had the furnace and
the electricity put in, and for once she blesses Frank's
habit of putting things off. She was after him for years
to take that stove to the dump. He cuts down the
dead elms, finally, and they burn them in the stove.

The telephone wires are blown down in a storm
and no one comes to fix them; or this is what Mrs.
Burridge deduces. At any rate, the phone goes dead.
Mrs. Burridge doesn't particularly mind, she never
liked using the phone much anyway, but it does
make her feel cut off.

About now men begin to appear on the back road,
the gravel road that goes past the gate, walking
usually by themselves, sometimes in pairs. They seem
to be heading north. Most of them are young, in their
twenties, Mrs. Burridge would guess. They are not
dressed like the men around here. It's been so long
since she has seen anyone *walking* along this road
that she becomes alarmed. She begins leaving the
dogs off their chains, she has kept them chained at
night ever since one of them bit a Jehovah's Witness
early one Sunday morning. Mrs. Burridge doesn't
hold with the Witnesses—she is United—but she
respects their perseverance, at least they have the
courage of their convictions which is more than you
can say for some members of her own church, and
she always buys a *Watchtower*. Maybe they have
been right all along.

It is about this time too that she takes one of the
guns, she thinks it will be the shotgun as she will have
a better chance of hitting something, and hides it,
along with the shells, under a piece of roofing behind
the barn. She does not tell Frank; he will have the
twenty-two. She has already picked out the spot.

They do not want to waste the little gasoline they
still have left in the pump so they do not make un-
necessary trips. They begin to eat the chickens, which
Mrs. Burridge does not look forward to. She hates
cleaning and plucking them, and the angriest she
ever got at Frank was the time he and Henry Clarke

decided to go into turkey farming. They did it too, despite all she had to say against it, and she had to cope with the turkeys escaping and scratching in the garden and impossible to catch, in her opinion they were the stupidest birds in God's creation, and she had to clean and pluck a turkey a week until luckily the blackhead wiped out a third of the flock, which was enough to discourage them, they sold off the rest at a loss. It was the only time she was actually glad to see Frank lose money on one of his ventures.

Mrs. Burridge will feel things are getting serious on the day the electricity goes off and does not come back on. She knows, with a kind of fatalism, that this will happen in November, when the freezer is full of the vegetables but before it is cold enough to keep the packages frozen outside. She stands and looks at the pliofilm bags of beans and corn and spinach and carrots, melting and sodden, and thinks, *Why couldn't they have waited till spring.* It is the waste, of food and also of her hard work, that aggravates her the most. She salvages what she can. During the Depression, she remembers, they used to say those on farms were better off than those in the city, because at least they had food; if you could keep the farm, that is; but she is no longer sure this is true. She feels beleaguered, isolated, like someone shut up inside a fortress, though no one has bothered them, in fact no one has passed their way for days, not even any of the solitary walking men.

With the electricity off they can no longer get the television. The radio stations, when they broadcast at all, give out nothing but soothing music, which Mrs. Burridge does not find soothing in the least.

One morning she goes to the back door and looks out and there are the columns of smoke, right where she's been expecting to see them, off to the south. She calls Frank and they stand watching. The smoke is thick and black, oily, as though something has exploded. She does not know what Frank is thinking; she herself is wondering about the children. She has had no news of them in weeks, but how could she? They stopped delivering mail some time ago.

Fifteen minutes later, Henry Clarke drives into the yard in his half-ton truck. This is very unusual as no one has been driving anywhere lately. There is another man with him, and Mrs. Burridge identifies him as the man three farms up who moved in four or five years ago. Frank goes out and talks with them, and they drive over to the gas pump and start pumping the rest of the previous gas into the truck. Frank comes back to the house. He tells her there's a little trouble down the road, they are going along to see about it and she isn't to worry. He goes into the back room, comes out with the twenty-two, asks her where the shotgun is. She says she doesn't know. He searches for it, fruitlessly—she can hear him swearing, he does not swear in her presence—until he gives up. He comes out, kisses her goodbye, which is unusual too, and says he'll be back in a couple of hours. She watches the three of them drive off in Henry Clarke's truck, towards the smoke; she knows he will not come back. She supposes she ought to feel more emotional about it, but she is well prepared, she has been saying goodbye to him silently for years.

She re-enters the house and closes the door. She is fifty-one, her feet hurt, and she does not know where she can go, but she realizes she cannot stay here. There will now be a lot of hungry people, those that can make it this far out of the cities will be young and tough, her house is a beacon, signalling warmth and food. It will be fought over, but not by her.

She goes upstairs, searches in the cupboard, and puts on her heavy slacks and her two thickest sweaters. Downstairs she gathers up all the food that will be light enough for her to carry: raisins, cooking chocolate, dried prunes and apricots, half a loaf of bread, some milk powder which she puts into a quart freezer bag, a piece of cheese. Then she unearths the shotgun from behind the barn. She thinks briefly of killing the livestock, the chickens, the heifers and the pig, so no one will do it who does not know the right way; but she herself does not know the right way, she has never killed anything in her life, Frank always did it, so she contents herself with opening the hen-house door and the gate into the back field. She hopes the animals will run away but she knows they probably will not.

She takes one last look around the house. As an afterthought, she adds her toothbrush to the bundle: she does not like the feel of unbrushed teeth. She does not go down into the cellar but she has an image of her carefully sealed bottles and jars, red and yellow and purple, shattered on the floor, in a sticky puddle that looks like blood. Those who come will be wasteful, what they cannot eat themselves they will destroy. She thinks about setting fire to the house herself, before anyone else can do it.

Mrs. Burridge sits at her kitchen table. On the back of her calendar page, it's for a Monday, she has written *Oatmeal*, in her evenly spaced public school handwriting that always got a star and has not changed very much since then. The dogs are a problem. After some thought she unchains them, but she does not let them past the gate: at a crucial moment they might give her away. She walks north in her heavy boots, carrying her parka because it is not yet cold enough to put it on, and her package of food and the shotgun which she has taken care to load. She passes the cemetery where her father and mother and her grandmother and grandfather are buried; the church used to be there but it burned down sixteen years ago and was rebuilt closer to the highway. Frank's people are in the other cemetery, his go back to the great-grandfather but they are Anglican, not that he kept it up. There is no one else on the road; she feels a little foolish. What if she is wrong and Frank comes back after all, what if nothing, really, is the matter? *Shortening*, she writes. She intends to make a lemon meringue pie for Sunday, when two of the children are coming up from the city for dinner.

It is almost evening and Mrs. Burridge is tired. She is in a part of the country she cannot remember, though she has stayed on the same road and it is a road she knows well; she has driven along it many times with Frank. But walking is not the same as driving. On one side there is a field, no buildings, on the other a woodlot; a stream flows through a culvert under the road. Mrs. Burridge kneels down to drink: the water is ice-cold and tastes of iron. Later there will be a frost, she can feel it. She puts on her parka and her gloves, and turns into the forest where she will not be seen. There she will eat some raisins and cheese and try to rest, waiting for the moon to rise so she can continue walking. It is now quite dark. She smells earth, wood, rotting leaves.

Suddenly her eye is caught by a flicker of red, and before she can turn back—how can this happen so quickly?—it takes shape, it is a small fire, off to the right, and two men are crouching near it. They have seen her, too: one of them rises and comes towards her. His teeth bare, he is smiling; he thinks she will be easy, an old woman. He says something but she cannot imagine what it is, she does not know how people dressed like that would talk.

They have spotted her gun, their eyes have fastened on it, they want it. Mrs. Burridge knows what she must do. She must wait until they are close enough and then she must raise the gun and shoot them, using one barrel for each, aiming at the faces. Otherwise they will kill her, she has no doubt about that. She will have to be fast, which is too bad because her hands feel thick and wooden; she is afraid, she does not want the loud noise or the burst of red that will follow, she has never killed anything in her life. She has no pictures beyond this point. You never know how you will act in a thing like that until it actually happens.

Mrs. Burridge looks at the kitchen clock. On her list she writes *Cheese*, they are eating more cheese now than they used to because of the price of meat. She gets up and goes to the kitchen door.

A Travel Piece

o o o

Annette is wiped right out. She never used to be this wiped out after a job; she supposes it's the medication. Any kind of a pill is a drain on the system, she doesn't like taking them but there you are.

She chews on one of the vacu-packed peanuts, thumbing through the travel brochure from the seat pocket, letting her mind drift among the coloured pictures. Thirty-six vacations in the sun, described in glowing terms, with the prices, all-inclusive it says but of course there are extras. *A gem of an island almost undiscovered by tourists, with brilliant white sand beaches and bluegreen lagoons complemented by the friendliness of the people.* Annette is returning from just such an island and she too writes pieces like this, but hers are not advertisements, they're for the newspaper and, when she gets lucky, for the glossy magazines as well, so the things she writes have to be less bland: little anecdotes, the personal touch, details on where to eat and how good the service is, jokes told by the barman if any, where to go shopping for bargains, all those straw hats and curios, out-of-the-way things you might do, such as climbing an extinct volcano or cooking a parrot-fish on a coral reef, if you had the energy and the desire. Increasingly she doesn't, but she puts herself through the paces anyway, she would consider it cheating to recommend these things without having done them. This is what makes her a good travel writer, among other things; and she has a knack for discovering local oddities, she knows what to look for, she has an eye for detail.

She's learned though that she has to strike the right balance between what she manages to notice, spontaneously and candidly—and she always takes a camera with her, just in case, though for the glossies they usually send down their own photographer—and what she chooses to leave out. For instance, by lifting her head slightly she can read: LIFE JEST INDER FRONT OF YOUR SEAT. It says LIFE JEST because the lettering, which is embroidered right into the cloth of the pocket, has been worn away by the outgoing and incoming thighs of countless passengers. It would strike a humorous note but she can't use it; the airline company would resent the implication that its planes were falling to pieces and that would be it for the complimentary tickets.

People, she found, did not want any hint of danger in the kind of articles it was her business to write. Even the ones who would never go to the places she described, who could not afford it, did not want to hear about danger or even unpleasantness; it was as if they wanted to believe that there was somewhere left in the world where all was well, where unpleasant things did not happen. An unspoiled Eden; that had been a useful phrase. Once, it seemed a long time ago, staying home meant safety, though tedium as well, and going to the places that were her specialty —the Caribbean, the northern half of South America, Mexico—meant adventure, threat, pirates, brigands, lawlessness. Now it was the reverse, home was the dangerous place and people went on vacation to snatch a few weeks of uneventfulness. If small black

beads of oil were appearing on the white sand
beaches, if the barman's niece had stabbed her husband, if things were stolen or it rained, they did not
want to know about it; if they felt like disasters or
crimes they could read about them in the other
pages of the newspaper. So she did not report such
things and she tried her best not to notice them.
There was that pig on the beach in Mexico, being
killed by a man who didn't know how to do it properly, because some tourist had wanted a Polynesian
feast. That was the sort of thing you had to filter out.
Her job was to be pleased, and she did this well, she
was evenly tanned and in trim physical shape, she
had direct blue eyes and a white smile and was good
at asking interested, polite questions and coping with
minor emergencies, such as lost suitcases, cheerfully
and without becoming irritated. She seldom had trouble; there was something about her, an air of profes-
sionalism, she was too thorough to be an ordinary
tourist; those in the industry sensed it would be bad
for business to upset her.

So she went her way undisturbed among the green
trees, along the white beaches, between the blue
sky and the indecently blue ocean, which more and
more lately had come to seem like a giant screen, flat
and with pictures painted on it to create the illusion
of solidity. If you walked up to it and kicked it, it
would tear and your foot would go right through,
into another space which Annette could only visualize
as darkness, a night in which something she did not
want to look at was hiding. Things were being kept
from her, she had begun to feel, especially in lobbies
and in cars taking her to and from airports; people
were watching her, as if they were aware of this. It
was the constant surveillance that was exhausting
her, and the effort she had been making not to find
out.

She attempted once to describe these feelings to
her husband, but the attempt was not a success. Her
capacity for being easily pleased, delighted even, had

pervaded their marriage as well as her job, and he reacted at first with a kind of restrained, offended outrage, as if she had complained to the maître d' about a wine. Very well, madam, it shall be replaced, and a look that says: Stupid bitch. Jeff seemed hurt that she was not totally and altogether happy, that she had been coming home from her trips too tired to go out for special little dinners with him, that she crawled into bed and remained there between her mock vacations, emerging only long enough to plod through the required exercises at the typewriter. When she said, "Sometimes I feel I'm not alive," he took it as a comment on his love-making, and she had to spend half an hour reassuring him, telling him that wasn't what she meant; she'd been talking about her job. But his view of her job was that it was a lucky accident, she was a very fortunate girl to have a job like that. He himself was interning at a hospital— she'd put him through medical school on her own salary—and he felt abused and overworked. He could not understand why she wanted to stay home more; finally he swiped the pills for her, telling her they would steady her nerves. Which they have, she supposes, but then her nerves have not been unsteady, quite the contrary. It's the unbroken calm, both within and without, that is getting to her. Real events happen to other people, she thinks, why not me? And then there's her conviction that they are happening, all around her, but that they're being kept from her.

Once she took Jeff along with her, to Bermuda, though they couldn't really afford it as his way had to be paid, of course. She thought it would be good for them, he would see what she really did and stop idealizing her; she felt that perhaps he had married her because of her tan, he found her glamorous. And it would be fun to get away together. But it hadn't been. All he'd wanted to do was lie in the sun and he'd refused to eat the pumpkin soup, he was a meat and potatoes man. "Relax," he kept telling her, "why

don't you just lie down beside me and relax?" He
hadn't understood why she needed to go shopping,
to explore the markets, to visit all the possible
beaches and restaurants. "It's my job," she told him,
to which he replied, "Some job, I should have a job
like that." "You're not suited for it," she said, thinking
of the fuss he had made over the fried plantain. He
could not understand that being pleased was hard
work, and he thought she was being too friendly
with the taxi drivers.

The plane starts to tilt down as Annette is finishing
her martini. Jeff told her she should go easy on mixing
the pills and liquor, but one wouldn't hurt, so dutifully she ordered only one. For a minute or two no
one notices; then the stewardesses are at their posts
and a blurred, alarmed voice is coming through the
intercom, but as usual it's inaudible, and half of it is
in French anyway. Hardly anyone is screaming. Annette takes off her high-heeled shoes, Cuban actually,
they're better for walking, slips them under the seat,
and rests her forehead on her knees, protecting it
with her arms. She's following the instructions on
the card tucked into the seat pocket; there's a diagram on it too, about how to blow up the life vest by
pulling the knobs. When the girls went through their
routine at the beginning of the flight she didn't
watch; she hasn't watched for a long time.

By twisting her head to the right she can see the
card sticking out of the pocket of the seat next to her,
and the edge of the vomit bag as well; they don't
say *vomit* but *discomfort*, which fits. Next to the
vomit bag is a man's knee. Nothing seems to be happening so Annette looks up to see what's going on.
A lot of the people don't have their heads down on
their knees the way they've been told, they're sitting
bolt upright, just staring, as if they're watching a
movie. The man next to Annette is white as a sheet.
She asks him if he wants a Rolaid, but he doesn't, so
she eats one herself. She carries a small arsenal of

patent medicines with her on these trips, laxatives, cold remedies, vitamin c, aspirins; everything you can get she's had a dose of at one time or another.

The plane is going down in a long glide, it's a lot easier than she would have expected. There's a faint smell of burning rubber, that's all, no explosions; she feels hardly any discomfort, though her ears are popping. The descent is silent too because the engines aren't working, and except for one woman who is still screaming half-heartedly and another who is crying, none of the passengers is making much noise.

"Where you from?" the man beside her says, abruptly, perhaps it's the only thing he can think of to say to a woman on an airplane, no matter what the circumstances; but before Annette can answer there's a jolt that knocks her teeth together, it isn't at all like hitting water. More like a slightly bumpy runway, as if the sea is hard, like cement.

It must have damaged the loudspeakers though, because the blurred voices have stopped. The passengers crowd into the aisles, released, their mingled voices rising excitedly, like children let out of school. Annette thinks they are being remarkably calm, though real panic, with stampeding feet and people being trampled on, is difficult when the aisle is so narrow. She always notes the locations of the emergency exits and tries to sit near one but she has not managed it this time, so she decides to wait in her seat until the jam is over. The back door appears to be stuck so everyone is shoving to the front. The man sitting beside her is trying to elbow his way into the lineup, which is like a supermarket queue, they even have bundles. Annette folds her hands and looks out through the oval porthole window but all she can see is the surface of the ocean, flat as a parking lot; there isn't even any smoke or flames.

When the aisle is clearer she stands up, lifts the seat as the instruction card has told her and takes out the life vest. She has noticed that many people, in their rush to get out, have been forgetting to do this.

She collects her coat from the overhead rack, which is still crammed with other coats, abandoned by their owners. The sun is shining as brightly as ever, but it may cool off at night. She has the coat with her because when she steps off the plane at the other end it will still be winter. She picks up her camera bag and her large purse, which doubles as a flight bag; she's familiar with the advantages of travelling light, she once did a fashion piece on crushable dresses.

Between the First Class cabin at the front and the Tourist Class is the tiny kitchen. As she goes through it, at the tail end of the line, Annette sees a rack of lunch trays, with plastic-wrapped sandwiches and desserts with snap-on lids. The drink trolley is there too, parked out of the way. She takes several of the sandwiches, three bottles of ginger ale and a handful of vacu-packed peanuts and stuffs them into her purse. She does this as much because she is hungry as for any other reason, but she is thinking, too, that they may need provisions. Though they will certainly be picked up soon, the plane must have sent out a distress signal. They will be rescued by helicopters. Still, it will be nice to have some lunch. She considers momentarily taking a bottle of liquor too, from the drink trolley, but rejects this as a bad idea. She remembers having read magazine articles about delirious sailors.

When she gets to the chute leading down from the open doorway she hesitates. The blue watery surface below her is dotted with round orange discs. Some of them have already made considerable headway, or have they been blown? From a distance the scene looks delightful, with the orange circles twirling on the sea like wading pools filled with happy children. Though she's a little disappointed; she knows this is an emergency but so far everything has been so uneventful, so orderly. Surely an emergency ought to feel like one.

She would like to take a picture of the scene, with the orange against the blue, two of her favourite colours. But someone at the bottom is calling to her to hurry up, so she sits on the chute, placing her knees together so her skirt won't blow up, holds her purse, her camera and her folded coat firmly on her lap, and pushes off. It's like going down a slide, the kind they used to have in parks.

Annette finds it odd that she should be the last one off the plane. Surely the captain and the stewardesses ought to have remained on board until all the passengers were safely off, but there is no sign of them. She doesn't have much time to think about this however, because the round boat is in a state of confusion, there seem to be a lot of people on it and someone is shouting orders. "Row," the voice says, "we've got to get away from here . . . the suction!"

Annette wonders what he is talking about. There are only two paddles in any case so she settles herself out of the way and watches while a couple of men, the owner of the voice and a younger man, paddle at either side of the boat as if their lives depended on it. The boat moves up and down with the waves, which are not large, it rotates—one of the men must be stronger than the other, Annette thinks—and it moves gradually away from the plane, in the direction of the afternoon sun. Annette feels as though she's being taken for a boat-ride; she leans back against the swelling rubber side of the boat and enjoys it. Behind them, the plane settles imperceptibly lower. Annette thinks it would be a good idea to get a picture of it, for use when they are rescued and she can write up the story, and she opens her camera bag, takes out her camera and adjusts the lens; but when she squirms around so she can get a better view, the plane is gone. She thinks it ought to have made a noise of some kind, but they are quite a distance from where it was.

"No sense in getting too far away from the crash site," says the man who has been giving the orders. There's something military about him, Annette decides; maybe it's the trimmed moustache or the fact that he's older. He and the other man ship their paddles and he begins to roll a cigarette, taking the papers and tobacco from his breast pocket. "I suggest we introduce ourselves," he says; he's used to directing.

There are not as many people in the boat as Annette at first supposed. There's the two men, the one who says he's in insurance (though Annette doubts this), and the younger one, who has a beard and claims to teach at a free school; the older man's wife, who is plump and kind-looking and keeps saying "I'm all right," although she isn't, she's been crying quietly to herself ever since they've been in the boat; an overly tanned woman of forty-five or so who gives no clue as to her occupation, and a boy who says he's a university student. When it comes to Annette's turn she says, "I write a food column for one of the newspapers." In fact she did this for a couple of months, before she got onto the travel page, so she knows enough about it to be able to back it up. Still, she is surprised at herself for lying and can't imagine why she did. The only reason she can think of is that she hasn't believed the stories of any of the others, except the plump, crying woman, who could not possibly be anything other than what she so obviously is.

"We've been damn lucky," says the older man, and they all agree.

"What are we supposed to do now?" says the tanned woman.

"Just sit around and wait to be rescued, I guess," the bearded schoolteacher says, with a nervous laugh. "It's an enforced vacation."

"It'll just be a matter of hours," says the older man. "They're more efficient about these things than they used to be."

Annette volunteers the information that she has some food and they all congratulate her for being so resourceful and foresighted. She provides the wrapped sandwiches and they divide them up equally; they pass around one of the bottles of ginger ale to wash them down. Annette doesn't say anything about the peanuts or the other two bottles of ginger ale. She does say, however, that she has some seasick pills if anyone needs one.

She's about to toss the plastic sandwich trays overboard, but the older man stops her. "No, no," he says, "can't throw those away. They might come in handy." She can't imagine what for, but she does as he says.

The plump woman has stopped crying and has become quite talkative; she wants to know all about the food column. In fact they are now a festive bunch, chattering away as if they are on a huge sofa in a recreation room, or in the waiting room of an airport where the flights have been temporarily held up. There's the same atmosphere of time being passed, from necessity but with superficial cheer. Annette is bored. For a moment she thought something real had happened to her but there is no danger here, it is as safe in this lifeboat as everywhere else, and the piece she would write about it would come out sounding the same as her other pieces. *For exploring the Caribbean, a round orange lifeboat strikes an unusual note. The vistas are charming, and you have a body-to-body contact with the sea which is simply not possible in any other kind of boat. Take some sandwiches and plan to stay out for lunch!*

The sun sets in its usual abrupt, spectacular fashion, and it's not until then that they begin to get worried. No helicopters have appeared, and none of the other lifeboats is in sight. Perhaps they paddled away too quickly. They haven't even heard any sounds of distant rescue operations. But "They'll be along, all right," the older man says, and his wife suggests they have a singsong. She begins with "You Are My Sunshine," warbling in a church soprano, and continues through a repertoire of once-popular favourites: "On Top Of Old Smokey," "Good Night Irene." The others join in, and Annette is momentarily amazed by the numbers of words to these songs that she herself can remember. She goes to sleep during one of the choruses, her winter coat pulled over her; she's glad she brought it.

She awakens feeling groggy and clogged. She can't believe they're all still on the boat, it's beginning to get annoying, and she is boiling hot under her coat. The rubber of the lifeboat is hot too and there's no wind, the sea is as flat as the palm of your hand with only a sickening groundswell. The others are sprawled listlessly around the boat's circumference, their legs in awkward tangles here and there. Annette thinks to herself they'd be better off with fewer people in the boat, but immediately censors this. The two women are still asleep; the plump one, the singer, lies with her mouth open, snoring slightly. Annette rubs her eyes; the lids feel dry and gritty. She seems to remember getting up in the night and squatting perilously over the edge of the boat; someone else must have made this effort and failed, or not made it at all, for there is a faint smell of urine. She is very thirsty.

The older man is awake, smoking in silence; so is the one with the beard. The student is drowsing still, curled in a heap, like a puppy.

"What should we do?" Annette asks.

"Stick it out till they come for us," says the older man. He doesn't look so military any more with his day's growth of stubble.

"Maybe they won't come," says the bearded man. "Maybe we're in the Bermuda whatchamacallit. You know, where those ships and planes vanish without a trace. What made the plane go down, anyway?"

Annette looks at the sky, which is more like a flat screen than ever. Maybe this is what has happened, she thinks, they've gone through the screen to the other side; that's why the rescuers can't see them. On this side of the screen, where she thought there would be darkness, there is merely a sea like the other one, with thousands of castaways floating around in orange lifeboats, lost and waiting to be rescued.

"The main thing," says the older man, "is to keep your mind occupied." He flicks his cigarette butt into the water. Annette expects to see a shark emerge and snap it up, but none does. "First off, we'll all get sunstroke if we aren't careful." He's right, they are all quite red.

He wakes the others and puts them to work constructing a shade, which they make from Annette's winter coat and the men's suit jackets, the buttons of one inserted into the buttonholes of the next. They prop it up with the paddles, lashing it on with neckties and stockings, and sit under it, with a fleeting sense of accomplishment. It's hot and stuffy, but it is out of the sun. Again at his suggestion the men turn out their pockets and the women empty their purses, "to see what we've got to work with," the older man says. Annette has forgotten everyone's name and suggests they introduce themselves again, which they do. Bill and Verna, Julia, Mike and Greg. Julia has a pounding headache and takes several of Annette's aspirins-with-codeine. Bill is going through the assortment of handkerchiefs, keys, compacts, lipsticks, travel-sized bottles of hand lotion, pills and chewing gum. He has appropriated the two remaining bottles of ginger ale and the peanuts, which he says will have to be rationed. For breakfast he lets them each have a Chiclet and a cough drop, to suck on. After that they take turns brushing their teeth, with Annette's toothbrush. She's the only one who has travelled light and thus has all her toiletries with her. The others used suitcases, which of course went down in the hold of the plane.

"If it rains," Bill says, "this boat is perfect for catching water," but it does not look like rain.

Bill has a lot of good ideas. In the afternoon he spends some time fishing, with a hook made from a safety-pin and a line of dental floss. He catches nothing. He says they could attract seagulls by flashing Annette's camera lens at them, if there were any seagulls. Annette is lethargic, although she keeps prodding herself, reminding herself that this is important, this may be the real thing, now that they have not been rescued.

"Were you in the war?" she asks Bill, who looks smug that she has noticed.

"You learn to be resourceful," he says. Towards evening they share out one of the bottles of ginger ale, and Bill allows them three peanuts each, telling them to scrape the salt off before eating them.

Annette goes to sleep thinking of a different story; it will have to be different now. She won't even have to write it, it will be her story As Told To, with a picture of herself, emaciated and sunburned but smiling bravely. Tomorrow she should take some pictures of the others.

During the night, which they spend under the sunshade, now a communal blanket, there is a scuffle. It's Greg the student and Bill, who has hit him and now claims he was making a try for the last bottle of ginger ale. They shout angrily at each other until Verna says it must have been a mistake, the boy was having a bad dream. All is quiet again but Annette is awake, she gazes up at the stars, you can't see stars like that in the city.

After a while there is heavy breathing, surely she's imagining it, but there's a distinct sound of furtive copulation. Who can it be? Julia and Mike, Julia and Greg? Not Verna, surely, in her corset which Annette is positive she has not taken off. Annette is a little disappointed that no one has made a pass at her, if that sort of thing is going around. But it was probably initiated by Julia, that suntanned solitary voyager, this must be what she goes on vacations for. Annette thinks of Jeff, wonders how he reacted to the fact that she is missing. She wishes he was here, he would be able to do something, though she doesn't know what. They could make love, anyway.

In the morning she scans their faces for signs, revealing clues as to who did what, but finds nothing. They brush their teeth once more, then rub hand lotion onto their faces, which is refreshing. Bill passes round a package of Tums and more cough drops; he's saving the peanuts and the ginger ale for the evening meal. He devises a strainer out of his shirt and trails it over the side of the boat, to catch plankton, he says. He brings in some messy green stuff, squeezes out the salt water, and chews a handful thoughtfully. The others each take a mouthful, except Julia who says she can't swallow it. Verna tries, but spits hers out. Annette gets it down; it's salty and tastes of fish. Later, Bill does manage to catch a small fish and they eat chunks of that also; the hot fish smell mingles with the other smells, unwashed bodies and slept-in clothes, which are rubbing against Annette's nerves. She's irritable, she's stopped taking the pills, maybe that's why.

Bill has a knife, and with it he slices the plastic sandwich trays in two, then cuts slits in them to make sun goggles, "like the Eskimos," he says. He has definite leadership ability. He unravels part of Verna's sweater, then twists the pink wool to make the strings to tie them with. They have abandoned the coat sunshade, it was too hot and the paddles had to be held upright all the time, so they fasten the plastic trays over their faces. They smear their noses and lips and the exposed parts of their foreheads with lipstick from the purse collection; Bill says it will be protection against sunburn. Annette is disturbed by the effect, these masks and bloody markings. What bothers her is that she can't tell any more who these people are, it could be anyone behind the white plastic faces with slit eyes. But she must look like that too. It is exotic though, and she is still functioning well enough to

think of taking a picture, though she doesn't take it.
She ought to, for the same reason she's kept her
watch conscientiously wound up, it would help morale by implying there is a future. But suddenly
there's no point.

About two o'clock Greg, the student, starts thrashing
around. He lunges for the side of the boat and tries to
get his head over into the sea. Bill throws himself on
top of him and after a minute Mike joins him. They
hold Greg down on the bottom of the boat. "He was
drinking sea water," Mike says, "I saw him, early this
morning." The boy is gasping like a fish, and he looks
like a fish too in his impersonal plastic face. Bill removes the mask, and the human features glare up into
his. "He's delirious," Bill says. "If we let him up, he'll
jump overboard." Bill's plastic mask turns, pointing itself toward the other members of the group. No one
says anything, but they are thinking, Annette knows
what they are thinking because she is thinking the
same thing. They can't hold him down forever. If they
let him up, he will die, and not only that, he will be
lost to them, wasted. They themselves are dying slowly of thirst. Surely it would be better to . . . Verna is
rummaging, slowly and painfully, like a crippled
bumblebee, in the heap of clothing and debris; what
is she looking for? Annette feels she is about to witness something mundane and horrible, doubly so because it will be bathed not in sinister blood-red
lightning but in the ordinary sunlight she has walked
in all her life; some tacky ritual put on for the tourists,
tacky because it is put on for tourists, for those who
are not responsible, for those who make the lives of
others their transient spectacle and pleasure. She is a
professional tourist, she works at being pleased and at
not participating; at sitting still and watching. But
they are going to slit his throat, like that pig on the
beach in Mexico, and for once she does not find it
quaint and unusual. "Stay out of it," the man in the
light-green suit had said to his wife, who was senti-

mental about animals. Could you stay out by wishing to?

I can always say it wasn't me, I couldn't help it, she thinks, visualizing the newspaper interview. But there may not be one, and she is therefore stuck in the present, with four Martians and one madman waiting for her to say something. So this is what goes on behind her back, so this is what it means to be alive, she's sorry she wondered. But the sky is not flat any more, it's bluer than ever and recedes away from her, clear but unfocused. You are my sunshine, Annette thinks; when skies are grey. The quality of the light has not changed. Am I one of them or not?

The Resplendent Quetzal

∘ ∘ ∘

Sarah was sitting near the edge of the sacrificial well. She had imagined something smaller, more like a wishing well, but this was huge, and the water at the bottom wasn't clear at all. It was mud-brown; a few clumps of reeds were growing over to one side, and the trees at the top dangled their roots, or were they vines, down the limestone walls into the water. Sarah thought there might be some point to being a sacrificial victim if the well were nicer, but you would never get her to jump into a muddy hole like that. They were probably pushed, or knocked on the head and thrown in. According to the guidebook the water was deep but it looked more like a swamp to her.

Beside her a group of tourists was being rounded up by the guide, who obviously wanted to get the whole thing over with so he could cram them back onto their pink and purple striped *turismo* bus and relax. These were Mexican tourists, and Sarah found it reassuring that other people besides Canadians and Americans wore big hats and sunglasses and took pictures of everything. She wished she and Edward could make these excursions at a less crowded time of

year, if they had to make them at all, but because of
Edward's teaching job they were limited to school
holidays. Christmas was the worst. It would be the
same even if he had a different job and they had children, though; but they didn't have any.

The guide shooed his charges back along the gravel
path as if they were chickens, which was what they
sounded like. He himself lingered beside Sarah, finishing his cigarette, one foot on a stone block, like a
conquistador. He was a small dark man with several
gold teeth, which glinted when he smiled. He was
smiling at Sarah now, sideways, and she smiled back
serenely. She liked it when these men smiled at her
or even when they made those juicy sucking noises
with their mouths as they walked behind her on the
street; so long as they didn't touch. Edward pretended not to hear them. Perhaps they did it so much
because she was blonde: blondes were rare here. She
didn't think of herself as beautiful, exactly; the word
she had chosen for herself some time ago was "comely." Comely to look upon. You would never use that
word for a thin woman.

The guide tossed his cigarette butt into the sacrificial well and turned to follow his flock. Sarah forgot
about him immediately. She'd felt something crawling up her leg, but when she looked nothing was
there. She tucked the full skirt of her cotton dress in
under her thighs and clamped it between her knees.
This was the kind of place you could get flea bites,
places with dirt on the ground, where people sat.
Parks and bus terminals. But she didn't care, her feet
were tired and the sun was hot. She would rather sit
in the shade and get bitten than rush around trying
to see everything, which was what Edward wanted
to do. Luckily the bites didn't swell up on her the way
they did on Edward.

Edward was back along the path, out of sight
among the bushes, peering around with his new Leitz
binoculars. He didn't like sitting down, it made him
restless. On these trips it was difficult for Sarah to sit

by herself and just think. Her own binoculars, which were Edward's old ones, dangled around her neck; they weighed a ton. She took them off and put them into her purse.

His passion for birds had been one of the first things Edward had confided to her. Shyly, as if it had been some precious gift, he'd shown her the lined notebook he'd started keeping when he was nine, with its awkward, boyish printing—*Robin, Bluejay, Kingfisher*—and the day and the year recorded beside each name. She'd pretended to be touched and interested, and in fact she had been. She herself didn't have compulsions of this kind; whereas Edward plunged totally into things, as if they were oceans. For a while it was stamps; then he took up playing the flute and nearly drove her crazy with the practising. Now it was pre-Columbian ruins, and he was determined to climb up every heap of old stones he could get his hands on. A capacity for dedication, she guessed you would call it. At first Edward's obsessions had fascinated her, since she didn't understand them, but now they merely made her tired. Sooner or later he'd dropped them all anyway, just as he began to get really good or really knowledgeable; all but the birds. That had remained constant. She herself, she thought, had once been one of his obsessions.

It wouldn't be so bad if he didn't insist on dragging her into everything. Or rather, he had once insisted; he no longer did. And she had encouraged him, she'd let him think she shared or at least indulged his interests. She was becoming less indulgent as she grew older. The waste of energy bothered her, because it was a waste, he never stuck with anything, and what use was his encyclopaedic knowledge of birds? It would be different if they had enough money, but they were always running short. If only he would take all that energy and do something productive with it, in his job for instance. He could be a principal if he wanted to, she kept telling him that. But he wasn't interested, he was content to poke along doing the same thing year after year. His Grade Six children adored him, the boys especially. Perhaps it was because they sensed he was a lot like them.

He'd started asking her to go birding, as he called it, shortly after they'd met, and of course she had gone. It would have been an error to refuse. She hadn't complained, then, about her sore feet or standing in the rain under the dripping bushes trying to keep track of some nondescript sparrow, while Edward thumbed through his *Peterson's Field Guide* as if it were the Bible or the bird was the Holy Grail. She'd even become quite good at it. Edward was nearsighted, and she was quicker at spotting movement than he was. With his usual generosity he acknowledged this, and she'd fallen into the habit of using it when she wanted to get rid of him for a while. Just now, for instance.

"There's something over there." She'd pointed across the well to the tangle of greenery on the other side.

"Where?" Edward had squinted eagerly and raised his binoculars. He looked a little like a bird himself, she thought, with his long nose and stilt legs.

"That thing there, sitting in that thing, the one with the tufts. The sort of bean tree. It's got orange on it."

Edward focused. "An oriole?"

"I can't tell from here. . . . Oh, it just flew." She pointed over their heads while Edward swept the sky in vain.

"I think it lit back there, behind us."

That was enough to send him off. She had to do this with enough real birds to keep him believing, however.

Edward sat down on the root of a tree and lit a cigarette. He had gone down the first side-path he'd come to; it smelled of piss, and he could see by the decomposing Kleenexes further along that this was one of the places people went when they couldn't make it back to the washroom behind the ticket counter.

He took off his glasses, then his hat, and wiped the sweat off his forehead. His face was red, he could feel it. Blushing, Sarah called it. She persisted in attributing it to shyness and boyish embarrassment; she hadn't yet deduced that it was simple rage. For someone so devious she was often incredibly stupid.

She didn't know, for instance, that he'd found out about her little trick with the birds at least three years ago. She'd pointed to a dead tree and said she saw a bird in it, but he himself had inspected that same tree only seconds earlier and there was nothing in it at all. And she was very careless: she described oriole-coloured birds behaving like kingbirds, woodpeckers where there would never be any woodpeckers, mute jays, neckless herons. She must have decided he was a total idiot and any slipshod invention would do.

But why not, since he appeared to fall for it every time. And why did he do it, why did he chase off after her imaginary birds, pretending he believed her? It was partly that although he knew what she was doing to him, he had no idea why. It couldn't be simple malice, she had enough outlets for that. He didn't want to know the real reason, which loomed in his mind as something formless, threatening and final. Her lie about the birds was one of the many lies that propped things up. He was afraid to confront her, that would be the end, all the pretences would come crashing down and they would be left standing in the rubble, staring at each other. There would be nothing left to say and Edward wasn't ready for that.

She would deny everything anyway. "What do you mean? Of course I saw it. It flew right over there. Why would I make up such a thing?" With her level gaze, blonde and stolid and immovable as a rock.

Edward had a sudden image of himself, crashing out of the undergrowth like King Kong, picking Sarah up and hurling her over the edge, down into the sacrificial well. Anything to shatter that imperturbable expression, bland and pale and plump and smug, like a Flemish Madonna's. Self-righteous, that's what it was.

Nothing was ever her fault. She hadn't been like that when he'd met her. But it wouldn't work: as she fell she would glance at him, not with fear but with maternal irritation, as if he'd spilled chocolate milk on a white tablecloth. And she'd pull her skirt down. She was concerned for appearances, always.

Though there would be something inappropriate about throwing Sarah into the sacrificial well, just as she was, with all her clothes on. He remembered snatches from the several books he'd read before they came down. (And that was another thing: Sarah didn't believe in reading up on places beforehand. "Don't you want to understand what you're looking at?" he'd asked her. "I'll see the same thing in any case, won't I?" she said. "I mean, knowing all those facts doesn't change the actual statue or whatever." Edward found this attitude infuriating; and now that they were here, she resisted his attempts to explain things to her by her usual passive method of pretending not to hear.

"That's a Chac-Mool, see that? That round thing on the stomach held the bowl where they put the hearts, and the butterfly on the head means the soul flying up to the sun."

"Could you get out the suntan lotion, Edward. I think it's in the tote bag, in the left-hand pocket."

And he would hand her the suntan lotion, defeated once again.)

No, she wouldn't be a fit sacrifice, with or without lotion. They only threw people in—or perhaps they jumped in, of their own free will—for the water god, to make it rain and ensure fertility. The drowned were messengers, sent to carry requests to the god. Sarah would have to be purified first, in the stone sweat-house beside the well. Then, naked, she would kneel before him, one arm across her breast in the attitude of submission. He added some ornaments: a gold necklace with a jade medallion, a gold circlet adorned with feathers. Her hair, which she usually wore in a braid coiled at the back of her head, would be hanging down. He thought of her body, which he made slimmer and more taut, with an abstract desire which was as unrelated as he could make it to Sarah herself. This was the only kind of desire he could feel for her any more: he had to dress her up before he could make love to her at all. He thought about their earlier days, before they'd married. It was almost as if he'd had an affair with another woman, she had been so different. He'd treated her body then as something holy, a white and gold chalice, to be touched with care and tenderness. And she had liked this; even though she was two years older than he was and much more experienced she hadn't minded his awkwardness and reverence, she hadn't laughed at him. Why had she changed?

Sometimes he thought it was the baby, which had died at birth. At the time he'd urged her to have another right away, and she'd said yes, but nothing had happened. It wasn't something they talked about. "Well, that's that," she said in the hospital afterwards. A perfect child, the doctor said; a freak accident, one of those things that happen. She'd never gone back to university either and she wouldn't get a job. She sat at home, tidying the apartment, looking over his shoulder, towards the door, out the window, as if she was waiting for something.

Sarah bowed her head before him. He, in the feathered costume and long-nosed, toothed mask of the high priest, sprinkled her with blood drawn with thorns from his own tongue and penis. Now he was supposed to give her the message to take to the god. But he couldn't think of anything he wanted to ask for.

And at the same time he thought: what a terrific idea for a Grade Six special project! He'd have them build scale models of the temples, he'd show the slides he'd taken, he'd bring in canned tortillas and tamales for a Mexican lunch, he'd have them make little Chac-Mools out of papier-mâché . . . and the ball game where the captain of the losing team had his head cut off, that would appeal to them, they were blood-thirsty at that age. He could see himself up there in front of them, pouring out his own enthusiasm, gesturing, posturing, acting it out for them, and their response. . . . Yet afterwards he knew he would be depressed. What were his special projects anyway but a substitute for television, something to keep them entertained? They liked him because he danced for them, a funny puppet, inexhaustible and a little absurd. No wonder Sarah despised him.

Edward stepped on the remains of his cigarette. He put his hat back on, a wide-brimmed white hat Sarah had bought for him at the market. He had wanted one with a narrower brim, so he could look up through his binoculars without the hat getting in his way; but she'd told him he would look like an American golfer. It was always there, that gentle, patronizing mockery.

He would wait long enough to be plausible; then he would go back.

Sarah was speculating about how she would be doing this whole trip if Edward had conveniently died. It wasn't that she wished him dead, but she couldn't imagine any other way for him to disappear. He was omnipresent, he pervaded her life like a kind of smell; it was hard for her to think or act except in reference to him. So she found it harmless and pleasant to walk herself through the same itinerary they were following now, but with Edward removed, cut neatly out of the picture. Not that she would be here at all if it wasn't for him. She would prefer to lie in a deck chair in, say, Acapulco, and drink cooling drinks. She threw in a few dark young men in bathing suits, but took them out: that would be too complicated and not relaxing. She had often thought about cheating on Edward—somehow it would serve him right, though she wasn't sure what for—but she had never actually done it. She didn't know anyone suitable, any more.

Suppose she was here, then, with no Edward. She would stay at a better hotel, for one thing. One that had a plug in the sink; they had not yet stayed in a hotel with a plug. Of course that would cost more money, but she thought of herself as having more money if Edward were dead: she would have all of his salary instead of just part of it. She knew there wouldn't be any salary if he really were dead, but it spoiled the fantasy to remember this. And she would travel on planes, if possible, or first-class buses, instead of the noisy, crowded second-class ones he insisted on taking. He said you saw more of the local colour that way and there was no point going to another country if you spent all your time with other tourists. In theory she agreed with this, but the buses gave her headaches and she could do without the closeup tour of squalor, the miserable thatched or tin-roofed huts, the turkeys and tethered pigs.

He applied the same logic to restaurants. There was a perfectly nice one in the village where they were staying, she'd seen it from the bus and it didn't look that expensive; but no, they had to eat in a seedy linoleum-tiled hutch, with plastic-covered tablecloths. They were the only customers in the place. Behind them four adolescent boys were playing dominoes and drinking beer, with a lot of annoying laughter, and some smaller children watched television, a program that Sarah realized was a re-run of *The Cisco Kid*, with dubbed voices.

On the bar beside the television set there was a crêche, with three painted plaster Wise Men, one on an elephant, the others on camels. The first Wise Man was missing his head. Inside the stable a stunted Joseph and Mary adored an enormous Christ Child which was more than half as big as the elephant. Sarah wondered how the Mary could possibly have squeezed out this colossus; it made her uncomfortable to think about it. Beside the crêche was a Santa Claus haloed with flashing lights, and beside that a radio in the shape of Fred Flintstone, which was playing American popular songs, all of them ancient.

"*Oh someone help me, help me, plee-ee-ee-eeze . . .*"

"Isn't that Paul Anka?" Sarah asked.

But this wasn't the sort of thing Edward could be expected to know. He launched into a defence of the food, the best he'd had in Mexico, he said. Sarah refused to give him the consolation of her agreement. She found the restaurant even more depressing than it should have been, especially the crêche. It was painful, like a cripple trying to walk, one of the last spastic gestures of a religion no one, surely, could believe in much longer.

Another group of tourists was coming up the path behind her, Americans by the sound of them. The guide was Mexican, though. He scrambled up onto the altar, preparing to give his spiel.

"Don't go too near the edge, now."

"Who me, I'm afraid of heights. What d'you see down there?"

"Water, what am I supposed to see?"

The guide clapped his hands for attention. Sarah only half-listened: she didn't really want to know anything more about it.

"Before, people said they threw nothing but virgins in here," the guide began. "How they could tell that, I do not know. It is always hard to tell." He waited for the expected laughter, which came. "But this is not true. Soon, I will tell you how we have found this out. Here we have the altar to the rain god Tlaloc . . ."

Two women sat down near Sarah. They were both wearing cotton slacks, high-heeled sandals and wide-brimmed straw hats.

"You go up the big one?"

"Not on your life. I made Alf go up, I took a picture of him at the top."

"What beats me is why they built all those things in the first place."

"It was their religion, that's what he said."

"Well, at least it would keep people busy."

"Solve the unemployment problem." They both laughed.

"How many more of these ruins is he gonna make us walk around?"

"Beats me. I'm about ruined out. I'd rather go back and sit on the bus."

"I'd rather go shopping. Not that there's much to buy."

Sarah, listening, suddenly felt indignant. Did they have no respect? The sentiments weren't that far from her own of a moment ago, but to hear them from these women, one of whom had a handbag decorated with tasteless straw flowers, made her want to defend the well.

"Nature is very definitely calling," said the woman with the handbag. "I couldn't get in before, there was such a lineup."

"Take a Kleenex," the other woman said. "There's no paper. Not only that, you just about have to wade in. There's water all over the floor."

"Maybe I'll just duck into the bushes," the first woman said.

Edward stood up and massaged his left leg, which had gone to sleep. It was time to go back. If he stayed away too long, Sarah would be querulous, despite the fact that it was she herself who had sent him off on this fool's expedition.

He started to walk back along the path. But then there was a flash of orange, at the corner of his eye. Edward swivelled and raised his binoculars. They were there when you least expected it. It was an oriole, partly hidden behind the leaves; he could see the breast, bright orange, and the dark barred wing. He wanted it to be a Hooded Oriole, he had not yet seen one. He talked to it silently, begging it to come out into the open. It was strange the way birds were completely magic for him the first time only, when he had never seen them before. But there were hundreds of kinds he would never see; no matter how many he saw there would always be one more. Perhaps this was why he kept looking. The bird was hopping further away from him, into the foliage. *Come back,* he called to it wordlessly, but it was gone.

Edward was suddenly happy. Maybe Sarah hadn't been lying to him after all, maybe she had really seen this bird. Even if she hadn't, it had come anyway, in answer to his need for it. Edward felt he was allowed to see birds only when they wanted him to, as if they had something to tell him, a secret, a message. The Aztecs thought hummingbirds were the souls of dead warriors, but why not all birds, why just warriors? Or perhaps they were the souls of the unborn, as some believed. "A jewel, a precious feather," they called an unborn baby, according to *The Daily Life of the Aztecs. Quetzal,* that was *feather.*

"This is the bird I want to see," Sarah said when they were looking through *The Birds of Mexico* before coming down.

"The Resplendent Quetzal," Edward said. It was a green and red bird with spectacular iridescent blue tail plumes. He explained to her that Quetzal Bird meant Feather Bird. "I don't think we're likely to see it," he said. He looked up the habitat. " '*Cloud forests.*' I don't think we'll be in any cloud forests."

"Well, that's the one I want," Sarah said. "That's the only one I want."

Sarah was always very determined about what she wanted and what she didn't want. If there wasn't anything on a restaurant menu that appealed to her, she would refuse to order anything; or she would permit him to order for her and then pick around the edges, as she had last night. It was no use telling her that this was the best meal they'd had since coming. She never lost her temper or her self-possession, but she was stubborn. Who but Sarah for instance would have insisted on bringing a collapsible umbrella to Mexico in the dry season? He'd argued and argued, pointing out its uselessness and the extra weight, but she'd brought it anyway. And then yesterday afternoon it had rained, a real cloudburst. Everyone else had run for shelter, huddling against walls and inside the temple doorways, but Sarah had put up her umbrella and stood under it, smugly. This had infuriated him. Even when she was wrong, she always managed, somehow, to be right. If only just once she would admit . . . what? That she could make mistakes. This was what really disturbed him: her assumption of infallibility.

And he knew that when the baby had died she had blamed it on him. He still didn't know why. Perhaps it was because he'd gone out for cigarettes, not expecting it to be born so soon. He wasn't there when she was told; she'd had to take the news alone.

"It was nobody's fault," he told her repeatedly. "Not the doctor's, not yours. The cord was twisted."

"I know," she said, and she had never accused him; nevertheless he could feel the reproach, hanging around her like a fog. As if there was anything he could have done.

"I wanted it as much as you did," he told her. And this was true. He hadn't thought of marrying Sarah at all, he'd never mentioned it because it had never occurred to him she would agree, until she told him she was pregnant. Up until that time, she had been the one in control; he was sure he was just an amusement for her. But the marriage hadn't been her suggestion, it had been his. He'd dropped out of Theology, he'd taken his public-school teaching certificate that summer in order to support them. Every evening he had massaged her belly, feeling the child move, touching it through her skin. To him it was a sacred thing, and he included her in his worship. In the sixth month, when she had taken to lying on her back, she had begun to snore, and he would lie awake at night listening to these gentle snores, white and silver they seemed to him, almost songs, mysterious talismans. . . . Unfortunately Sarah had retained this habit, but he no longer felt the same way about it.

When the child had died, he was the one who had cried, not Sarah. She had never cried. She got up and walked around almost immediately, she wanted to get out of the hospital as quickly as possible. The baby clothes she'd been buying disappeared from the apartment; he never found out what she'd done with them, he'd been afraid to ask.

Since that time he'd come to wonder why they were still married. It was illogical. If they'd married because of the child and there was no child, and there continued to be no child, why didn't they separate? But he wasn't sure he wanted this. Maybe he was still hoping something would happen, there would be another child. But there was no use demanding it. They came when they wanted to, not when you wanted them to. They came when you least expected it. A jewel, a precious feather.

"Now I will tell you," said the guide. "The archaeologists have dived down into the well. They have dredged up more than fifty skeletons, and they have found that some of them were not virgins at all but men. Also, most of them were children. So as you can see, that is the end of the popular legend." He made an odd little movement from the top of the altar, almost like a bow, but there was no applause. "They do not do these things to be cruel," he continued. "They believe these people will take a message to the rain god, and live forever in his paradise at the bottom of the well."

The woman with the handbag got up. "Some paradise," she said to her friend. "I'm starting back. You coming?"

In fact the whole group was moving off now, in the scattered way they had. Sarah waited until they had gone. Then she opened her purse and took out the plaster Christ Child she had stolen from the crèche the night before. It was inconceivable to her that she had done such a thing, but there it was, she really had.

She hadn't planned it beforehand. She'd been standing beside the crêche while Edward was paying the bill, he'd had to go into the kitchen to do it as they were very slow about bringing it to the table. No one was watching her: the domino-playing boys were absorbed in their game and the children were riveted to the television. She'd just suddenly reached out her hand, past the Wise Men and through the door of the stable, picked the child up and put it into her purse.

She turned it over in her hands. Separated from the dwarfish Virgin and Joseph, it didn't look quite so absurd. Its diaper was cast as part of it, more like a tunic, it had glass eyes and a sort of page-boy haircut, quite long for a newborn. A perfect child, except for the chip out of the back, luckily where it would not be noticed. Someone must have dropped it on the floor.

You could never be too careful. All the time she was pregnant, she'd taken meticulous care of herself, counting out the vitamin pills prescribed by the doctor and eating only what the books recommended. She had drunk four glasses of milk a day, even though she hated milk. She had done the exercises and gone to the classes. No one would be able to say she had not done the right things. Yet she had been disturbed by the thought that the child would be born with something wrong, it would be a mongoloid or a cripple, or a hydrocephalic with a huge liquid head like the ones she'd seen taking the sun in their wheelchairs on the lawn of the hospital one day. But the child had been perfect.

She would never take that risk, go through all that work again. Let Edward strain his pelvis till he was blue in the face; "trying again," he called it. She took the pill every day, without telling him. She wasn't going to try again. It was too much for anyone to expect of her.

What had she done wrong? She hadn't done anything wrong, that was the trouble. There was nothing and no one to blame, except, obscurely, Edward; and he couldn't be blamed for the child's death, just for not being there. Increasingly since that time he had simply absented himself. When she no longer had the child inside her he had lost interest, he had deserted her. This, she realized, was what she resented most about him. He had left her alone with the corpse, a corpse for which there was no explanation.

"*Lost*," people called it. They spoke of her as having lost the child, as though it was wandering around looking for her, crying plaintively, as though she had neglected it or misplaced it somewhere. But where? What limbo had it gone to, what watery paradise? Sometimes she felt as if there had been some mistake, the child had not been born yet. She could still feel it moving, ever so slightly, holding on to her from the inside.

Sarah placed the baby on the rock beside her. She stood up, smoothing out the wrinkles in her skirt. She was sure there would be more flea bites when she got back to the hotel. She picked up the child and walked slowly towards the well, until she was standing at the very brink.

Edward, coming back up the path, saw Sarah at the well's edge, her arms raised above her head. *My God*, he thought, *she's going to jump*. He wanted to shout to her, tell her to stop, but he was afraid to startle her. He could run up behind her, grab her . . . but she would hear him. So he waited, paralyzed, while Sarah stood immobile. He expected her to hurtle downwards, and then what would he do? But she merely drew back her right arm and threw something into the well. Then she turned, half stumbling, towards the rock where he had left her and crouched down.

"Sarah," he said. She had her hands over her face; she didn't lift them. He kneeled so he was level with her. "What is it? Are you sick?"

She shook her head. She seemed to be crying, behind her hands, soundlessly and without moving. Edward was dismayed. The ordinary Sarah, with all her perversity, was something he could cope with, he'd invented ways of coping. But he was unprepared for this. She had always been the one in control.

"Come on," he said, trying to disguise his desperation, "you need some lunch, you'll feel better." He realized as he said this how fatuous it must sound, but for once there was no patronizing smile, no indulgent answer.

"This isn't like you," Edward said, pleading, as if that was a final argument which would snap her out of it, bring back the old calm Sarah.

Sarah took her hands away from her face, and as she did so Edward felt cold fear. Surely what he would see would be the face of someone else, someone entirely different, a woman he had never seen before in his life. Or there would be no face at all. But (and this was almost worse) it was only Sarah, looking much as she always did.

She took a Kleenex out of her purse and wiped her nose. *It is like me,* she thought. She stood up and smoothed her skirt once more, then collected her purse and her collapsible umbrella.

"I'd like an orange," she said. "They have them, across from the ticket office. I saw them when we came in. Did you find your bird?"

Training

o o o

It must have taken Rob several minutes to notice that the sun was in her eyes. When he did notice, because she was squinting, he moved her sideways a little so she could see better. He felt the padded arms of the chair, where her thin bare arms were kept at rest by the leather straps, to make sure they were not overheated. She should have a hat, they were always being warned about sunburn. So far it had always been sunny during the day, though there had been a thunderstorm the night before. But no hat had been wheeled out with her.

"They forgot your hat," he said to her. "That was stupid of them, wasn't it?" Then he offered her another piece of the wooden puzzle, giving her time to consider it and to look also at the half-finished puzzle on the tray.

"This way?" he said. He watched her left hand for the slight movement towards him that would say *yes*. It was one of the few controlled movements she could make.

He also watched her eyes and face. She could move her eyes, though her head jerked around if she tried

171

to swivel it too fast. But she had little control of the
muscles of her face, so he could never tell if she was
trying to smile or whether the contortion of her mouth
was caused by the spontaneous knotting and unknot-
ting of her jumpy flesh, the body that would not respond to the enormous will he saw, or thought he saw,
sealed up in her eyes like some small fierce animal
captured in a metal net. She couldn't get out! She
was strapped into the wheelchair, prisoned in her
cage of braces, trays, steel wheels, but only because
she was strapped into her own body as into some
bumpy, sickening carnival ride. Let out of her chair,
she would thrash, topple, flail, hurtle through space. It
was one of the worst cases they'd ever taken, Pam the
physiotherapist had told him.

But everyone agreed she was bright, very bright; it
was amazing really what she could do. She could say
yes by moving her left hand, and therefore she could
play games, answer questions, indicate what she
wanted. It just needed more work than usual on the
part of the counsellor, and you had to do a lot of
guessing. It took time, but after she had beaten him
twice in a row at chequers, with no collusion on his
part, Rob was willing to spend the time. He wondered about teaching her to play chess. But there
were too many pieces, too many moves, a game
would take weeks. He thought of her, sitting impatiently inside her body, waiting for him to get to the
piece she wanted to move and figure out where she
wanted to move it.

She hadn't said anything. He turned the puzzle
piece around. *Yes*, her hand said immediately, and he
fitted it in. It was a giraffe, two giraffes, a funny-ani-
mal picture, a caricature. It struck him that she might
not know what a giraffe was; she might never have
seen a real one or even a picture of one.

"Is this puzzle boring?" he asked her. *Yes*, she said.
"How about a game of chequers?"

That was fine with her. "Okay, killer," he said, "but

this time I'm going to beat you." Her blue eyes stared at him; her mouth wavered. He wished she could smile. He wheeled her off to get out the chequers and return the puzzle.

It was her brightness that fascinated him. It was amazing, but it was horrible too, that mind trapped and strangling. Maybe she was a genius; who could ever tell? Surely she knew things and could sense things that would escape other people. When she looked at him with her ice-blue eyes, clear and cold, hard like mint candies, it was as if she could see into him, past the desperately cheerful kind-uncle act he knew was only an act. He had to be careful what he thought about when he was with her. She would pick it up, and for some reason it mattered what she felt about him.

Sometimes he thought she would be better off if she were like some of the others. The hydrocephalics, for instance, with their watery pumpkin heads and infant's bodies; there were three of them at the camp right now, and they could all talk, but they weren't very bright. Or the muscular dystrophy cases, who looked so normal the first time you saw them, slumped in their wheelchairs, wan and limp as orphans. They would be dead soon; some of them would be dead even before the next summer. Rob found the camp song so painful he could not bring himself to sing it.

> Where do you find the girls and boys
> Who grow to be women and men?
> Eff ay eye ar
> EE—ee—dee-ee en!

The tune was the Mickey Mouse song, which made it worse for Rob by conjuring up an image of the Mouseketeers, those plump, pert children with functional arms and legs who had chosen to use their normal, beautiful bodies for *that*, for prancing and jiggling and acting on television. He would stand looking down, looking away, looking anywhere but at the rows of doomed children ranged in the auditorium, brought there so Bert the Assistant Director could finger his accordion and generate what he called "camp spirit." But the children sang the song with gusto. They liked to sing. Those who could clapped their hands.

Jordan could not clap. But on the other hand, she would live a long time. You didn't die from what she had. She was only nine years old.

GAMES was in the right-hand half of the cabin nearest the main house. The front window had been enlarged and fitted with an awning, a wooden shutter for when it rained, and a counter. Jo-Anne Johnson, who had the shift this week, was sitting behind the counter on a high stool, reading a paperback. She was wearing a white terry T-shirt with an anchor on the left breast and red short-shorts, and she had her legs crossed. Rob looked at the line on her thigh where the tan ended, then switched to the shelves behind her where the volleyballs and baseball bats were stored. She had brown hair, in a pony-tail held with a gold clip, and tortoise-shell sunglasses. When she walked she limped a little. She was one of the former campers who had come back as a counsellor. Rob thought of her as a nice girl; at least she was always nice to him.

"We'd like to exchange this puzzle," he told her. "We'd like to get out some chequers."

"Chequers again, eh?" she said. "You must be sick of chequers. That's the fourth time this week."

Rob didn't like the way some people talked in front of Jordan as if she couldn't hear. "Oh no," he said. "I'm playing Jordan. She's beaten me twice."

Jo-Anne smiled at him as if they shared a secret. Then she smiled down at Jordan, who stared back at her, not moving much. "Yes, I've heard she's a real whiz," she said. She crossed out the puzzle in the lined notebook on the counter and wrote in the chequer set opposite his name. "See you later," she said. "Have a good game."

"Let's find some shade," Rob said to Jordan. He wheeled her along the cement pathway, beside the row of cabins. The cabins were white, neat, identical. Each one had a front ramp instead of a doorstep; inside them were the special beds, the special toilets, and the curious smell that was not like the smell of children but was sweeter, heavier and more humid, and reminded him of a greenhouse. A smell of warm earth and baby powder, of things mouldering slightly. Of course there was always a lot of laundry, sitting in bags, waiting to be taken away. Some of the children wore diapers, grotesque when you saw them on a twelve-year-old. In the mornings, before the beds had been changed, the smell was stronger. It took a long time to get everyone ready for the day. The girl counsellors were forbidden to lift the children out of the beds or out of the wheelchairs; only the boys could do that. Rob lifted his own cabin and two girls' cabins, Number Seven and Number Eight, Jordan's cabin. With her Dutch-boy haircut and tough wilful little face, she looked out of place in the frilled pink nightgowns they put on her. He wondered if she were ever allowed to help choose her own clothes.

They reached the corner of the walk and turned left. From the open windows of the auditorium, which doubled as a gym, came the sound of recorded music and a woman's voice: "No, back to your places and try again. You can do it, Susie." Now they had reached the end of the boys' side. The girls' side was across the central field, where there was a baseball game going on, as there had been the day he had arrived. The camp van had stopped in the circular driveway. From the front, the main house could have been a rich man's mansion, and in fact it once had been. Some figures that looked at first like grandmothers in rocking chairs were placed at intervals along the wide verandah. The Director had greeted them and had deputized Bert to give them the tour

for new counsellors. Around the corner was the baseball game, and Rob had thought, *Well, it's not going
to be so bad,* because from a distance, on the green
field, in the full sunlight that seemed to have been
shining ever since, the game had seemed almost normal.

The strange thing about it was the silence. Boys
that age ought to be shouting, that was part of the
game; but games here were played with quiet concentration. These were mostly children who could
walk, with the aid of braces or crutches; some could
even run. But a few of the players were double, one
boy being pushed around the bases in a wheelchair
by another. Rob knew from having played that the
games were conducted with a politeness and consider-
ation that he found eerie. During baseball games
these children behaved as adults were always telling
children to behave. The only noisy one at the moment was Bert, the umpire, who was waving his arms
and yelling encouragement as Dave Snider, paralyzed by polio from the waist down, knocked the ball
straight out past second base. Two outfielders on
crutches hobbled after it while Dave spun onto first.

Rob knew he should be volunteering for more
sports and supervision, but he wanted to spend the
time with Jordan. Besides, he hated baseball. It was
his family's game, the one he was expected to excel at
as a matter of course, just as he was expected to become a doctor. His father was the one who insisted on
the games, with some echo in his mind perhaps of
the golden Kennedys, as featured recently in *Life*
magazine playing touch football. Joseph Kennedy and
his three fine boys. His father wore a T-shirt with
CHAMP on it, given to him by his mother. His two
older brothers were good players, and so were the
Miller boys. Dr. Miller was a surgeon too, like his
father; they had the place next door. His father did
hearts, Dr. Miller did brains, and both of the Miller
boys were going to be doctors, too.

They played on the beach, and for Rob the sense

of hopelessness and failure that went with these games went also with blue skies, full sunlight and waves breaking on sand. These things, that for other people meant carefree vacations, meant for him an almost intolerable bondage. To refuse to play would have been unthinkable. If he'd been a better player, he would have been able to say he didn't feel like a game, but, as it was, the cries of spoilsport and poor loser would have been too truthful. No one held it against him that he was so wretched a player, that he could barely hit the ball, because of his bad eyesight perhaps, the sunlight glinting into his eyes from the frames of his glasses, that he would not see the ball when it came hurtling towards him out of the sizzling blue sky like an assassin's bomb, numbing his fingers when he raised his hands to fend it off, knocking him on the head or neck, or, even more humiliating, ignoring him so completely so that he had to run after it, chase it down the beach or into the lake. His family treated him as a joke, even, and especially, his mother. "What did you hurt today?" she would ask him, as she doled out the snacks afterwards on the patio deck above the boathouse, sandwiches and Cokes for the boys, beers for the men. In the city his father drank Scotch, but at the cottage, which he called his "summer place," he drank beer. The others would tell funny stories about Rob's blunderings, his losing duels with the demonic white ball, while he would grin. The grin was obligatory, to show he was a good sport and didn't mind. "You have to be able to take it," his father was fond of saying, without being too specific about what *it* was. He also said, after almost every game, that competitive sports were good for you because they taught you how to handle failure. Rob knew his father was only trying to make him feel better; nevertheless, he felt like answering that he'd had enough practice at that and he wouldn't mind being taught how to handle success.

But he had to be careful about saying things like that. "He's the sensitive one," his mother was in the habit of telling her friends, half proud, half rueful. Her favourite picture of him was the one in his choir-boy surplice, taken the year before his voice cracked. His oldest brother was supposed to be the handsome one, his middle brother was the smart one, Rob was the sensitive one. For this reason it was necessary, he knew, to appear as insensitive as possible. Lately he had begun to succeed, and his mother was now complaining that he never talked to her any more. He found even her moments of solicitous interest painful.

She trusted the others to make their own way, but she didn't trust him, and secretly Rob agreed with her estimate. He knew he could never be a doctor, although he felt he wanted to. He wanted to be good at baseball too, but he wasn't, and all he could see ahead for himself at Medical School was catastrophe. How to confess that even the drawings in his father's medical books, those interiors of bodies abstract as plaster models, made him queasy, that he'd actually fainted—though no one knew, because he'd been ly-ing down anyway—when he'd given blood this year at the clinic and had seen for the first time the hot purple worm of his own blood inching through the clear tube across his bare arm? His father thought it was a great treat for his boys to be allowed into the observation bubble at the hospital while he was doing open heart surgery, but Rob was unable to turn down the offer or admit his nausea. (*Red rubber, it's only red rubber*, he would repeat to himself over and over, closing his eyes when his brothers weren't watching.) He would come away from these or-deals with his knees jellied and his palms scored with the marks of his jagged, bitten nails. He couldn't do it, he could never do it.

James, the handsome one, was already interning, and the family made jokes at the Sunday dinner table about pretty nurses. Adrian was cleaning up the top marks in third year. Both of them fit so easily into the definitions that had been provided for them. And who was he supposed to be, what had been left over for

him when they were dishing out the roles? The bum-
bling third son in a fairy tale, with no princess and no
good luck. But friendly and generous, kind to old
women and dwarves in the forest. He despised his
own generosity, which he felt was mostly cowardice.

Rob was supposed to go into Pre-Meds in the fall,
and dutifully he would do it. But sooner or later he
would be forced to drop out, and what then? He saw
himself on top of a boxcar like some waif from the
thirties, penniless, fleeing his family's disappointment,
heading for some form of oblivion so foreign to him he
could not even picture it. But there was no one he
could talk to about his knowledge of his own doom. A
year ago his father had taken him aside for the pep-
talk Rob was sure he'd had with both of the others.
Medicine wasn't just a job, he told Rob. It was a
calling, a vocation. One of the noblest things a man
could do was to dedicate his life selflessly to the saving of others. His father's eyes gleamed piously: was
Rob worthy? (Speedboat, Rob thought, summer place
on the bay, two cars, Forest Hill house.) "Your grandfather was a doctor," his father said, as if this was the
clincher. His grandfather had been a doctor, but he'd
been a country doctor, driving a sleigh and team
through blizzards to deliver babies. They had often
heard these heroic stories. "He wasn't very good at
collecting his bills," Rob's father would say, shaking
his head with a mixture of admiration and indulgent
contempt. This was not one of his own weaknesses.
"During the Depression we lived on chickens; the
farmers gave them to us instead of money. I had
only one pair of shoes." Rob thought of the shoe rack
that ran the length of his father's triple-doored closet,
the twinkling shoes arranged on it like testimonials.

He would not be able to take the scene when they
found out, he would just disappear. He thought of the
final catastrophe as happening in a classroom. They
would all be dissecting a cadaver, and he would suddenly begin to scream. He would run out of the room
and down the corridor, reeking of formaldehyde, he

would forget his coat and the galoshes that were a
fetish of his mother's, it would be snowing. He would
wake up the next morning in a greenish-grey hotel
room, with no recollection of what he had done.

It was his family who had chosen this job, this
camp. They felt it would be good practice for him to
spend the summer with crippled children; it would be
part of the *it* he had to learn to take. His father knew
the Director, and it was all arranged before Rob was
told about it. His father and mother had been so
enthusiastic, so full of their sense of the wonderful
opportunity they'd arranged for him, how could he
refuse? "Use your powers of observation," his father
had said to him at the train station. "I wish I'd had
this chance when I was your age."

For the first week Rob had had nightmares. The
dreams were of bodies, pieces of bodies, arms and legs
and torsos, detached and floating in mid-air; or he
would feel he couldn't move, couldn't breathe, and
he would wake up with his skin wet from effort. He
found the sight of the children, especially the younger
ones, unbearably painful, and he didn't understand
how the other staff members could go around all day
with expressions of such bluff professional cheer. Except that he did it himself. Though apparently with
less success than he'd thought, since Pam the physiotherapist had come over to sit beside him in the staff
lounge after the second-day orientation meeting. She
had dull blonde hair held back by a velvet band
that matched the blue of her plaid Bermuda shorts.
She was pretty, but Rob felt she had too many teeth.
Too many and too solid. "It's rough working with kids
like this," she said, "but it's so rewarding." Rob
nodded dutifully: what did she mean, rewarding? He
still felt sick to his stomach. He'd been on shift for
dinner that evening, and he could barely stand the
milk dribbling from the bent plastic feeding tubes, the
chair trays splattered with food ("Let them do as
much for themselves as they can"), the slurps and
suction noises. Pam lit a cigarette and Rob watched

the red fingernails on her strong, competent hands. "It doesn't do *them* any good for you to be depressed," she said. "They'll use it against you. A lot of them don't know the difference. They've never been any other way." She was going to do this for a living, she was going to do this for the rest of her life! "You'll get used to it," she said, and patted his arm in a way that Rob found insulting. *She's trying to be nice*, he corrected himself quickly.

"I know your brother James," she said, smiling again with her solid teeth. "I met him on a double-date. He's quite the boy."

Rob excused himself and got up. She was older than him anyway, she was probably twenty.

But she'd been right, he was getting used to it. The nightmares had gone away, though not before he'd aroused the interest of the boys in his cabin. They nicknamed him "The Groaner." They had nick-names for everyone in the camp.

"Hey, ya hear the Groaner last night?"

"Yeah. *Uh. Uh.* Getting his rocks off good."

"Ya have a good time, Groaner?"

Rob, blushing, would mumble, "I was having a nightmare," but they would hoot with laughter.

"Oh yeah. *We* heard ya. Wish I had nightmares like that." They were the oldest boys' cabin, fourteen to sixteen-year-olds, and he'd had trouble with them from the first. They weren't like the younger children, polite, eager to enjoy themselves in whatever way they could, grateful for help. Instead they were cyni-cal about the camp, about the Director, about Bert (whom they nicknamed "Bert the Nert") and about themselves and their lives. They drank beer, when they could get hold of it; they smoked furtive ciga-rettes. They kept girlie magazines hidden under their mattresses, and they told some of the foulest jokes Rob had ever heard. They divided the world into two camps, the "crips" and the "norms," and for the most part they accepted only the crips. The norms were seen as their oppressors, the dimwits who would never understand, who would never get it right, and whom it was their duty to war against and exploit. It gave them a bitter pleasure to outrage norm sensibility whenever possible, and they'd found Rob an easy target.

"Hey, Pete," Dave Snider would start. He'd be sitting in his chair, wearing one of the T-shirts with the cut-off arms that displayed his overdeveloped biceps to advantage. He had a Charles Atlas set at home, Rob knew, and subscribed to bodybuilding magazines.

"Yeah, Dave?" Pete would answer. They both had classic ducktails, which they wore covered with grease. They found Rob's private-school English-style haircut ludicrous. Pete was paralyzed from the neck down, but he'd somehow gained second place in the cabin's pecking order. Dave combed his duck's ass for him.

"What's black and crawls and catches flies?"

"Roy Campanello!"

Raucous laughter, in which the rest of the cabin joined while Rob blushed. "I don't think that's very nice," he'd said the first time.

"He doesn't think it's very *nice*," Dave mimicked. "What weighs two thousand pounds and twitches?"

"Moby Spaz!"

They called these jokes "spaz jokes." What bothered Rob most about them was that they reminded him of the kinds of jokes his brothers and their medical-student friends would tell, having a game of pool in their father's rec room, to relax after classes. ("Bring your friends over anytime, boys. You too, Rob.") Except that theirs were supposed to be true stories. They played endless practical jokes on each other, most of them involving parts of cadavers they would cut off during dissection: eyeballs in the teacup, hands in the coat pocket.

"Hey, we were doing this old guy, and I thought, *What the hell*, and I cut off his tool, it's all brown and shrivelled up, like they get, and I slipped it into my briefcase. So I go down to the Babloor, and I have a few beers, and I go into the can and I open my fly, but I stick this old guy's dork out instead of my own. So I stand there like I'm pissing, and I wait till another guy comes in, and I shake it and it comes off in my hand. So I throw it down and I say, 'Damn thing never worked anyway.' You should've seen the look on his face!"

They related rumours from Emergency at the hospital, most of which seemed to involve women with broken Coke bottles stuck in them or men who had been masturbating with the hot water tap. "Had to get a plumber to saw him out. Came in with the tap still on and two feet of pipe." "I heard of one with a crayon. Got stuck in the bladder. He came in because he was pissing blue and he couldn't figure out why."

"I heard about one with a snake."

"Why do you tell those stories?" Rob asked them one night when he felt courageous.

"Why do you listen to them?" James grinned.

"You'll do it, too," Adrian told him. "Wait and see." Then, after the others had gone home, he said, more seriously, "You have to tell them. I know you think it's pretty gross, but you don't know what it's like. It's real life out there. You have to laugh or go crazy." Rob tried to reject this, but it haunted him. Real life would be too much for him, he would not be able to take it. He would not be able to laugh. He would go crazy. He would run out into the snow with no galoshes, he would vanish, he would be lost forever.

"What weighs two thousand pounds and has an exploding head?"

"Moby Hydrocephalic!"

"That's enough!" Rob said, trying to assert his authority.

"Look, Groaner," Dave said. "You're here to see we have a good time, right? Well, we're having a good time."

"Yeah," Pete said. "You don't like it, you can beat me up."

"Sure, go on," Dave said. "Do your Boy Scout good deed for the week. Kill a cripple." Bullying him with his own guilt.

It didn't help that the other counsellor, Gordon Holmes, encouraged them. He smuggled beer and cigarettes into the cabin for them, ogled their girlie magazines, and told them which of the girl counsellors were "easy outs."

"Hey, make out last night?" Dave would ask him in the morning.

"Not bad, not bad."

"She go down for ya?"

Gordon's secretive smile. Patting Old Spice on the back of his neck.

"Who was it, Pammer the Slammer?"

"Every time she pounds my back I get a bone on."

"Hey, was it Jo-Anne?"

"Naw, she's a crip. Gord wouldn't take out a crip, would ya, Gord?"

"You got to go along with them," Gordon told Rob. "Kid them a little. They're frustrated, they got normal emotions just like you and me." He punched Rob on the shoulder. "Take it easy, man, you think too much."

Gordon went to a public high school in East York. His mother and father were divorced and he lived with his mother, whom he called "the old lady." He'd got the job with the camp through the Big Brothers. He wasn't a juvenile delinquent, and Rob could think of many good points about him, but he couldn't bear to be around him for long. It did no good for Rob to tell himself that Gord would probably end up as a garage mechanic, that the kind of girls he talked about so freely were what his own mother would call "cheap," that he would get one of them pregnant and have to get married and end up in a dingy, overcrowded apartment, drinking beer in front of the TV while his wife nagged him about the laundry. He was

envious anyway, listening despite himself to the sagas
of back seats and forbidden mickeys at the drive-in, of
heavy petting, forays into undergarments by Gord's
daring fingers, triumphs over hostile elastic straps,
conquests of breasts. He resented this sleazy freedom
even though he knew he wouldn't enjoy it himself,
wouldn't know what to say or where to put his hands.
He himself had never taken out anyone but his
mother's friends' daughters, pallid little girls who
needed to be escorted to their own private-school
dances and didn't know anyone else to ask. He bought
them wrist corsages and steered them swiftly, correct-
ly, around the floor in their dresses like layers of pas-
tel toilet paper, their small wired bosoms pressing
lightly into his chest, his hands against their backs
feeling the rows of hooks that might conceivably be
undone; but no, that would be too embarrassing.
Though he'd sometimes felt his crotch tighten during
the joyless foxtrots (he stood out the few chaste rock
numbers the hired band would attempt), he hadn't
liked any of these girls, though he tried to make sure
they had a good time. He had even kissed one of
them goodnight, because he felt she was expecting it.
It was three years ago, when he was still wearing
bands on his teeth. So was the girl, and when he'd
kissed her harder than he'd intended, their teeth had
locked painfully together, at her front door, in full
view of the entire street. Anyone watching would
have thought it was a passionate embrace, but he
could still remember the panic in her eyes, though
he'd repressed her name.

Rob turned Jordan right, onto the Nature Walk
that run in a meandering oval through the small
woods behind the boys' cabins. It was paved, like all
the other walks. The trees were labelled, and there
was a little glass case at the far end of the oval
where Bert the Nert, who was a nature buff, put a
new exhibit every day. He'd taken Jordan on the Na-

ture Walk several times before, stopping to read the
labels on the trees, pointing out chipmunks and once
a stray cat. Hardly anyone else seemed to go on it. He
liked to wheel her along through the trees, whistling
or singing songs to her. He wasn't shy about his
voice when there was no one else but her, he even
sang songs from Bert's repertoire that stuck in his
throat when the assembled children sang them, led
by red-faced Bert, his master-of-ceremonies smile,
and his energetic accordion.

Jordan River is chilly and cold,
Hallelujah,
Chills the body but not the soul,
Hallelujah.

"Your name is the name of a famous river," he told
her. He hoped she would be pleased by that. He
wondered if her parents had known about her, about
what she was going to be like, when they named
her, and whether they'd felt later that the expensive-
sounding name was wasted because she would never
match it, never sip cocktails on a terrace or smile
like Grace Kelly in cool lipstick. But they must have
known; it said in her file that it was a birth defect. She
had one brother and one sister, both normal, and her
father was something in a bank.

Sometimes, thinking of the catastrophe ahead of
him, his failure and his flight, he thought about taking
her with him. That was her clinging to his neck as
he scrambled up the boxcar (but she couldn't cling!),
she was with him in the hotel room when he woke up,
sitting in her chair (how had he got her there?), looking into his eyes with her icy blue ones, her face mi-
raculously still. Then she would open her mouth and
words would come out, she would stand up, he would
somehow have cured her. . . . Sometimes, very quickly
(and he would repress it immediately) he would see
both of them hurtling from the top of a building. *An*

accident, an accident, he would tell himself. I don't mean that.

Jordan River is chilly and wide,
Hallelujah,

Rob crooned. He was heading for a bench, there was one up ahead, where he could sit and they could have their game of chequers.

"Hey, look at this." It was Bert's glass case. *"Shelf fungus,"* he read from the typed card. *"There are several species of shelf fungus. The shelf fungus is a saprophyte which feeds on decaying vegetable matter and can often be found growing on dead trees.* You can write your name on the bottom with a stick," he said. He used to do that at the cottage, without removing the fungus from the tree, and it gave him pleasure to think of his name growing in secret, getting a little bigger every year. It was hard to tell whether or not she was interested.

He found the bench, turned Jordan to face it and unfolded the board. "I was red last time," he said, "so you get it this time, okay?" There was one chequer missing, on her side. "We'll use something else," he said. He looked around for a flat stone, but there wasn't one. Finally he pulled a button off his shirtsleeves. "That okay?" he said.

Jordan's hand moved *yes.* He began the laborious trial-and-error process of determining how she wanted to move. He would point at each chequer in turn until she signalled. Then he would point to each possible square. They could get through a game a lot faster now that he was used to playing this way. Her face would fold and unfold, screw itself up, twitch, movements he found distressing in other CP children still, but not in her. Concentrating made her worse.

They had hardly gone through the opening moves when the bell sounded from the main building. That meant the Play Period was over and it was time for the afternoon group activities. Jordan, he knew, had swimming with the rest of her cabin. She couldn't swim, but someone held her in the water, where her movements, they said, were more controlled than on land. He himself was supposed to help with Occupational Therapy. "Mud pies," the boys in his cabin called it. They liked making obscene statues out of clay in order to shock Wilda, the OT instructor, who wanted so much to be able to tell them they were being creative.

Rob put his shirt button into his pocket. He took out the notebook they used and marked down their respective positions. "We'll finish it tomorrow," he told Jordan. He wheeled her along the path in the same direction they'd been going, which would get them back sooner, since they were three-quarters of the way around the oval already.

To the north side of the cement path there was a clearing, a stretch of grass and across it the silver of water: the stream that was always there, usually a sluggish trickle but swollen now by last night's rain. Rob thought, *She's probably never felt grass before, she's probably never had her hand in a real stream.* He suddenly wanted to give her something that no one else ever had, that no one else would ever think of.

"I'm going to take you out," he told her. "I'm going to put you down on the grass, so you can feel it. Okay?"

There was a hesitation before she signalled *yes.* She was looking into his face; perhaps she didn't understand. "It's fun," he told her, "it feels nice," thinking of the many times he had sprawled on the lawn of the back garden, eight or ten years ago, chewing on the white soft ends of grass blades and reading the almost-forbidden Captain Marvel comic books.

He unbuckled the straps that held her in and lifted her thin body. She was so light, lighter even than she looked, a creature of balsa wood and paper. But tough, he told himself. She could take it, you could see it in her eyes. He put her down on the grass, on her side, where she could see the flowing stream.

"There," he said. He knelt beside her, took her left hand and put it into the cold stream. "That's real water, not like a swimming pool." He smiled, feeling magnanimous, a giver, a healer; but she had closed her eyes, and from somewhere a curious sound, a whine, a growl . . . Her body was limp, her arm jerking; suddenly her leg shot out and her foot in its steel-crusted boot kicked him in the shin.

"Jordan," he said. "Are you all right?" More growling: was it joy or terror? He couldn't tell, and he was frightened. Maybe this was too much for her, too exciting. He wrapped his arms around her, pulling her up to put her back into the chair. The grass had been damper than he'd thought, and the right side of her face was streaked with mud.

"What the hell are you doing with that child?" Pam's voice behind him. Rob turned, still holding Jordan, who was thrashing her arms like a propeller gone crazy. Pam was standing on the cement walk, hands on her hips, the posture of an accusing mother coming upon the children playing Doctor in the bushes. Her face was red, her hair mussed, as if she'd been running. There was a twig dangling above her ear.

"Nothing," Rob said, "I was just. . . ." *She thinks I'm some kind of a pervert,* he saw, and felt himself blushing. "I thought she would like to see what the grass felt like," he said.

"You know that's dangerous," Pam said. "You know she isn't supposed to be taken out. She could hit her head, injure herself. . . ."

"I was watching her the whole time," Rob said. Who was she to be bossing him around like this?

"I think you spend far too much time with that child," Pam said, less angry now but definitely not convinced by his explanation. "You should spend more time with some of the others. It's not good for *them,* you know, forming . . . attachments . . . that can't possibly be kept up after camp." Jordan's eyes were open now; she was looking at Rob.

"What the hell are you talking about?" Rob said, almost shouted. "How do *you* know, you don't know . . ." She was accusing him, in advance, of betraying Jordan, abandoning her.

"Don't get your girdle in a knot about it," Pam said. "But I think you should have a word with Bert, after Staff Lounge tonight. I've discussed this problem with him already."

She turned away from him and walked quickly off towards the main house. On the back of her Bermuda shorts there was a small patch of wet mud.

Rob buckled Jordan back into the chair. *This problem.* Why was it a problem? There wasn't much time, he would be assigned to other children, discouraged from seeing her, and she would think. . . . What could he say to her, how convince her? He knelt in front of her, resting his arms on the chair tray, and took hold of her left hand.

"I'm sorry if it frightened you, being on the ground," he said. "Did it?" Her hand did not move. "Don't pay any attention to what Pam just said. I'm going to write you letters after camp, lots of letters." Would he? "And someone at your house can read them to you." But of course they might forget, or lose the letters. In Pre-Meds, dissecting corpses, would he have time to remember her? Her eyes watched his face. She could see through him.

"I'm going to give you something special," he told her, casting around desperately for something to give. He searched his pocket with his free hand. "This is my button, and it's magic. I wore it on my shirt cuff like that just to keep it disguised." He placed it in her hand, folded the fingers around it. "I'm giving it to you, and whenever you see it. . . ." No, that wouldn't do; someone was bound to find it in her pocket and throw it out, and she would have no way of explaining. "You don't even have to see it, because it's invisible sometimes. All you have to do is think about it. And every time you think about it, you'll know I'm thinking specially about you. Okay?" He'd tried to make it as convincing as possible, but she was probably too old and too bright, she probably knew he was just trying to reassure her. In any case, she moved her hand *yes*. Whether it was real belief or embarrassed kindness he could never know.

After or Rob went back to his own cabin, to help with the pre-dinner change into clean clothes that Bert felt was good for morale. The boys were unusually boisterous, but it was probably only his own anxiety and need for peace that made them seem that way. Or it might have been the show that was being put on that evening, by a number of the seniors. All of these boys were in it, even Pete, who was going to be the MC, with a mike strapped to his shoulder near his mouth. None of the ordinary counsellors were involved; they and the younger children were to be the audience, while Scott and Martina, Drama and Dance respectively, ran the show. Rob knew the boys had been practising for two weeks at least, but he had not been interested enough to ask them what the show was about.

"Lemme borrow your zit cream."

"Wouldn't do you any good, pusface."

"Yeah, he's got pimples on his pimples."

"You spaz!" A scuffle.

"Cut that out, prickhead!"

Rob wondered if he would be transferred to another cabin. He was helping Dave Snider into his clean shirt, a pink one with charcoal stripes ("Cheap," his mother's voice said), when Gordon strolled into the cabin, late. Rob suspected him of thumbing into town for a quick drink in the beer-parlour, which wasn't choosy about your age. He had been late a number of times recently, leaving Rob to attempt control of the cabin single-handed. He looked very smug; he didn't reply to the admiring mock cheers that always accompanied his entrances, but dug into his pocket and, very casual, very cool, draped something over his bedpost. A pair of black panties, with red lace edges.

"Hey! Wow! Hey, Gord, whose are they?"

Out with the comb, patting the blond pompadour into place. "That's for me to know and you to find out."

"Hey, come on, Gord, eh Gord?"

"Hey, no fair, Gord! But you stole em from the laundry!"

"Take a look, smart boy. They're not from any laundry."

Dave wheeled over and grabbed the panties. He stuck them on his head and circled the cabin floor. "Mickey Mouse, Mickey Mouse," he sang. "Forever let us hold our whammers high. . . . Hey Groaner, you wanna try em on? Bet they'd fit, you got a big head."

Other hands snatched at the panties. Rob left the room, went down the hall into the washroom. They must have been in the woods, near him, near Jordan. Her outrage, lecturing him like that with the twigs still in her hair, what gave her the right? Mud on her rump.

His face, his nice face, bland and freckled, framed in neatly trimmed sandy hair, watched him from the mirror. He would have preferred a scar, a patch over one eye, sunburned wrinkles, a fang. How untouched he looked, like the fat on uncooked bacon: nobody's fingerprints on him, no dirt, and he despised this purity. At the same time he could never be like the others, gloat over some woman's musky underpants. *Maybe I'm not normal,* he thought with gloomy pride.

After the chaos and mess of dinner had been endured, Rob went to the auditorium with the others. The stage, which was like a school stage except for the ramps at either side, had its red curtains closed. There were no chairs. Those in wheelchairs didn't need them, and the others sat on the floor, wherever

they liked. Rob sought out Jordan and moved closer
to her. He prepared to applaud, dutifully, whatever
was set before him.

The lights in the room dimmed, there was some
fumbling behind the curtains, and Pete in his chair
was pushed out by several pairs of hands. The audience clapped, some cheered. Pete was quite popular.

"Don't push me off the edge, you spaz," he said into
the mike, which got a laugh from some of the older
boys. He was wearing a vaudeville straw hat with a
red crepe-paper band, and someone had glued a
false moustache unevenly to his upper lip.

"Ladies and gents," he said. He made his moustache wiggle at one side, then at the other, and the
younger children giggled. At that moment Rob almost
liked him. "This here is the Fair-Eden Follies, and
you better believe it, anyways, we all did a lot of falling down practising it." His voice went serious.
"We've all worked hard to make this a good show,
and I want you to give a big hand to the first number,
which is—a square dance, by the Fair-Eden Wheel-
er Dealers. Thank you."

Pete was jerked backwards, became briefly en-
tangled, and disappeared. After a pause the curtains
parted haltingly. In front of a brown-paper backdrop
with a poster-painted apple tree and a cow, four boys
and four girls faced each other in standard square
dance formation. They were all in wheelchairs, without the trays.

The girls were two polio cases and two paraplegic
CPs. They were wearing lipstick and had red paper
bows at the necks of their white blouses; their emaciated legs and braces were hidden by long printed
cotton skirts, and one of them, the one without the
glasses, was astonishingly pretty. Dave Snider was
the front corner boy. Like the others, he had on a
Western string tie and a cardboard cowboy hat. The
dancers looked self-conscious, but proud. None of
them was smiling.

Martina was off to the side, with the primitive record player. "Now," she prompted, and the scratchy fiddle music started up. She clapped her hands in time. "Honour your partners," she called, and the two lines bowed to each other from the waist. "Honour your corners!" Then the two opposite corners shot forward, met each other in the centre of the square, passed, and by quick hand-turnings of their wheels executed a perfect do-si-do.

Jesus, Rob thought. *They must have practised for hours.* He saw the concentration in Dave Snider's face and thought for a brief second, *He cares about it,* and, triumphantly, *Now I've got something on him.* Immediately he was ashamed of himself. The dancers whizzed out again, locked wheels and arms, and swung, careening dangerously. They seemed to have forgotten about the audience: their attention was held entirely by the rhythm and by the intricate manipulations of the wheels needed at such close quarters.

Rob looked over at Jordan. She was sitting almost still, her arms moving slightly, aimlessly, under the leather straps. He wanted her to turn her eyes so he could smile at her, but she was gazing straight at the dancers, her eyes shining with what he saw, with a quick jolt of his heart, were tears. She had never cried before: he hadn't known she could, he'd thought of her as a little changeling, not quite human. What was wrong? He tried to see as she was seeing, and, of course, it wasn't anything he could give her that she wanted. She wanted something she could imagine, something almost possible for her, she wanted to do this! A square dance in a wheelchair. She longed to be able to do just this much, this particular dance, that would be wonderful. And it was wonderful. He had wasted himself, his body, why couldn't he have moved with such abandon, such joy in precision, during those interminable formal dances when his legs went stiff as wood, his feet compressed themselves to clumsy blocks inside his polished shoes. . . .

But it was grotesque, he saw also, he couldn't help seeing. It was a mockery, of themselves and of the dance; who had ever allowed them to do it? All their effort, their perfection even, amounted to this: they were ludicrous in their cumbersome machines. They danced like comic robots. They danced like him.

Rob felt something inside him, coming up, bursting out. He doubled over, his hands clenched to his mouth. He was laughing. He tried to hold the laughter back, stifle it, turn it to coughing, but it was no use. He was red with shame and shaking all over; he couldn't stop. He crouched towards the door, hands across his face, stumbled through it, and collapsed onto the grass of the baseball field. He hoped they would think he was being sick to his stomach. That's what he would tell them afterwards. How could he, how could he have been so incredibly callous and rude? But he was still laughing so hard his stomach hurt. And she had seen him, she had turned her wet eyes and seen him just as it happened, she would think he had betrayed her.

Rob took off his glasses and wiped his eyes. Then he pressed his forehead into the grass, which was damp and cool with dew. From the open windows of the auditorium the tinny music ground on, to the rumble of wheels. *I'll have to leave, I can't explain, I'll never be able to face them.* But then he realized that nobody had really seen but her, and she couldn't tell. He was safe. And who was that, in the bright room at the back of his room, that man in the green gown and the mask, under the glass bubble, raising the knife?

Lives of the Poets

∘ ∘ ∘

Lying on the bathroom floor of this anonymous hotel room, my feet up on the edge of the bathtub and a cold wet washcloth balled at the back of my neck. Bloody nosebleed. A good adjective, it works, as the students say in those creative writing classes that are sometimes part of the package. So colourful. Never had a nosebleed before, what are you supposed to do? An icecube would be nice. Image of the Coke-and-ice machine at the end of the hall, me streaking toward it, a white towel over my head, the bloodstain spreading through it. A hotel guest opens his roomdoor. Horrors, an accident. Stabbed in the nose. Doesn't want to get involved, the roomdoor shuts, my quarter jams the machine. I'll stick with the washcloth.

The air's too dry, that must be it, nothing to do with me or the protests of the soggy body. Osmosis. Blood to the outside because there's not enough water vapour; they keep the radiators going full blast and no switch to shut them off. Cheapskates, why couldn't I stay at the Holiday Inn? Instead it's this one, pseudo-Elizabethan motifs tacked to a mouse-eaten frame, somebody's last-ditch attempt to make something out of this corner of the woods. The outskirts of Sudbury, nickel-smelting capital of the world. Can we show you around, they said. I'd like to see the slagheaps, and the places where the vegetation has all been scorched off. Oh, ha ha, they said. It's growing back, they raised the stacks. It's turning into quite a, you know, civilized place. I used to like it, I said, it looked like the moon. There's something to be said for a place where absolutely nothing grows. Bald. Dead. Clean as a bone. Know what I mean? Furtive glances at one another, young beardy faces, one pipe-smokes, they write footnotes, on their way up, why do we always get stuck with the visiting poet? Last one threw up on the car rug. Just wait till we get tenure.

Julia moved her head. The blood trickled gently down the back of her throat, thick and purple-tasting. She had been sitting there in front of the phone, trying to figure out the instructions for calling long distance through the hotel operator, when she'd sneezed and the page in front of her had been suddenly spattered with blood. Totally unprovoked. And Bernie would be hanging around at home, waiting for her to call. In two hours she had to give the reading. A gracious introduction, she would rise and move to the microphone, smiling, she would open her mouth and blood would start to drip from her nose. Would they clap? Would they pretend not to notice? Would they think it was part of the poem? She would have to start rooting around in her purse for a Kleenex, or, better still, she'd faint, and someone else would have to cope. (But everyone would think she was drunk.) How upsetting for the committee. Would they pay her anyway? She could imagine them discussing it.

She raised her head a little, to see if it had stopped. Something that felt like a warm slug crawled down towards her upper lip. She licked, tasting salt. How was she going to get to the phone? On her back, creeping supine across the floor, using her elbows and pushing with her feet, a swimming motion, like a giant aquatic insect. She shouldn't be calling Bernie, she should be calling a doctor. But it wasn't serious enough. Something like this always happened when she had to give a reading, something painful but too minor for a doctor. Besides, it was always out of town, she never knew any doctors. Once it was a bad cold; her voice had sounded as if it was coming through a layer of mud. Once her hands and ankles had swelled up. Headaches were standard: she never got headaches at home. It was as if something was against these readings and was trying to keep her from giving them. She was waiting for it to take a more drastic form, paralysis of the jaw muscles, temporary blindness, fits. This was what she thought about during the introductions, always: herself on a stretcher, the waiting ambulance, then waking up, safe and cured, with Bernie sitting beside the bed. He would smile at her, he would kiss her forehead, he would tell her—what? Some magical thing. They had won the Wintario Lottery. He'd been left a lot of money. The gallery was solvent. Something that would mean she didn't have to do this any more.

That was the problem: they needed the money. They had always needed the money, for the whole four years they had lived together, and they still needed it. At first it hadn't seemed so important. Bernie was on a grant then, painting, and after that he got a renewal. She had a part-time job, cataloguing in a library. Then she had a book published, by one of the medium-sized houses, and got a grant herself. Of course she quit her job, to make the best use of the time. But Bernie ran out of money, and he had trouble selling paintings. Even when he did sell one, the dealer got most of it. The dealer system was wrong, he told her, and he and two other painters opened a co-operative artists' gallery which, after a lot of talk, they decided to call *The Notes From Underground*. One of the other painters had money, but they didn't want to take advantage of him; they would go strict thirds. Bernie explained all this to her, and he was so enthusiastic it had seemed natural to lend him half of her grant money, just to get things going. As soon as they began to show a profit, he said, he would pay her back. He even gave her two shares in the gallery. They hadn't started to show a profit yet, though, and, as Bernie pointed out, she didn't really need the money back right at the moment. She could get some more. She now had a reputation; a small one, but still, she could earn money easier and faster than he could, travelling around and giving readings on college campuses. She was "promising," which meant that she was cheaper than those who were more than promising. She got enough invitations to keep them going, and though she debated the merits of each one with Bernie, hoping he would veto, he had never yet advised her to turn one down. But to be fair, she had never told him quite how much she hated it, the stares of the eyes, her own voice detached and floating, the one destructive question that was sure to lurk there among all the blank ones. *I mean, do you really think you have anything to say?*

Deep in February, deep in the snow, bleeding on the tiles of this bathroom floor. By turning her head she could see them, white hexagons linked like a honeycomb, with a single black tile at regular intervals.

For a measly hundred and twenty-five dollars—but it's half the rent, don't forget that—and twenty-five a day for expenses. Had to take the morning plane, no seats in the afternoon, who the hell goes to Sudbury in February? A bunch of engineers. Practical citizens, digging out the ore, making a bundle, two cars and a swimming pool. They don't stay at this place, anyway. Dining room at lunchtime almost empty. Just me and a very old man who talked to himself out loud. What's wrong with him? I said to the waitress. Is he crazy? In a whisper I said it. It's okay, he's deaf, she said. No, he's just lonely, he's been real lonely ever since his wife died. He lives here. I guess it's better than an old-age home, you know? There are more people here in the summertime. And we get a lot of men who're separating from their wives. You can always tell them, by what they order.

Didn't pursue that. Should have though, now I'll never know. What they order. Was looking as usual for the cheapest thing on the menu. Need that whole hundred and twenty-five, why waste it on food? This food. The menu a skewed effort to be Elizabethan, everything spelled with an "e" at the end. Got the Anne Boleyn Special, a hamburger with no bun, garnished with a square of red Jello and followed by "a glass of skime milke." Do they know that Anne Boleyn's head was cut off? Is that why the hamburger has no bun? What goes on in people's minds? Everyone thinks writers must know more about the inside of the human head, but that's wrong. They know less, that's why they write. Trying to find out what everyone else takes for granted. The symbolism of the menu, for god's sake, why am I even thinking about it? The menu has no symbolism, it's just some dimwit's ill-informed attempt to be cute. Isn't it?

You're too complicated, Bernie used to tell her, when they were still stroking and picking at each other's psyches. You should take it easy. Lie back. Eat an orange. Paint your toenails.

All very well for him.

Maybe he wasn't even up yet. He used to take naps in the afternoons, he'd be lying there under the heaped-up blankets of their Queen Street West apartment (over the store that had once sold hardware but was now a weaving boutique, and the rent was climbing), face down, arms flung out to either side, his socks on the floor where he'd discarded them, one after the other, like deflated feet or stiffened blue footprints leading to the bed. Even in the mornings he would wake up slowly and fumble his way to the kitchen for some coffee, which she would already have made. That was one of their few luxuries, real coffee. She'd have been up for hours, crouching at the kitchen table, worrying away at a piece of paper, gnawing words, shredding the language. He would place his mouth, still full of sleep, on hers, and perhaps pull her back into the bedroom and down into the bed with him, into that liquid pool of flesh, his mouth sliding over her, furry pleasure, the covers closing over them as they sank into weightlessness. But he hadn't done that for some time. He had been waking earlier and earlier; she, on the other hand, had been having trouble getting out of bed. She was losing that compulsion, that joy, whatever had nagged her out into the cold morning air, driven her to fill all those notebooks, all those printed pages. Instead she would roll herself up in the blankets after Bernie got up, tucking in all the corners, muffling herself in wool. She had begun to have the feeling that nothing was waiting for her outside the bed's edge. Not emptiness but nothing, the zero with legs in the arithmetic book.

"I'm off," he'd say to her groggy bundled back. She'd be awake enough to hear this; then she would lapse back into a humid sleep. His absence was one more reason for not getting up. He would be going to *The Notes From Underground,* which was where he seemed to spend most of his time now. He was pleased with the way it had been going, they'd had several interviews in the papers, and it was easy for her to understand how something could be thought of as a qualified success and still not make money, since the same thing had happened to her book. But she worried a little because he wasn't doing very much painting any more. His last picture had been a try at Magic Realism. It was her, sitting at the kitchen table, wrapped in the plaid rug off the foot of the bed, with her hair in a sleazy bun at the back of her neck, looking like some kind of famine victim. Too bad the kitchen was yellow; it made her skin green. He hadn't finished it though. Paper work, he would say. That

was what he spent his mornings at the gallery doing,
that and answering the phone. The three of them were
supposed to take turns and he should have been off at
twelve, but he usually ended up there in the afternoons, too. The gallery had attracted a few younger
painters, who sat around drinking plastic cups of Nes-
café and cans of beer and arguing about whether or
not anyone who bought a share in the gallery should
be able to have a show there and whether the gallery
should take commissions, and if not how it was going
to survive. They had various schemes, and they'd recently hired a girl to do public relations, posters
and mailings and bothering the media. She was free-
lance and did it for two other small galleries and one
commercial photographer. She was just starting out,
Bernie said. She talked about building them up. Her
name was Marika; Julia had met her at the gallery,
back in the days when she'd been in the habit of dropping around in the afternoons. That seemed a long
time ago.

Marika was a peach-cheeked blonde, about twenty-
two or three, anyway no more than five or six years
younger than Julia. Although her name suggested the
exotic, a Hungarian perhaps, her accent was flat Ontario and her last name was Hunt. Either a fanciful
mother or a name-changing father, or perhaps Marika
had adopted the name herself. She had been very
friendly to Julia. "I've read your book," she said. "I
don't find time to read too many books, but I got yours
out of the library because of Bernie. I didn't think I
was going to like it, but actually it's quite good." Julia
was grateful, Bernie said too grateful, to people who
said they liked her work or who had even read it.
Nevertheless, she heard a voice inside her head saying, *Piss right off*. It was the way Marika offered her
compliment: like a biscuit to a dog, part reward, part
bribe, and condescending.

Since then they'd had coffee together several times.
It was always Marika who dropped over, on some er-
rand or other from Bernie. They sat in the kitchen and

talked, but no real connections were made. They were like two mothers at a birthday party, sitting on the sidelines while their children whooped and gobbled: they were polite to each other, but the real focus of their attention was elsewhere. Once Marika had said, "I've always thought I might like to write myself," and Julia had felt a small red explosion at the back of her neck and had almost thrown her cup of coffee at her, until she realized Marika didn't mean it that way, she was just trying to appear interested. "Aren't you afraid you'll run out of material?"

"Not material, energy," she'd said, making it sound like a joke; but it had been true, that was her fear. Weren't they the same thing? "According to Einstein," she said, and Marika, having missed the connection, gave her a funny look and changed the subject to films.

The last time Marika came over, Julia wasn't even out of bed. She had no excuse, no explanation. She almost told her to go away, but Bernie needed his black notebook, the one with the phone numbers, so she had to let her in. Marika leaned in the bedroom doorway, trim in her little layered look, dangling her handwoven bag, while Julia, with unwashed hair straggling over the shoulders of her nightgown, mossmouthed and blurryminded, knelt on the floor and scrabbled through Bernie's discarded pockets. For the first time in their life she wished he would bloody well pick up his clothes. She felt exposed by them, though she shouldn't, they weren't her clothes, she hadn't dropped them. Marika exuded surprise, embarrassment and a certain glee, as if Bernie's dirty socks and trampled jeans were Julia's soft underbelly, which she'd always wanted to get a look at.

"I don't know where he's put it," Julia said, irritated. "He's supposed to pick them up himself," and added, far too defensively she knew, "We share everything."

"Of course, with your work and all," Marika said. She was scanning the room, the greyish bed, Julia's sweater slumped in the corner chair, the avocado with brown-edged leaves on the windowsill, their only plant. She'd grown it from the pit of a celebration avocado—she could no longer remember the reason for the rejoicing—but there was something wrong with it. Tea-leaves, you were supposed to put tea-leaves on them, or was it charcoal?

The notebook was finally under the bed. Julia pulled it out; a dustball clung to it. She saw in her mind a small plaque, like the ones on historical houses: DUSTBALL. *Once the property of Julia Morse, Poetess.* With a few bored schoolchildren looking at it through the glass of a case. That was the future, if there was a future, if she kept on writing, if she became at least marginally significant, an obligatory footnote in someone's thesis. Fragments left over after the general decay, classified, gathering dust, like the vertebrae of dinosaurs. Bloodless.

She handed the notebook over. "Would you like some coffee?" she asked, in a voice meant to discourage.

"I don't want to put you out," Marika said, but she had some anyway, chatting brightly about their plans for a collective show, to be called "Up From Under." Her eyes shifted around the kitchen, taking in the dripping tap, the smelly J cloth draped over it, the ancient toaster with the crumbs around its base like the debris from a tiny landslide. "I'm really glad we can be friends," she said just before leaving. "Bernie says we have nothing in common, but I think we get on real well. They're mostly men down there." This could have been some ersatz variety of women's lib, Julia thought, but it wasn't: Marika's voice stank of bridge club. "Real well." How incongruous, with those three-inch platforms, that trendy bum. Marika's visits made her feel like a welfare case. She wondered how she could get her to stop coming, without being too rude. She begrudged the time, too, she could be using it for work. Though increasingly there was no work.

Bernie didn't seem to notice that she was doing next to nothing. He no longer asked to read what she might have written during the day. When he came home for dinner he would talk obsessively about the gallery, eating plate after plate of spaghetti and, it seemed to her, whole loaves of bread. His appetite had increased, and they had recently begun to argue about the food bills and who was supposed to do the cooking and shopping. In the beginning they had shared everything, that was the agreement. Julia wanted to point out that since he was now eating twice as much as she was, he really ought to do more of the shopping and pay more than half, but she felt it would be mingy of her to say this. Especially since, whenever they talked about money, he would say, "Don't worry, you'll get paid off," as if she begrudged him the gallery loan. Which she supposed she did.

What time is it? Lift the wrist: six-thirty. The blood seems to have slowed down, but it's still there, a thickening like sludge at the back of the throat. A teacher, once, in public school, who came into the classroom with her teeth outlined in blood. She must have been to the dentist and then not checked in the mirror, but we were all so afraid of her none of us said anything and we spent the afternoon drawing three tulips in a vase, presided over by that bloodthirsty smile. Have to remember to brush my teeth and clean my face carefully, a drop of blood on the chin might be disturbing to the audience. Blood, the elemental fluid, the juice of life, byproduct of birth, prelude to death. The red badge of courage. The people's flag. Maybe I could get a job writing political speeches, if all else fails. But when it comes out of your nose, not magic or even symbolic, just ridiculous. Pinned by the nose to the geometric net of this bathroom floor. Don't be completely stupid, get started. Stand up carefully: if the blood keeps flowing, call off the reading and get on the plane. (Leaving a trail of clots?) I could be home tonight. Bernie's there now, waiting for me to call, it's past the time.

She pulled herself up, slowly, holding onto the sink, and walked into the bedroom with her head tilted back precariously. She groped for the phone and picked it up. She dialled 0 and got the operator to place the call for her. She listened to the outer-space noises the phone made, anticipating Bernie's voice, feeling his tongue already on the inside of her mouth. They would go to bed and after that they would have a late supper, the two of them in the kitchen with the gas oven lit and open to keep them warm, the way they used to. (Her mind skipped the details of what they would eat. She knew there had been nothing in the refrigerator when she left but a couple of aging weiners. Not even any buns.) Things would get better, time would reverse itself, they would talk, she would tell him how much she had missed him (for surely she had been away much longer than a day), silence would open, language would flow again.

The line was busy.

She did not want to think about her disappointment. She would phone later. There was no more blood, though she could feel it crusted inside her head. So she would stay, she would do the reading, she would collect the fee and use it to pay the rent. What else was possible?

It was dinnertime and she was hungry, but she couldn't afford another meal. Sometimes they took the poet out for dinner, sometimes they gave a party afterwards where she could fill up on crackers and cheese. Here there was nothing. They picked her up at the airport, that was it. She could tell there had been no posters, no advance publicity. A small audience, nervous because they were there and nobody else was, caught out attending the wrong reading. And she didn't even look like a poet, she was wearing a neat navy-blue pantsuit, easy for stairs and cars. Maybe a robe would help, something flowing and ethereal. Bangles, a scarf?

She sat on the edge of the straightbacked chair, facing a picture of two dead ducks and an Irish setter.

There was time to be filled. No television set. Read the Gideon Bible? No, nothing too strenuous, she didn't want to start bleeding again. In half an hour they would come to pick her up. Then the eyes, the polite hands, the fixed smiles. Afterwards everyone would murmur. "Don't you feel exposed up there?" a young girl had asked her once. "No," she'd said, and she didn't, it wasn't her, she read only her most soothing poems, she didn't want to disturb anyone. But they distrusted her anyway. At least she never got drunk beforehand the way a lot of the others did. She wanted to be nice, and everyone approved of that.

Except the few hungry ones, the ones who wanted to know the secret, who believed there was a secret. They would straggle up afterwards, she knew, hanging around the edges, behind the murmuring committee members, clutching little packets of poems, extending them to her gingerly, as if the pages were raw flesh they could not bear to have touched. She could remember when she had felt like that. Most of the poems would be dismal, but now and then there would be one that had something, the energy, the thing that could not be defined. *Don't do it*, she wanted to tell them, *don't make the mistake I made*. But what was her mistake? Thinking she could save her soul, no doubt. By the word alone.

Did I really believe that? Did I really believe that language could seize me by the hair and draw me straight up, out into the free air? But if you stop believing, you can't do it any longer, you can't fly. So I'm stuck here on this chair. *A sixty-year-old smiling public man*. Crisis of faith? Faith in what? Resurrection, that's what is needed. Up from under. Get rid of these haunts, these fictions, *he said, she said*, counting up points and grievances; the dialogues of shadows. Otherwise there will be nothing left but the rest of my life. Something is frozen.

Bernie, save me.

He was so nice this morning, before she left.

The phone again, the voice flies through the darkness of space. Hollow ringing, a click.

"Hi." A woman's voice, Marika, she knew who it would be.

"Could I please speak to Bernie?" Stupid to act as though she didn't recognize the voice.

"Hi, Julia," Marika said. "Bernie's not here right now. He had to go away for a couple of days, but he knew you'd be calling tonight so he asked me to come over. So you wouldn't worry or anything. He said to have a good reading, and don't forget to water the plant when you get back."

"Oh, thanks, Marika," she said. As if she was his secretary, leaving her with messages for the idiot wife while he. . . . She couldn't ask where he had gone. She herself went away, why couldn't he? If he wanted her to know where, he'd tell her. She said goodbye. As she put down the phone, she thought she heard something. A voice, a laugh?

He hasn't gone anywhere. He's there, in the apartment, I can see it, it must have been going on for weeks, months, down at the gallery, *I've read your book*, checking out the competition. I must be feebleminded, everyone knew but me. Trotting over to have coffee with me, casing the joint. Hope they have the grace to change the sheets. Didn't have the guts to talk to me himself, water the plant my ass, it's dead anyway. Melodrama in a parking lot, long stretches of asphalt with here and there a splotch of crushed animal, is that what my life has become?

Rock bottom in this room among the slagheaps, outer space, on the dead moon, with two slaughtered ducks and a stuffed dog, why did you have to do it that way, when I'm out here, you know it cripples me, these ordeals, walking through the eyes, couldn't you have waited? You set it up so well, I'll come back and yell and scream, and you'll deny it all, you'll look at me, very cool, and say, *What are you talking about?*

And what will I be talking about, maybe I'm wrong, I'll never know. Beautiful.

It's almost time.

They will arrive, the two young men who are polite and who do not yet have tenure. She will get into the front seat of their Volvo, and all the way to the reading, as they drive between the snowdrifts piled halfway up the telephone poles, the two young men will discuss the virtues of this car and the relative virtues of the car belonging to the one who is not driving but who is sitting in the back seat with his legs doubled like a grasshopper's.

She will not be able to say anything at all. She will watch the snow coming at the windshield and being wiped away by the windshield wipers, and it will be red, it will be like a solid red wall. A violation, this is what she hates, they had promised never to lie.

Stomach full of blood, head full of blood, burning red, she can feel it at last, this rage that has been going on for a long time, energy, words swarming behind her eyes like spring bees. Something is hungry, something is coiling itself. A long song coils and uncoils itself just in front of the windshield, where the red snow is falling, bringing everything to life. They park the virtuous car and she is led by the two young men into the auditorium, grey cinderblock, where a gathering of polite faces waits to hear the word. Hands will clap, things will be said about her, nothing astonishing, she is supposed to be good for them, they must open their mouths and take her in, like vitamins, like bland medicine. No. No sweet identity, she will clench herself against it. She will step across the stage, words coiled, she will open her mouth and the room will explode in blood.

Dancing Girls

∘ ∘ ∘

The first sign of the new man was the knock on the door. It was the landlady, knocking not at Ann's door, as she'd thought, but on the other door, the one east of the bathroom. Knock, knock, knock; then a pause, soft footsteps, the sound of unlocking. Ann, who had been reading a book on canals, put it down and lit herself a cigarette. It wasn't that she tried to overhear: in this house you couldn't help it.

"Hi!" Mrs. Nolan's voice loud, overly friendly. "I was wondering, my kids would love to see your native costume. You think you could put it on, like, and come down?"

A soft voice, unintelligible.

"Gee, that's great! We'd sure appreciate it!"

Closing and locking, Mrs. Nolan slip-slopping along the hall in, Ann knew, her mauve terry-cloth scuffies and flowered housecoat, down the stairs, hollering at her two boys. "You get into this room right now!" Her voice came up through Ann's hot air register as if the grate were a PA system. *It isn't those kids who want to see him,* she thought. *It's her.* She put out the cigarette, reserving the other half for later, and opened her book again. What costume? Which land, this time?

Unlocking, opening, soft feet down the hall. They sounded bare. Ann closed the book and opened her own door. A white robe, the back of a brown head, moving with a certain stealth or caution toward the stairs. Ann went into the bathroom and turned on the light. They would share it; the person in that room always shared her bathroom. She hoped he would be better than the man before, who always seemed to forget his razor and would knock on the door while Ann was having a bath. You wouldn't have to worry about getting raped or anything in this house though, that was one good thing. Mrs. Nolan was better than any burglar alarm, and she was always there.

That one had been from France, studying Cinema. Before him there had been a girl, from Turkey, studying Comparative Literature. Lelah, or that was how it was pronounced. Ann used to find her beautiful long auburn hairs in the washbasin fairly regularly; she'd run her thumb and index finger along them, enviously, before discarding them. She had to keep her own hair chopped off at ear level, as it was brittle and broke easily. Lelah also had a gold tooth, right at the front on the outside where it showed when she smiled. Curiously, Ann was envious of this tooth as well. It and the hair and the turquoise-studded earrings Lelah wore gave her a gypsy look, a wise look that Ann, with her beige eyebrows and delicate mouth, knew she would never be able to develop, no matter how wise she got. She herself went in for "classics," tailored skirts and Shetland sweaters; it was the only look she could carry off. But she and Lelah had been friends, smoking cigarettes in each other's rooms, commiserating with each other about the difficulties of their courses and the loudness of Mrs. Nolan's voice. So Ann was familiar with that room; she knew what it looked like inside and how much it cost. It was no luxury suite, certainly, and she wasn't surprised at the high rate of turnover. It had an even more direct

pipeline to the sounds of the Nolan family than hers
had. Lelah had left because she couldn't stand the
noise.

The room was smaller and cheaper than her room,
though painted the same depressing shade of green.
Unlike hers, it did not have its own tiny refrigerator,
sink and stove; you had to use the kitchen at the front
of the house, which had been staked out much earlier
by a small enclave of mathematicians, two men and
one woman, from Hong Kong. Whoever took that
room either had to eat out all the time or run the
gamut of their conversation, which even when not in
Chinese was so rarefied as to be unintelligible. And
you could never find any space in the refrigerator, it
was always full of mushrooms. This from Lelah; Ann
herself never had to deal with them since she could
cook in her own room. She could see them, though,
as she went in and out. At mealtimes they usually sat
quietly at their kitchen table, discussing surds, she
assumed. Ann suspected that what Lelah had really
resented about them was not the mushrooms: they
simply made her feel stupid.

Every morning, before she left for classes, Ann
checked the bathroom for signs of the new man—
hairs, cosmetics—but there was nothing. She hardly
ever heard him; sometimes there was that soft, bare-
footed pacing, the click of his lock, but there were no
radio noises, no coughs, no conversations. For the first
couple of weeks, apart from that one glimpse of a tall,
billowing figure, she didn't even see him. He didn't
appear to use the kitchen, where the mathematicians
continued their mysteries undisturbed; or if he did,
he cooked while no one else was there. Ann would
have forgotten about him completely if it hadn't been
for Mrs. Nolan.

"He's real nice, not like some you get," she said to
Ann in her piercing whisper. Although she shouted at
her husband, when he was home, and especially at her
children, she always whispered when she was talking
to Ann, a hoarse, avid whisper, as if they shared dis-

reputable secrets. Ann was standing in front of her door with the room key in her hand, her usual location during these confidences. Mrs. Nolan knew Ann's routine. It wasn't difficult for her to pretend to be cleaning the bathroom, to pop out and waylay Ann, Ajax and rag in hand, whenever she felt she had something to tell her. She was a short, barrel-shaped woman: the top of her head came only to Ann's nose, so she had to look up at Ann, which at these moments made her seem oddly childlike.

"He's from one of them Arabian countries. Though I thought they wore turbans, or not turbans, those white things, like. He just has this funny hat, sort of like the Shriners. He don't look much like an Arab to me. He's got these tattoo marks on his face. . . . But he's real nice."

Ann stood, her umbrella dripping onto the floor, waiting for Mrs. Nolan to finish. She never had to say anything much; it wasn't expected. "You think you could get me the rent on Wednesday?" Mrs. Nolan asked. Three days early; the real point of the conversation, probably. Still, as Mrs. Nolan had said back in September, she didn't have much of anyone to talk to. Her husband was away much of the time and her children escaped outdoors whenever they could. She never went out herself except to shop, and for Mass on Sundays.

"I'm glad it was you took the room," she'd said to Ann. "I can talk to you. You're not, like, foreign. Not like most of them. It was his idea, getting this big house to rent out. Not that he has to do the work or put up with them. You never know what they'll do."

Ann wanted to point out to her that she was indeed foreign, that she was just as foreign as any of the others, but she knew Mrs. Nolan would not understand. It would be like that fiasco in October. *Wear your native costumes.* She had responded to the invitation out of a sense of duty, as well as one of irony. Wait till they get a load of my native costume, she'd thought, contemplating snowshoes and a parka but actually putting on her good blue wool suit. There was only one thing *native costume* reminded her of: the cover picture on the Missionary Sunday School paper they'd once handed out, which showed children from all the countries of the world dancing in a circle around a smiling white-faced Jesus in a bedsheet. That, and the poem in the *Golden Windows Reader*:

> Little Indian, Sioux or Cree,
> Oh, don't you wish that you were me?

The awful thing, as she told Lelah later, was that she was the only one who'd gone. "She had all this food ready, and not a single other person was there. She was really upset, and I was so embarrassed for her. It was some Friends of Foreign Students thing, just for women: students and the wives of students. She obviously didn't think I was foreign enough, and she couldn't figure out why no one else came." Neither could Ann, who had stayed far too long and had eaten platefuls of crackers and cheese she didn't want in order to soothe her hostess' thwarted sense of hospitality. The woman, who had tastefully-streaked ash-blonde hair and a livingroom filled with polished and satiny traditional surfaces, had alternately urged her to eat and stared at the door, as if expecting a parade of foreigners in their native costumes to come trooping gratefully through it.

Lelah smiled, showing her wise tooth. "Don't they know any better than to throw those things at night?" she said. "Those men aren't going to let their wives go out by themselves at night. And the single ones are afraid to walk on the streets alone, I know I am."

"I'm not," Ann said, "as long as you stay on the main ones, where it's lighted."

"Then you're a fool," Lelah said. "Don't you know there was a girl murdered three blocks from here? Left her bathroom window unlocked. Some man climbed through the window and cut her throat."

"I always carry my umbrella," Ann said. Of course

there were certain places where you just didn't go.
Scollay Square, for instance, where the prostitutes
hung out and you might get followed, or worse. She
tried to explain to Lelah that she wasn't used to this,
to any of this, that in Toronto you could walk all over
the city, well, almost anywhere, and never have any
trouble. She went on to say that no one here seemed
to understand that she wasn't like them, she came
from a different country, it wasn't the same; but Lelah
was quickly bored by this. She had to get back to Tol-
stoy, she said, putting out her cigarette in her un-
finished cup of instant coffee. (*Not strong enough for
her, I suppose*, Ann thought.)

"You shouldn't worry," she said. "You're well off. At
least your family doesn't almost disown you for doing
what you want to do." Lelah's father kept writing her
letters, urging her to return to Turkey, where the family had decided on the perfect husband for her. Lelah
had stalled them for one year, and maybe she could
stall them for one more, but that would be her limit.
She couldn't possibly finish her thesis in that time.

Ann hadn't seen much of her since she'd moved out.
You lost sight of people quickly here, in the ever-shift-
ing population of hopeful and despairing transients.

No one wrote her letters urging her to come home,
no one had picked out the perfect husband for her.
On the contrary. She could imagine her mother's defeated look, the greying and sinking of her face, if she
were suddenly to announce that she was going to
quit school, trade in her ambitions for fate, and get
married. Even her father wouldn't like it. *Finish what
you start*, he'd say, *I didn't and look what happened
to me*. The bungalow at the top of Avenue Road, beside a gas station, with the roar of the expressway
always there, like the sea, and fumes blighting the
Chinese elm hedge her mother had planted to conceal
the pumps. Both her brothers had dropped out of high
school; they weren't the good students Ann had been.
One worked in a print shop now and had a wife; the
other had drifted to Vancouver, and no one knew

what he did. She remembered her first real boyfriend, beefy, easygoing Bill Decker, with his two-tone car that kept losing the muffler. They'd spent a lot of time parked on side streets, rubbing against each other through all those layers of clothes. But even in that sensual mist, the cocoon of breath and skin they'd spun around each other, those phone conversations that existed as a form of touch, she'd known this was not something she could get too involved in. He was probably flabby by now, settled. She'd had relationships with men since then, but she had treated them the same way. *Circumspect*.

Not that Mrs. Nolan's back room was any step up. Out one window there was a view of the funeral home next door; out the other was the yard, which the Nolan kids had scraped clean of grass and which was now a bog of half-frozen mud. Their dog, a mongrelized German Shepherd, was kept tied there, where the kids alternately hugged and tormented it. ("Jimmy! Donny! Now you leave that dog alone!" "Don't do that, he's filthy! Look at you!" Ann covering her ears, reading about underground malls.) She'd tried to fix the room up, she'd hung a Madras spread as a curtain in front of the cooking area, she'd put up several prints, Braque still-lifes of guitars and soothing Cubist fruit, and she was growing herbs on her windowsill; she needed surroundings that at least tried not to be ugly. But none of these things helped much. At night she wore earplugs. She hadn't known about the scarcity of good rooms, hadn't realized that the whole area was a student slum, that the rents would be so high, the available places so dismal. Next year would be different; she'd get here early and have the pick of the crop. Mrs. Nolan's was definitely a leftover. You could do much better for the money; you could even have a whole apartment, if you were willing to live in the real slum that spread in narrow streets of three-storey frame houses, fading mustard yellow and soot grey, nearer the river. Though Ann didn't think she was quite up to that. Something in one of the good old houses, on a quiet back street, with a little stained glass, would be more like it. Her friend Jetske had a place like that.

But she was doing what she wanted, no doubt of that. In high school she had planned to be an architect, but while finishing the preliminary courses at university she had realized that the buildings she wanted to design were either impossible—who could afford them?—or futile. They would be lost, smothered, ruined by all the other buildings jammed inharmoniously around them. This was why she had decided to go into Urban Design, and she had come here because this school was the best. Or rumoured to be the best. By the time she finished, she intended to be so well-qualified, so armoured with qualifications, that no one back home would dare turn her down for the job she coveted. She wanted to rearrange Toronto. Toronto would do for a start.

She wasn't yet too certain of the specific details. What she saw were spaces, beautiful green spaces, with water flowing through them, and trees. Not big golf-course lawns, though; something more winding, something with sudden turns, private niches, surprising vistas. And no formal flower beds. The houses, or whatever they were, set unobtrusively among the trees, the cars kept . . . where? And where would people shop, and who would live in these places? This was the problem: she could see the vistas, the trees and the streams or canals, quite clearly, but she could never visualize the people. Her green spaces were always empty.

She didn't see her next-door neighbour again until February. She was coming back from the small local supermarket where she bought the food for her cheap, carefully balanced meals. He was leaning in the doorway of what, at home, she would have called a vestibule, smoking a cigarette and staring out at the rain, through the glass panes at the side of the front door. He should have moved a little to give Ann room to put

down her umbrella, but he didn't. He didn't even look
at her. She squeezed in, shook her deflated umbrella
and checked her mail box, which didn't have a key.
There weren't usually any letters in it, and today was
no exception. He was wearing a white shirt that was
too big for him and some greenish trousers. His feet
were not bare, in fact he was wearing a pair of pro-
saic brown shoes. He did have tattoo marks, though,
or rather scars, a set of them running across each
cheek. It was the first time she had seen him from the
front. He seemed a little shorter than he had when
she'd glimpsed him heading towards the stairs, but
perhaps it was because he had no hat on. He was
curved so listlessly against the doorframe, it was almost as if he had no bones.

There was nothing to see through the front of Mrs.
Nolan's door except the traffic, sizzling by the way it
did every day. He was depressed, it must be that. This
weather would depress anyone. Ann sympathized
with his loneliness, but she did not wish to become
involved in it, implicated by it. She had enough
trouble dealing with her own. She smiled at him,
though since he wasn't looking at her this smile was
lost. She went past him and up the stairs.

As she fumbled in her purse for her key, Mrs. Nolan
stumped out of the bathroom. "You see him?" she
whispered.

"Who?" Ann said.

"*Him.*" Mrs. Nolan jerked her thumb. "Standing
down there, by the door. He does that a lot. He's
bothering me, like. I don't have such good nerves."

"He's not doing anything," Ann said.

"That's what I mean," Mrs. Nolan whispered omi-
nously. "He never does nothing. Far as I can tell, he
never goes out much. All he does is borrow my vacuum cleaner."

"Your vacuum cleaner?" Ann said, startled into re-
sponding.

"That's what I said." Mrs. Nolan had a rubber plun-
ger which she was fingering. "And there's more of

them. They come in the other night, up to his room.
Two more, with the same marks and everything, on
their faces. It's like some kind of, like, a religion or
something. And he never gave the vacuum cleaner
back till the next day."

"Does he pay the rent?" Ann said, trying to switch
the conversation to practical matters. Mrs. Nolan was
letting her imagination get out of control.

"Regular," Mrs. Nolan said. "Except I don't like the
way he comes down, so quiet like, right into my house.
With Fred away so much."

"I wouldn't worry," Ann said in what she hoped was
a soothing voice. "He seems perfectly nice."

"It's always that kind," Mrs. Nolan said.

Ann cooked her dinner, a chicken breast, some peas,
a digestive biscuit. Then she washed her hair in the
bathroom and put it up in rollers. She had to do that,
to give it body. With her head encased in the plastic
hood of her portable dryer she sat at her table, drinking instant coffee, smoking her usual half cigarette,
and attempting to read a book about Roman aqueducts, from which she hoped to get some novel ideas
for her current project. (An aqueduct, going right
through the middle of the obligatory shopping centre?
Would anyone care?) Her mind kept flicking, though,
to the problem of the man next door. Ann did not often try to think about what it would be like to be a
man. But this particular man . . . Who was he, and
what was happening to him? He must be a student,
everyone here was a student. And he would be intelligent, that went without saying. Probably on scholarship. Everyone here in the graduate school was on
scholarship, except the real Americans, who sometimes
weren't. Or rather, the women were, but some of the
men were still avoiding the draft, though President
Johnson had announced he was going to do away with
all that. She herself would never have made it this far
without scholarships; her parents could not have af-
forded it.

So he was here on scholarship, studying something

practical, no doubt, nuclear physics or the construction
of dams, and, like herself and the other foreigners, he
was expected to go away again as soon as he'd learned
what he'd come for. But he never went out of the
house; he stood at the front door and watched the
brutish flow of cars, the winter rain, while those back
in his own country, the ones that had sent him, were
confidently expecting him to return some day,
crammed with knowledge, ready to solve their
lives. . . . *He's lost his nerve*, Ann thought. *He'll fail.*
It was too late in the year for him ever to catch up.
Such failures, such paralyses, were fairly common
here, especially among the foreigners. He was far
from home, from the language he shared, the wearers
of his native costume; he was in exile, he was drowning. What did he do, alone by himself in his room at
night?

Ann switched her hair dryer to COOL and wrenched
her mind back to aqueducts. She could see he was
drowning but there was nothing she could do. Unless
you were good at it you shouldn't even try, she was
wise enough to know that. All you could do for the
drowning was to make sure you were not one of them.

The aqueduct, now. It would be made of natural
brick, an earthy red; it would have low arches, in the
shade of which there would be ferns and, perhaps,
some delphiniums, in varying tones of blue. She must
learn more about plants. Before entering the shopping
complex (trust him to assign a shopping complex; before that he had demanded a public housing project), it would flow through her green space, in which,
she could now see, there were people walking. Children? *But not children like Mrs. Nolan's.* They would
turn her grass to mud, they'd nail things to her
trees, their mangy dogs would shit on her ferns, they'd
throw bottles and pop cans into her aqueduct. . . .
And Mrs. Nolan herself, and her Noah's Ark of seedy,
brilliant foreigners, where would she put them? For
the houses of the Mrs. Nolans of this world would
have to go; that was one of the axioms of Urban De-

sign. She could convert them to small offices, or single-floor apartments; some shrubs and hanging plants and a new coat of paint would do wonders. But she knew this was temporizing. Around her green space, she could see, there was now a high wire fence. Inside it were trees, flowers and grass, outside the dirty snow, the endless rain, the grunting cars and the half-frozen mud of Mrs. Nolan's drab backyard. That was what *exclusive* meant, it meant that some people were excluded. Her parents stood in the rain outside the fence, watching with dreary pride while she strolled about in the eternal sunlight. Their one success.

Stop it, she commanded herself. *They want me to be doing this.* She unwound her hair and brushed it out. Three hours from now, she knew, it would be limp as ever because of the damp.

The next day, she tried to raise her new theoretical problem with her friend Jetske. Jetske was in Urban Design, too. She was from Holland, and could remember running through the devastated streets as a child, begging small change, first from the Germans, later from the American soldiers, who were always good for a chocolate bar or two.

"You learn how to take care of yourself," she'd said. "It didn't seem hard at the time, but when you are a child, nothing is that hard. We were all the same, nobody had anything." Because of this background, which was more exotic and cruel than anything Ann herself had experienced (what was a gas pump compared to the Nazis?), Ann respected her opinions. She liked her also because she was the only person she'd met here who seemed to know where Canada was. There were a lot of Canadian soldiers buried in Holland. This provided Ann with at least a shadowy identity, which she felt she needed. She didn't have a native costume, but at least she had some heroic dead bodies with which she was connected, however remotely.

"The trouble with what we're doing . . . ," she said to Jetske, as they walked towards the library under

Ann's umbrella. "I mean, you can rebuild one part, but what do you do about the rest?"

"Of the city?" Jetske said.

"No," Ann said slowly. "I guess I mean of the world."

Jetske laughed. She had what Ann now thought of as Dutch teeth, even and white, with quite a lot of gum showing above them and below the lip. "I didn't know you were a socialist," she said. Her cheeks were pink and healthy, like a cheese ad.

"I'm not," Ann said. "But I thought we were supposed to be thinking in total patterns."

Jetske laughed again. "Did you know," she said, "that in some countries you have to get official permission to move from one town to another?"

Ann didn't like this idea at all. "It controls the population flow," Jetske said. "You can't really have Urban Design without that, you know."

"I think that's awful," Ann said.

"Of course you do," Jetske said, as close to bitterness as she ever got. "You've never had to do it. Over here you are soft in the belly, you think you can always have everything. You think there is freedom of choice. The whole world will come to it. You will see." She began teasing Ann again about her plastic headscarf. Jetske never wore anything on her head.

Ann designed her shopping complex, putting in a skylight and banks of indoor plants, leaving out the aqueduct. She got an A.

In the third week of March, Ann went with Jetske and some of the others to a Buckminster Fuller lecture. Afterwards they all went to the pub on the corner of the Square for a couple of beers. Ann left with Jetske about eleven o'clock and walked a couple of blocks with her before Jetske turned off towards her lovely old house with the stained glass. Ann continued by herself, warily, keeping to the lighted streets. She carried her purse under her elbow and held her furled umbrella at the ready. For once it wasn't raining.

When she got back to the house and started to climb the stairs, it struck her that something was different. Upstairs, she knew. Absolutely, something was out of line. There was curious music coming from the room next door, a high flute rising over drums, thumping noises, the sound of voices. The man next door was throwing a party, it seemed. *Good for him*, Ann thought. He might as well do something. She settled down for an hour's reading.

But the noises were getting louder. From the bathroom came the sound of retching. There was going to be trouble. Ann checked her door to make sure it was locked, got out the bottle of sherry she kept in the cupboard next to the oven, and poured herself a drink. Then she turned out the light and sat with her back against the door, drinking her sherry in the faint blue light from the funeral home next door. There was no point in going to bed: even with her earplugs in, she could never sleep.

The music and thumpings got louder. After a while there was a banging on the floor, then some shouting, which came quite clearly through Ann's hot-air register. "I'm calling the police! You hear? I'm calling the police! You get them out of here and get out yourself!" The music switched off, the door opened, and there was a clattering down the stairs. Then more footsteps —Ann couldn't tell whether they were going up or down—and more shouting. The front door banged and the shouts continued on down the street. Ann undressed and put on her nightgown, still without turning on the light, and crept into the bathroom. The bathtub was full of vomit.

This time Mrs. Nolan didn't even wait for Ann to get back from classes. She waylaid her in the morning as she was coming out of her room. Mrs. Nolan was holding a can of Drano and had dark circles under her eyes. Somehow this made her look younger. *She's probably not much older than I am*, Ann thought. Until now she had considered her middle-aged.

"I guess you saw the mess in there," she whispered.

"Yes, I did," Ann said.

"I guess you heard all that last night." She paused.

"What happened?" Ann asked. In fact she really wanted to know.

"He had some dancing girls in there! Three dancing girls, and two other men, in that little room! I thought the ceiling was gonna come right down on our heads!"

"I did hear something like dancing," Ann said.

"Dancing! They was jumping, it sounded like they jumped right off the bed onto the floor. The plaster was coming off. Fred wasn't home, he's not home yet. I was afraid for the kids. Like, with those tattoos, who knows what they was working themselves up to?" Her sibilant voice hinted of ritual murders, young Jimmy and runny-nosed Donny sacrificed to some obscure god.

"What did you do?" Ann asked.

"I called the police. Well, the dancing girls, as soon as they heard I was calling the police, they got out of here, I can tell you. Put on their coats and was down the stairs and out the door like nothing. You can bet they didn't want no trouble with the police. But not the others, they don't seem to know what police means."

She paused again, and Ann asked, "Did they come?"

"Who?"

"The police."

"Well, you know around here it always takes the police a while to get there, unless there's some right outside. I know that, it's not the first time I've had to call them. So who knows what they would've done in the meantime? I could hear them coming downstairs, like, so I just grabs the broom and I chased them out. I chased them all the way down the street."

Ann saw that she thought she had done something very brave, which meant that in fact she had. She really believed that the man next door and his friends were dangerous, that they were a threat to her children. She had chased them single-handedly, yelling with fear and defiance. But he had only been throwing a party.

"Heavens," she said weakly.

"You can say that again," said Mrs. Nolan. "I went in there this morning, to get his things and put them out front where he could get them without me having to see him. I don't have such good nerves, I didn't sleep at all, even after they was gone. Fred is just gonna have to stop driving nights, I can't take it. But you know? He didn't have no things in there. Not one. Just an old empty suitcase?"

"What about his native costume?" Ann said.

"He had it on," Mrs. Nolan said. "He just went running down the street in it, like some kind of a loony. And you know what else I found in there? In one corner, there was this pile of empty bottles. Liquor. He must've been drinking like a fish for months, and never threw out the bottles. And in another corner, there was this pile of burnt matches. He could've burnt the house down, throwing them on the floor like that. But the worst thing was, you know all the times he borrowed my vacuum cleaner?"

"Yes," Ann said.

"Well, he never threw away the dirt. There it all was, in the other corner of the room. He must've just emptied it out and left it there. I don't get it." Mrs. Nolan, by now, was puzzled rather than angry.

"Well," Ann said. "That certainly is strange."

"Strange?" Mrs. Nolan said. "I'll tell you it's strange. He always paid the rent though, right on time. Never a day late. Why would he put the dirt in a corner like that, when he could've put it out in a bag like everyone else? It's not like he didn't know. I told him real clear which were the garbage days, when he moved in."

Ann said she was going to be late for class if she didn't hurry. At the front door she tucked her hair under her plastic scarf. Today it was just a drizzle, not heavy enough for the umbrella. She started off, walking quickly along beside the double line of traffic.

She wondered where he had gone, chased down the street by Mrs. Nolan in her scuffies and flowered housecoat, shouting and flailing at him with a broom. She must have been at least as terrifying a spectacle to him as he was to her, and just as inexplicable. Why would this woman, this fat crazy woman, wish to burst in upon a scene of harmless hospitality, banging and raving? He and his friends could easily have overpowered her, but they would not even have thought about doing that. They would have been too frightened. What unspoken taboo had they violated? What would these cold, mad people do next?

Anyway, he did have some friends. They would take care of him, at least for the time being. Which was a relief, she guessed. But what she really felt was a childish regret that she had not seen the dancing girls. If she had known they were there, she might even have risked opening her door. She knew they were not real dancing girls, they were probably just some whores from Scollay Square. Mrs. Nolan had called them that as a euphemism, or perhaps because of an unconscious association with the word *Arabian*, the vaguely Arabian country. She never had found out what it was. Nevertheless, she wished she had seen them. Jetske would find all of this quite amusing, especially the image of her backed against the door, drinking sherry in the dark. It would have been better if she'd had the courage to look.

She began to think about her green space, as she often did during this walk. The green, perfect space of the future. She knew by now that it was cancelled in advance, that it would never come into being, that it was already too late. Once she was qualified, she would return to plan tasteful mixes of residential units and shopping complexes, with a lot of underground malls and arcades to protect people from the snow. But she could allow herself to see it one last time.

The fence was gone now, and the green stretched out endlessly, fields and trees and flowing water, as far as she could see. In the distance, beneath the arches of the aqueduct, a herd of animals, deer or something, was grazing. (She must learn more about animals.) Groups of people were walking happily among the trees, holding hands, not just in twos but in threes, fours, fives. The man from next door was there, in his native costume, and the mathematicians, they were all in their native costumes. Beside the stream a man was playing the flute; and around him, in long flowered robes and mauve scuffies, their auburn hair floating around their healthy pink faces, smiling their Dutch smiles, the dancing girls were sedately dancing.

Giving Birth

∘ ∘ ∘

But who gives it? And to whom is it given? Certainly it doesn't feel like giving, which implies a flow, a gentle handing over, no coercion. But there is scant gentleness here, it's too strenuous, the belly like a knotted fist, squeezing, the heavy trudge of the heart, every muscle in the body tight and moving, as in a slow motion shot of a high-jump, the faceless body sailing up, turning, hanging for a moment in the air, and then—back to real time again—the plunge, the rush down, the result. Maybe the phrase was made by someone viewing the result only: in this case, the rows of babies to whom birth has occurred, lying like neat packages in their expertly wrapped blankets, pink or blue, with their labels scotch-taped to their clear plastic cots, behind the plate-glass window.

No one ever says *giving death*, although they are in some ways the same, events, not things. And *delivering*, that act the doctor is generally believed to perform: who delivers what? Is it the mother who is delivered, like a prisoner being released? Surely not; nor is the child delivered to the mother like a letter through a slot. How can you be both the sender and

the receiver at once? Was someone in bondage, is
someone made free? Thus language, muttering in its
archaic tongues of something, yet one more thing, that
needs to be re-named.

It won't be by me, though. These are the only words
I have, I'm stuck with them, stuck in them. (That
image of the tar sands, old tableau in the Royal Ontario Museum, second floor north, how persistent it is.
Will I break free, or will I be sucked down, fossilized,
a sabre-toothed tiger or lumbering brontosaurus who
ventured out too far? Words ripple at my feet, black,
sluggish, lethal. Let me try once more, before the sun
gets me, before I starve or drown, while I can. It's
only a tableau after all, it's only a metaphor. See, I
can speak, I am not trapped, and you on your part can
understand. So we will go ahead as if there were no
problem about language.)

This story about giving birth is not about me. In order to convince you of that I should tell you what I
did this morning, before I sat down at this desk—a
door on top of two filing cabinets, radio to the left,
calendar to the right, these devices by which I place
myself in time. I got up at twenty-to-seven, and, halfway down the stairs, met my daughter, who was as-
cending, autonomously she thought, actually in the
arms of her father. We greeted each other with hugs
and smiles; we then played with the alarm clock and
the hot water bottle, a ritual we go through only on
the days her father has to leave the house early to
drive into the city. This ritual exists to give me the
illusion that I am sleeping in. When she finally decided it was time for me to get up, she began pulling
my hair. I got dressed while she explored the bathroom scales and the mysterious white altar of the toilet. I took her downstairs and we had the usual struggle over her clothes. Already she is wearing miniature
jeans, miniature T-shirts. After this she fed herself:
orange, banana, muffin, porridge.

We then went out to the sunporch, where we recognized anew, and by their names, the dog, the cats

and the birds, bluejays and goldfinches at this time of year, which is winter. She puts her fingers on my lips as I pronounce these words; she hasn't yet learned the secret of making them. I am waiting for her first word: surely it will be miraculous, something that has never yet been said. But if so, perhaps she's already said it and I, in my entrapment, my addiction to the usual, have not heard it.

In her playpen I discovered the first alarming thing of the day. It was a small naked woman, made of that soft plastic from which jiggly spiders and lizards and the other things people hang in their car windows are also made. She was given to my daughter by a friend, a woman who does props for movies, she was supposed to have been a prop but she wasn't used. The baby loved her and would crawl around the floor holding her in her mouth like a dog carrying a bone, with the head sticking out one side and the feet out the other. She seemed chewy and harmless, but the other day I noticed that the baby had managed to make a tear in the body with her new teeth. I put the woman into the cardboard box I use for toy storage.

But this morning she was back in the playpen and the feet were gone. The baby must have eaten them, and I worried about whether or not the plastic would dissolve in her stomach, whether it was toxic. Sooner or later, in the contents of her diaper, which I examine with the usual amount of maternal brooding, I knew I would find two small pink plastic feet. I removed the doll and later, while she was still singing to the dog outside the window, dropped it into the garbage. I am not up to finding tiny female arms, breasts, a head, in my daughter's disposable diapers, partially covered by undigested carrots and the husks of raisins, like the relics of some gruesome and demented murder.

Now she's having her nap and I am writing this story. From what I have said, you can see that my life (despite these occasional surprises, reminders of another world) is calm and orderly, suffused with that

warm, reddish light, those well-placed blue highlights
and reflecting surfaces (mirrors, plates, oblong window panes) you think of as belonging to Dutch genre
paintings; and like them it is realistic in detail and
slightly sentimental. Or at least it has an aura of
sentiment. (Already I'm having moments of muted
grief over those of my daughter's baby clothes which
are too small for her to wear any more. I will be a
keeper of hair, I will store things in trunks, I will weep
over photos.) But above all it's solid, everything here
has solidity. No more of those washes of light, those
shifts, nebulous effects of cloud, Turner sunsets, vague
fears, the impalpables Jeannie used to concern herself
with.

I call this woman Jeannie after the song. I can't
remember any more of the song, only the title. The
point (for in language there are always these "points,"
these reflections; this is what makes it so rich and
sticky, this is why so many have disappeared beneath
its dark and shining surface, why you should never
try to see your own reflection in it; you will lean
over too far, a strand of your hair will fall in and
come out gold, and, thinking it is gold all the way
down, you yourself will follow, sliding into those
outstretched arms, towards the mouth you think is
opening to pronounce your name but instead, just
before your ears fill with pure sound, will form a word
you have never heard before . . .)

The point, for me, is in the hair. My own hair is
not light brown, but Jeannie's was. This is one difference between us. The other point is the dreaming,
for Jeannie isn't real in the same way that I am real.
But by now, and I mean your time, both of us will
have the same degree of reality, we will be equal:
wraiths, echoes, reverberations in your own brain. At
the moment though Jeannie is to me as I will some
day be to you. So she is real enough.

Jeannie is on her way to the hospital, to give birth,
to be delivered. She is not quibbling over these
terms. She's sitting in the back seat of the car, with

her eyes closed and her coat spread over her like a blanket. She is doing her breathing exercises and timing her contractions with a stopwatch. She has been up since two-thirty in the morning, when she took a bath and ate some lime Jello, and it's now almost ten. She has learned to count, during the slow breathing, in numbers (from one to ten while breathing in, from ten to one while breathing out) which she can actually see while she is silently pronouncing them. Each number is a different colour and, if she's concentrating very hard, a different typeface. They range from plain Roman to ornamented circus numbers, red with gold filigree and dots. This is a refinement not mentioned in any of the numerous books she's read on the subject. Jeannie is a devotee of handbooks. She has at least two shelves of books that cover everything from building kitchen cabinets to auto repairs to smoking your own hams. She doesn't do many of these things, but she does some of them, and in her suitcase, along with a washcloth, a package of lemon lifesavers, a pair of glasses, a hot water bottle, some talcum powder and a paper bag, is the book that suggested she take along all of these things.

(By this time you may be thinking that I've invented Jeannie in order to distance myself from these experiences. Nothing could be further from the truth. I am, in fact, trying to bring myself closer to something that time has already made distant. As for Jeannie, my intention is simple: I am bringing her back to life.)

There are two other people in the car with Jeannie. One is a man, whom I will call A., for convenience. A. is driving. When Jeannie opens her eyes, at the end of every contraction, she can see the back of his slightly balding head and his reassuring shoulders. A. drives well and not too quickly. From time to time he asks her how she is, and she tells him how long the contractions are lasting and how long there is between them. When they stop for gas he buys them each a styrofoam container of coffee. For months he has helped her with the breathing exercises, pressing on her knee as recommended by the book, and he will be present at the delivery. (Perhaps it's to him that the birth will be given, in the same sense that one gives a performance.) Together they have toured the hospital maternity ward, in company with a small group of other pairs like them: one thin solicitous person, one slow bulbous person. They have been shown the rooms, shared and private, the sitz-baths, the delivery room itself, which gave the impression of being white. The nurse was light-brown, with limber hips and elbows; she laughed a lot as she answered questions.

"First they'll give you an enema. You know what it is? They take a tube of water and put it up your behind. Now, the gentlemen must put on this—and these, over your shoes. And these hats, this one for those with long hair, this for those with short hair."

"What about those with no hair?" says A.

The nurse looks up at his head and laughs. "Oh, you still have some," she said. "If you have a question, do not be afraid to ask."

They have also seen the film made by the hospital, a full-colour film of a woman giving birth to, can it be a baby? "Not all babies will be this large at birth," the Australian nurse who introduces the movie says. Still, the audience, half of which is pregnant, doesn't look very relaxed when the lights go on. ("If you don't like the visuals," a friend of Jeannie's has told her, "you can always close your eyes.") It isn't the blood so much as the brownish-red disinfectant that bothers her. "I've decided to call this whole thing off," she says to A., smiling to show it's a joke. He gives her a hug and says, "Everything's going to be fine."

And she knows it is. Everything will be fine. But there is another woman in the car. She's sitting in the front seat, and she hasn't turned or acknowledged Jeannie in any way. She, like Jeannie, is going to the hospital. She too is pregnant. She is not going to the hospital to give birth, however, because the word, the words, are too alien to her experience, the experience she is about to have, to be used about it at all. She's wearing a cloth coat with checks in maroon and brown, and she has a kerchief tied over her hair. Jeannie has seen her before, but she knows little about her except that she is a woman who did not wish to become pregnant, who did not choose to divide herself like this, who did not choose any of these ordeals, these initiations. It would be no use telling her that everything is going to be fine. The word in English for unwanted intercourse is rape, but there is no word in the language for what is about to happen to this woman.

Jeannie has seen this woman from time to time throughout her pregnancy, always in the same coat, always with the same kerchief. Naturally, being pregnant herself has made her more aware of other pregnant women, and she has watched them, examined them covertly, every time she has seen one. But not every other pregnant woman is this woman. She did not, for instance, attend Jeannie's pre-natal classes at the hospital, where the women were all young, younger than Jeannie.

"How many will be breast-feeding?" asks the Australian nurse with the hefty shoulders.

All hands but one shoot up. A modern group, the new generation, and the one lone bottle-feeder, who might have (who knows?) something wrong with her breasts, is ashamed of herself. The others look politely away from her. What they want most to discuss, it seems, are the differences between one kind of disposable diaper and another. Sometimes they lie on mats and squeeze each other's hands, simulating contractions and counting breaths. It's all very hopeful. The Australian nurse tells them not to get in and out of the bathtub by themselves. At the end of an hour they are each given a glass of apple juice.

There is only one woman in the class who has already given birth. She's there, she says, to make sure they give her a shot this time. They delayed it last time and she went through hell. The others look at her with mild disapproval. *They* are not clamouring for shots, they do not intend to go through hell. Hell comes from the wrong attitude, they feel. The books talk about *discomfort*.

"It's not discomfort, it's pain, baby," the woman says.

The others smile uneasily and the conversation slides back to disposable diapers.

Vitaminized, conscientious, well-read Jeannie, who has managed to avoid morning sickness, varicose veins, stretch marks, toxemia and depression, who has had no aberrations of appetite, no blurrings of vision —why is she followed, then, by this other? At first it was only a glimpse now and then, at the infants' clothing section in Simpson's Basement, in the super-market lineup, on streetcorners as she herself slid by in A.'s car: the haggard face, the bloated torso, the kerchief holding back the too-sparse hair. In any case, it was Jeannie who saw her, not the other way around. If she knew she was following Jeannie she gave no sign.

As Jeannie has come closer and closer to this day, the unknown day on which she will give birth, as time has thickened around her so that it has become some-thing she must propel herself through, a kind of slush, wet earth underfoot, she has seen this woman more and more often, though always from a distance. De-pending on the light, she has appeared by turns as a young girl of perhaps twenty to an older woman of forty or forty-five, but there was never any doubt in Jeannie's mind that it was the same woman. In fact it did not occur to her that the woman was not real in the usual sense (and perhaps she was, originally, on the first or second sighting, as the voice that causes an echo is real), until A. stopped for a red light dur-ing this drive to the hospital and the woman, who had been standing on the corner with a brown pa-per bag in her arms, simply opened the front door of

the car and got in. A. didn't react, and Jeannie knows
better than to say anything to him. She is aware that
the woman is not really there: Jeannie is not crazy.
She could even make the woman disappear by opening her eyes wider, by staring, but it is only the
shape that would go away, not the feeling. Jeannie
isn't exactly afraid of this woman. She is afraid for her.

When they reach the hospital, the woman gets out
of the car and is through the door by the time A. has
come around to help Jeannie out of the back seat. In
the lobby she is nowhere to be seen. Jeannie goes
through Admission in the usual way, unshadowed.

There has been an epidemic of babies during the
night and the maternity ward is overcrowded. Jeannie waits for her room behind a dividing screen.
Nearby someone is screaming, screaming and mum-
bling between screams in what sounds like a foreign
language. Portuguese, Jeannie thinks. She tells herself that for them it is different, you're supposed to
scream, you're regarded as queer if you don't scream,
it's a required part of giving birth. Nevertheless she
knows that the woman screaming is the other woman
and she is screaming from pain. Jeannie listens to
the other voice, also a woman's, comforting, reassuring: her mother? A nurse?

A. arrives and they sit uneasily, listening to the
screams. Finally Jeannie is sent for and she goes for
her prep. *Prep school,* she thinks. She takes off her
clothes—when will she see them again?—and puts on
the hospital gown. She is examined, labelled around
the wrist, and given an enema. She tells the nurse
she can't take Demerol because she's allergic to it,
and the nurse writes this down. Jeannie doesn't know
whether this is true or not but she doesn't want Demerol, she has read the books. She intends to put up a
struggle over her pubic hair—surely she will lose her
strength if it is all shaved off—but it turns out the
nurse doesn't have very strong feelings about it. She
is told her contractions are not far enough along to
be taken seriously, she can even have lunch. She puts

on her dressing gown and rejoins A., in the freshly vacated room, eats some tomato soup and a veal cutlet, and decides to take a nap while A. goes out for supplies.

Jeannie wakes up when A. comes back. He has brought a paper, some detective novels for Jeannie, and a bottle of Scotch for himself. A. reads the paper and drinks Scotch, and Jeannie reads *Poirot's Early Cases*. There is no connection between Poirot and her labour, which is now intensifying, unless it is the egg-shape of Poirot's head and the vegetable marrows he is known to cultivate with strands of wet wool (placentae? umbilical cords?). She is glad the stories are short; she is walking around the room now, between contractions. Lunch was definitely a mistake.

"I think I have back labour," she says to A. They get out the handbook and look up the instructions for this. It's useful that everything has a name. Jeannie kneels on the bed and rests her forehead on her arms while A. rubs her back. A. pours himself another Scotch, in the hospital glass. The nurse, in pink, comes, looks, asks about the timing, and goes away again. Jeannie is beginning to sweat. She can only manage half a page or so of Poirot before she has to clamber back up on the bed again and begin breathing and running through the coloured numbers.

When the nurse comes back, she has a wheelchair. It's time to go down to the labour room, she says. Jeannie feels stupid sitting in the wheelchair. She tells herself about peasant women having babies in the fields, Indian women having them on portages with hardly a second thought. She feels effete. But the hospital wants her to ride, and considering the fact that the nurse is tiny, perhaps it's just as well. What if Jeannie were to collapse, after all? After all her courageous talk. An image of the tiny pink nurse, ant-like, trundling large Jeannie through the corridors, rolling her along like a heavy beachball.

As they go by the check-in desk a woman is

wheeled past on a table, covered by a sheet. Her eyes
are closed and there's a bottle feeding into her arm
through a tube. Something is wrong. Jeannie looks
back—she thinks it was the other woman—but the
sheeted table is hidden now behind the counter.

In the dim labour room Jeannie takes off her dressing gown and is helped up onto the bed by the nurse.
A. brings her suitcase, which is not a suitcase actually
but a small flight bag; the significance of this has not
been lost on Jeannie, and in fact she now has some of
the apprehensive feelings she associates with planes,
including the fear of a crash. She takes out her Lifesavers, her glasses, her washcloth and the other
things she thinks she will need. She removes her
contact lenses and places them in their case, reminding A. that they must not be lost. Now she is
purblind.

There is something else in her bag that she doesn't
remove. It's a talisman, given to her several years ago
as a souvenir by a travelling friend of hers. It's a
rounded oblong of opaque blue glass, with four yellow and white eye shapes on it. In Turkey, her friend
has told her, they hang them on mules to protect
against the Evil Eye. Jeannie knows this talisman
probably won't work for her, she is not Turkish and
she isn't a mule, but it makes her feel safer to have it
in the room with her. She had planned to hold it in
her hand during the most difficult part of labour but
somehow there is no longer any time for carrying out
plans like this.

An old woman, a fat old woman dressed all in
green, comes into the room and sits beside Jeannie.
She says to A., who is sitting on the other side of Jeannie, "That is a good watch. They don't make watches
like that any more." She is referring to his gold pocket
watch, one of his few extravagances, which is on the
night table. Then she places her hand on Jeannie's
belly to feel the contraction. "This is good," she says;
her accent is Swedish or German. "This, I call a con-

traction. Before, it was nothing." Jeannie can no longer remember having seen her before. "Good. Good."

"When will I have it?" Jeannie asks, when she can talk, when she is no longer counting.

The old woman laughs. Surely that laugh, those tribal hands, have presided over a thousand beds, a thousand kitchen tables . . . "A long time yet," she says. "Eight, ten hours."

"But I've been *doing* this for twelve hours already," Jeannie says.

"Not hard labour," the woman says. "Not good, like this."

Jeannie settles into herself for the long wait. At the moment she can't remember why she wanted to have a baby in the first place. That decision was made by someone else, whose motives are now unclear. She remembers the way women who had babies used to smile at one another, mysteriously, as if there was something they knew that she didn't, the way they would casually exclude her from their frame of reference. What was the knowledge, the mystery, or was having a baby really no more inexplicable than having a car accident or an orgasm? (But these too were indescribable, events of the body, all of them; why should the mind distress itself trying to find a language for them?) She has sworn she will never do that to any woman without children, engage in those passwords and exclusions. She's old enough, she's been put through enough years of it to find it tiresome and cruel.

But—and this is the part of Jeannie that goes with the talisman hidden in her bag, not with the part that longs to build kitchen cabinets and smoke hams —she is, secretly, hoping for a mystery. Something more than this, something else, a vision. After all she is risking her life, though it's not too likely she will die. Still, some women do. Internal bleeding, shock, heart failure, a mistake on the part of someone, a nurse, a doctor. She deserves a vision, she deserves to be allowed to bring something back with her from this dark place into which she is now rapidly descending.

She thinks momentarily about the other woman. Her motives, too, are unclear. Why doesn't she want to have a baby? Has she been raped, does she have ten other children, is she starving? Why hasn't she had an abortion? Jeannie doesn't know, and in fact it no longer matters why. *Uncross your fingers*, Jeannie thinks to her. Her face, distorted with pain and terror, floats briefly behind Jeannie's eyes before it too drifts away.

Jeannie tries to reach down to the baby, as she has many times before, sending waves of love, colour, music, down through her arteries to it, but she finds she can no longer do this. She can no longer feel the baby as a baby, its arms and legs poking, kicking, turning. It has collected itself together, it's a hard sphere, it does not have time right now to listen to her. She's grateful for this because she isn't sure anyway how good the message would be. She no longer has control of the numbers either, she can no longer see them, although she continues mechanically to count. She realizes she has practised for the wrong thing, A. squeezing her knee was nothing, she should have practised for this, whatever it is.

"Slow down," A. says. She's on her side now, he's holding her hand. "Slow it right down."

"I can't, I can't do it, I can't do this."

"Yes you can."

"Will I sound like that?"

"Like what?" A. says. Perhaps he can't hear it: it's the other woman, in the room next door or the room next door to that. She's screaming and crying, screaming and crying. While she cries she is saying, over and over, "It hurts. It hurts."

"No, you won't," he says. So there is someone, after all.

A doctor comes in, not her own doctor. They want her to turn over on her back.

"I can't," she says. "I don't like it that way." Sounds have receded, she has trouble hearing them. She turns over and the doctor gropes with her rubber-gloved hand. Something wet and hot flows over her thighs.

"It was just ready to break," the doctor says. "All I had to do was touch it. Four centimetres," she says to A.

"Only *four?*" Jeannie says. She feels cheated; they must be wrong. The doctor says her own doctor will be called in time. Jeannie is outraged at them. They have not understood, but it's too late to say this and she slips back into the dark place, which is not hell, which is more like being inside, trying to get out. *Out*, she says or thinks. Then she is floating, the numbers are gone, if anyone told her to get up, go out of the room, stand on her head, she would do it. From minute to minute she comes up again, grabs for air.

"You're hyperventilating," A. says. "Slow it down." He is rubbing her back now, hard, and she takes his hand and shoves it viciously farther down, to the right place, which is not the right place as soon as his hand is there. She remembers a story she read once, about the Nazis tying the legs of Jewish women together during labour. She never really understood before how that could kill you.

A nurse appears with a needle. "I don't want it," Jeannie says.

"Don't be hard on yourself," the nurse says. "You don't have to go through pain like that." *What pain?* Jeannie thinks. When there is no pain she feels nothing, when there is pain, she feels nothing because there is no *she*. This, finally, is the disappearance of language. *You don't remember afterwards*, she has been told by almost everyone.

Jeannie comes out of a contraction, gropes for control. "Will it hurt the baby?" she says.

"It's a mild analgesic," the doctor says. "We wouldn't allow anything that would hurt the baby."

Jeannie doesn't believe this. Nevertheless she is jabbed, and the doctor is right, it is very mild, because it doesn't seem to do a thing for Jeannie, though A. later tells her she has slept briefly between contractions.

Suddenly she sits bolt upright. She is wide awake and lucid. "You have to ring that bell right now," she says. "This baby is being born."

A. clearly doesn't believe her. "I can feel it, I can feel the head," she says. A. pushes the button for the call bell. A nurse appears and checks, and now everything is happening too soon, nobody is ready. They set off down the hall, the nurse wheeling. Jeannie feels fine. She watches the corridors, the edges of everything shadowy because she doesn't have her glasses on. She hopes A. will remember to bring them. They pass another doctor.

"Need me?" she asks.

"Oh no," the nurse answers breezily. "Natural childbirth."

Jeannie realizes that this woman must have been the anaesthetist. "What?" she says, but it's too late now, they are in the room itself, all those glossy surfaces, tubular strange apparatus like a science fiction movie, and the nurse is telling her to get onto the delivery table. No one else is in the room.

"You must be crazy," Jeannie says.

"Don't push," the nurse says.

"What do you mean?" Jeannie says. This is absurd. Why should she wait, why should the baby wait for them because they're late?

"Breathe through your mouth," the nurse says. "Pant," and Jeannie finally remembers how. When the contraction is over she uses the nurse's arm as a lever and hauls herself across onto the table.

From somewhere her own doctor materializes, in her doctor suit already, looking even more like Mary Poppins than usual, and Jeannie says, "Bet you weren't expecting to see me so soon!" The baby is being born when Jeannie said it would, though just three days ago the doctor said it would be at least another week, and this makes Jeannie feel jubilant and smug. Not that she knew, she'd believed the doctor.

She's being covered with a green tablecloth, they are taking far too long, she feels like pushing the baby out now, before they are ready. A. is there by her head, swathed in robes, hats, masks. He has forgotten her glasses. "Push now," the doctor says. Jeannie grips with her hands, grits her teeth, face, her whole body together, a snarl, a fierce smile, the baby is enormous, a stone, a boulder, her bones unlock, and, once, twice, the third time, she opens like a birdcage turning slowly inside out.

A pause; a wet kitten slithers between her legs. "Why don't you look?" says the doctor, but Jeannie still has her eyes closed. No glasses, she couldn't have seen a thing anyway. "Why don't you look?" the doctor says again.

Jeannie opens her eyes. She can see the baby, who has been wheeled up beside her and is fading already from the alarming birth purple. *A good baby,* she thinks, meaning it as the old woman did: *a good watch,* well-made, substantial. The baby isn't crying; she squints in the new light. Birth isn't something that has been given to her, nor has she taken it. It was just something that has happened so they could greet each other like this. The nurse is stringing beads for her name. When the baby is bundled and tucked beside Jeannie, she goes to sleep.

As for the vision, there wasn't one. Jeannie is conscious of no special knowledge; already she's forgetting what it was like. She's tired and very cold; she is shaking, and asks for another blanket. A. comes back to the room with her; her clothes are still there. Everything is quiet, the other woman is no longer screaming. Something has happened to her, Jeannie knows, Is she dead? Is the baby dead? Perhaps she is one of those casualties (and how can Jeannie herself be sure, yet, that she will not be among them) who will go into postpartum depression and never come out. "You see, there was nothing to be afraid of," A. says before he leaves, but he was wrong.

The next morning Jeannie wakes up when it's light. She's been warned about getting out of bed the first time without the help of a nurse, but she decides to do it anyway (peasant in the field! Indian on the portage!). She's still running on adrenalin; she's also weaker than she thought, but she wants very much to look out the window. She feels she's been inside too long, she wants to see the sun come up. Being awake this early always makes her feel a little unreal, a little insubstantial, as if she's partly transparent, partly dead.

(It was to me, after all, that the birth was given, Jeannie gave it, I am the result. What would she make of me? Would she be pleased?)

The window is two panes with a venetian blind sandwiched between them; it turns by a knob at the side. Jeannie has never seen a window like this before. She closes and opens the blind several times. Then she leaves it open and looks out.

All she can see from the window is a building. It's an old stone building, heavy and Victorian, with a copper roof oxidized to green. It's solid, hard, darkened by soot, dour, leaden. But as she looks at this building, so old and seemingly immutable, she sees that it's made of water. Water, and some tenuous jellylike substance. Light flows through it from behind (the sun is coming up), the building is so thin, so fragile, that it quivers in the slight dawn wind. Jeannie sees that if the building is this way (a touch could destroy it, a ripple of the earth, why has no one noticed, guarded it against accidents?) then the rest of the world must be like this too, the entire earth, the rocks, people, trees, everything needs to be protected, cared for, tended. The enormity of this task defeats her; she will never be up to it, and what will happen then?

Jeannie hears footsteps in the hall outside her door.

She thinks it must be the other woman, in her brown and maroon checked coat, carrying her paper bag, leaving the hospital now that her job is done. She has seen Jeannie safely through, she must go now to hunt through the streets of the city for her next case. But the door opens, it's only a nurse, who is just in time to catch Jeannie as she sinks to the floor, holding onto the edge of the air-conditioning unit. The nurse scolds her for getting up too soon.

After that the baby is carried in, solid, substantial, packed together like an apple. Jeannie examines her, she is complete, and in the days that follow Jeannie herself becomes drifted over with new words, her hair slowly darkens, she ceases to be what she was and is replaced, gradually, by someone else.

ABOUT THE AUTHOR

MARGARET ATWOOD was born in Ottawa and grew up in northern Ontario, Quebec, and Toronto. She has lived in many other cities, including Boston, Vancouver, Montreal, and London, England, and has travelled extensively.

She is the author of more than twenty volumes of poetry, fiction, and non-fiction, including the novels, *The Edible Woman*, *Surfacing*, *Lady Oracle*, *Life Before Man*, *Bodily Harm*, and *The Handmaid's Tale*, and for her two collections of short fiction, *Dancing Girls*, and *Bluebeard's Egg*. Her work has been published in more than twenty countries. Her new novel is *Cat's Eye*.

Margaret Atwood lives in Toronto with novelist Graeme Gibson and their daughter Jess.

SEAL BOOKS

Offers you a list of outstanding fiction, non-fiction, and classics of Canadian literature in paperback by Canadian authors, available at all good bookstores throughout Canada.

THE BACK DOCTOR	Hamilton Hall
THE IVORY SWING	Janette Turner Hospital
NEVER CRY WOLF	Farley Mowat
THE KITE	W. O. Mitchell
A BIRD IN THE HOUSE	Margaret Laurence
ANNE OF GREEN GABLES	Lucy Maud Montgomery
BEST CANADIAN SHORT STORIES	John Stevens, Ed.
LADY ORACLE	Margaret Atwood
BORDERLINE	Janette Turner Hospital
AND NO BIRDS SANG	Farley Mowat
STONE ANGEL	Margaret Laurence
STRAIGHT FROM THE HEART	Jean Chretien
BLUEBEARD'S EGG	Margaret Atwood
JOSHUA THEN AND NOW	Mordecai Richler
MY DISCOVERY OF AMERICA	Farley Mowat
A CERTAIN MR. TAKAHASHI	Ann Ireland
THE CANADIAN ESTABLISHMENT	Peter C. Newman
A JEST OF GOD	Margaret Laurence
HOW I SPENT MY SUMMER HOLIDAYS	W. O. Mitchell
SEA OF SLAUGHTER	Farley Mowat
THE HANDMAID'S TALE	Margaret Atwood
THE CANADIANS (seven volumes)	Robert E. Wall
JACOB TWO TWO MEETS THE HOODED FANG	Mordecai Richler
HEART OF A STRANGER	Margaret Laurence
THE DOG WHO WOULDN'T BE	Farley Mowat
WHO HAS SEEN THE WIND	W. O. Mitchell
DOWNFALL PEOPLE	Jo Anne Williams Bennett
CONTROLLING INTEREST	Diane Francis
THE STORY GIRL	Lucy Maud Montgomery
JACKRABBIT PAROLE	Stephen Reid
NO FIXED ADDRESS	Aritha Van Herk
THE GOLDEN ROAD	Lucy Maud Montgomery
THE SUSPECT	L. R. Wright
DIVORCED PARENTING	Dr. Sol Goldstein
HUNTING HUMANS	Elliott Leyton

The Mark of Canadian Bestsellers